Dan

Enjoy!

Kathryn Young

I hadn't done anything wrong, so why was I being arrested?

I reached the back doorway when my phone buzzed. Fishing it out of my pocket, I read the number displayed and smiled. "Hey, Deena."

"Thank goodness you answered."

I hooked my arm around the nearest chair and pulled it toward me. I eased into it before asking, "What's wrong?" I remembered Nash's warning that Deena's fate was on me.

"If you're at the bar, you want to leave soon, real soon. Like right this minute," Deena said, keeping her voice soft and low.

I grew exasperated. "Why, Deena?"

"Sheriff and his deputy are coming to arrest you," she hissed.

"What?" I shouted and popped out of my chair. Nash stopped wiping the counter to frown at me while Cisco peeked around the doorway. I waved my arm at both men to go on about their business. Turning my back to them, I whispered into the phone. "What are you talking about?"

"I can't say much because somebody might come in the bathroom and hear me. I'm on probation, you know."

I sensed my composure falling apart, and my patience. "Yeah, I do. But, Deena, can we get back to the part about me getting arrested?"

"I heard Parker tell the deputy there was evidence about the case and how it tied to you, something on the body. It's probably physical evidence linking you to the crime, you know?"

Research assistant Sarah Mackenzie loves working for her uncle, collecting information for his local history projects. However, when she stumbles upon an uncovered grave in Cornplanter Cemetery, it's like staring into the face of a ghost. The body reminds her of someone she knew, someone she believed died ten years ago. Her discovery leads to more unpleasant surprises and definitely not the kind Sarah likes to collect.

The local sheriff learns about Sarah's strained relationship with the victim, and the clues keep dropping to shift suspicion to her as the prime suspect. As the murders escalate and one becomes three, Sarah confronts her fears and searches for the truth, venturing into the world of Seneca Indian culture. Confronted with mysteries from the past as well as the present, she must find their common link to discover the identity of the Grave Maker and stop his killing spree.

KUDOS for *Buried in Sin*

"Kathryn Long delivers a can't-put-down, thoroughly enjoyable read from the first captivating sentence to the last heart-pounding chapter." ~ Jane Ann Turzillo, Agatha nominee for *Wicked Women of Ohio*

"With excellent character development, an intriguing mystery, and plenty of suspense, this is one you won't be able to put down." ~ Taylor Jones, The Review Team of Taylor Jones & Regan Murphy

"Combining superb character development, a complex and intriguing mystery, a hint of romance, a little paranormal, and plenty of nail-biting suspense, *Buried in Sin* is a page turner you'll enjoy reading more than once." ~ Regan Murphy, The Review Team of Taylor Jones & Regan Murphy

ACKNOWLEDGMENTS

First off, I'd like to thank all the wonderful staff at Black Opal Books. You made this whole process so much easier! Your help and dedication to your authors is a true blessing. A special thanks goes to Faith. You made editing an almost painless job!

None of this writing journey would be possible if not for my family's support. I can be a total mess at times, but you all turn me around to think on the positive side with your words of encouragement. Thank you for that.

Of course, no one understands writers better than other writers. That's why I look forward to each month when our Author Brainstorm group meets. What a great bunch of ladies! Sharing and caring—we do it all! So, thank you, Julie, Jane, Cari, Shelly, Wendy, and Heather. You lift me up!

Also, I need to mention a great group of people who helped give me feedback about my title choice. It's nice including others like them in this whole writing process.

In years past, I have attended the Mohican Indian Pow-wow in Loudonville, Ohio. Watching the dance competition, feasting on fry bread, listening to folklore tales, and perusing the tents filled with Indian relics have given me a wealth of experience for which I am grateful. I was able to include these details in the description of the Salamanca pow-wow.

Finally, much of my inspiration and knowledge about the setting and details in this book come from personal experience. On Roper Hollow Road you'll find our family cabin. It has been there for over sixty years. I've spent plenty of summer vacations there, visiting the surrounding cities and sites such as Kinzua Bridge and Cornplanter Cemetery. As a child, I watched the Allegheny River and the river road change geographically when the Kinzua Dam and Reservoir were built, though at the time I hardly knew how devastating this was to the Seneca people, many who lost their homes. Plenty of cabins and homes have been built along Roper Hollow Road since then. Rather than it taking a week for a dozen cars to pass by our place, the weekend traffic swells as boaters drive down to the dock and disrupt the silence. Still, the place remains quiet most of time as nature keeps a tight hold of our little sanctuary atop the hill, deep inside the Allegheny Forest.

When personal experience wasn't enough, I used several sources to discover more. Those being numerous online sites and two reference books from my reference library.

The Allegany Senecas and Kinzua Dam: Forced Relocation through Two Generations – Joy A. Bilharz

Cornplanter: Chief Warrior of the Allegany Senecas (The Iroquois and Their Neighbors) – Thomas S. Abler

Buried

in

Sin

A Mackenzie Blue Mystery

Kathryn Long

A Black Opal Books Publication

GENRE: MYSTERY-DETECTIVE/WOMEN SLEUTHS

BURIED IN SIN ~ A MACKENZIE BLUE MYSTERY
Copyright © 2019 by Kathryn long
Cover Design by Kathryn Long
All cover art copyright © 2019
All Rights Reserved
Print ISBN: 9781644371114

First Publication: MARCH 2019

Published by Black Opal Books **http://www.blackopalbooks.com**

DEDICATION

To a true man of nature, a passionate explorer who traveled across many miles of northwest Pennsylvania's Allegheny Forest, River, and Kinzua country, a native who loved every detail of his home state, from the history to the geography to the people, the one who taught me to love and respect the land—he's the real-life Chaz Mackenzie. Dad, this one's for you.

John Henry Schake
1905-1994

Chapter 1

*N*obody *dies twice. I imagine it's what most folks believe*. I did, until the day I found him in Cornplanter Cemetery, when morning had shifted into afternoon and the sweet smell of warm grass and the chirping of cicadas made everything seem normal.

I knelt between the rows, admiring the limestone marker battle-scarred with age, my gaze solemn. Squiggles and crevices wormed their way in and out and through its engraved surface. With brush in hand, I delicately stroked the stone to swipe away the powdery gray dirt and uncover the name and dates. Pushing back a loose strand of unruly black hair, I then rubbed both hands on my pant legs to remove the sweat before taking hold of the voice recorder. Placing it close to my mouth, I read the information. "Jordan Corydon, born 1863, died 1898."

I stood and winced as knees cracked under pressure and overuse from the morning's trial that now dipped into afternoon. Blistering heat sparked while brilliant sunlight streamed and fanned its rays across the rows of stones. With a twist of an arm, I glanced at my watch warning of the need to leave soon. A sigh escaped. I glanced from one row to the next. After five hours, I'd barely made a dent. Three hundred and fifty-seven stone markers, and only ninety-eight of them recorded.

After gulping several ounces of water, I doused my face with the rest of the bottle. The temperature had reached close to ninety by noon. Not exactly the best weather for this sort of work. A curse or two escaped my lips. A time later in the week, after the mountain rains had cooled the air, would have suited me.

"Half dozen more, Chaz Mackenzie. That's all you'll get." Through griping, I struggled to my feet and moved to the next marker. I swiped the stone clean with my brush.

One-hundred and thirty-nine cemeteries were located in Warren County, ten of them in Elk Township alone, and they varied in size from a family plot of less than a handful to hundreds. Some sites had been transplanted from their original location, like Cornplanter's. Of course, that one had a story all its own, burdened with a rich and tragic history. I knew all of this and more because I re-searched it.

"Jacob Bluehawk, born 1898, died…1899." I reread the inscription in silence and resisted any tears. The lump in my throat was harder to swallow. I turned away to make the call. "Hey, Uncle Chaz."

"About time, Miss Sarah."

"Sorry." I shivered, gripped by a longing to escape and be among the living. "This will take a while. How you feeling today?"

"Above dirt, I expect. Find any matches?"

"Sort of. There are several Corydons and Bluehawks and Pierces, but none of the Clearwater clan." I tired of reciting even a handful of so many names. Sweat dribbled down my neck. The heat got to me, and somehow I was left with an inconsolable sadness. All those many souls gone to another place where the living couldn't follow until fate or some spiritual power chose to take them there. With a firm click, I turned off the recorder once more and pocketed the device. Enough for one day. My armored defense to stave off emotion had dissolved.

I strolled between two rows of markers to reach shade under a canopy of trees.

"Not nearly good enough," Uncle Chaz said. "I need a solid, documented connection between at least two families."

"For once, try being more optimistic, will you? If I can manage to get a hold of the genealogy records at some other courthouse or library, I believe that could be our break," I reasoned with him, for what good it would do.

His voice rose: "I need the information now, not tomorrow or next week."

I raked fingers through my hair. My patience, along with my physical strength, was weakening by the second. "Please don't take an attitude with me. I can't help it if the only records to come up in my web search failed to provide anything prior to the fifties. But I'm not about to stop looking. You know me. There're bound to be other ones. I only have to find them. So, calm yourself before you pass out or worse."

I stopped at the tree line. Grateful to be in the shade, I leaned against a thick-trunked oak and breathed in cooler air. I loved my uncle deeply, but blood ties or not, he taxed my patience. The son and grandson of coal miners hardened by life's cruel nature, Chaz was demanding, gruff, and often made unreasonable requests. However, I'd made a promise to Aunt Grace the day she left him to return home to Export.

Here we were, five years later. Chaz Blue Mackenzie

still dished out his salty meanness while I, Sarah Blue Mackenzie, continued to care for him. I tightened my grip on the phone while listening to his persistent complaints. Why could he never make it easy?

"And that's more time than I have," he griped. "Holy saints, I'm stuck four-feet deep in a mud hole with writin' this book and ain't about to dig my way out."

I pushed away from the trunk to stand straight then took quick steps along the tree line, the pace of my feet rapid enough to match my heartbeat. If I glanced in the mirror, I'd surely see the fire sparking in my eyes. "Look, Uncle Chaz, I'm doing the best I can with what little I have to go on, but your sour mood is not helping me to—" My voice broke off and I stilled. There was a fresh mound of dirt piled high next to a good-sized hole that rested ten or so yards ahead.

"I'm sorry, child. I should've never considered takin' on this project. The historical society spun quite an appealin' story, you know? Shoot. Problems and headaches, that's all it is. Don't you agree? Sarah? You still there?"

"Ah, yeah. Hold on," I said, once more moving forward. A fresh grave in a cemetery. This wasn't anything unusual. Somebody who died would need burying. However, no one had been buried in Cornplanter's since the first half of the twentieth century.

My pace slowed to a crawl as I sniffed a foul odor. The harsh chatter of crows perched in the tree above startled me, enough that I lost my balance. I gasped, and my arms flailed wildly until I found my feet planted on the ground once more. Counting to ten, I took a deep breath. Another step. One more, and I reached the edge of the hole. "Okay, Mac, you can do this," I whispered before leaning in to take a peek.

With a loud gasp, I stumbled backward. Doubling over at the waist, I coughed and tried to hold down the bitter taste rising up through my stomach and into my throat.

"What in blue blazes is all that noise you're makin'?"

My legs weakened, and I crumbled to the ground. In another minute, maybe longer, I put the phone back to my ear. "I have to go, Uncle Chaz. There's a body…in a grave. I need to call the sheriff."

Chaz laughed. "What did you expect? Land sakes. You're in a cemetery."

I shook my head, hard enough to make myself dizzy. My voice came out breathy and weak. "This one's different. I'll talk to you when I get home." I ended the call, despite his sputtering protests. My knuckles blanched as I tightened the grip on the phone.

To be certain the long day with its heat and burning sunlight hadn't played games with my eyes, I walked back to the grave once more. Another quick look told me this was no delusion. A man lay in the grave, a red-stained hole through the middle of his chest. For a brief moment, though it seemed insane, the face appeared strangely familiar. Somebody from my past. But that was impossible, wasn't it?

As I began to turn away, something else caught my eye. A rather large, flat stone rested at the head of the grave, as if placed there with deliberate intent. Curious, I edged closer to examine the stone with steps distanced enough to keep from slipping into the hole. The smoothly polished surface was marred by crude lettering engraved in its center. I bent to read and puzzled over what I saw. "Sins of the soul," I whispered aloud.

I forced my trembling hand to hold steady as I pushed buttons on the phone to call the Warren authorities. A tiny whimper escaped my lips as I stole another glimpse at the grave and tombstone. Twirling on my heel,

I faced the other way. I took several steps from the grave and my heartbeat evened. As I waited for someone to pick up, my mind tossed around the insane idea of how familiar the face was and the conclusion it pushed me to form.

I fought the urge to look again, but it taunted me, as if I needed convincing to give me some kind of reassurance. Instead, I continued in the other direction and moved toward the front of the cemetery where Jacob Bluehawk rested. There I stopped. Taking one hand, I rubbed it harshly over my face, struggling to erase the image of the body. Reese Logan was dead. He'd died almost ten years ago. He wasn't the man in the open grave.

"Warren Sheriff's Department, Paula Yelkin speaking."

The sound disrupted my thoughts. A sudden chill passed through me, and I trembled. "Hi, Paula. It's Mac. I need to speak to the sheriff about..." I paused to catch my breath. "It's urgent. Please."

"Are you okay?"

"I'm fine." But someone else sure wasn't. "Can you get the sheriff for me?"

"You bet. Hold on a sec."

I chewed on my thumbnail and waited until a deep growl came across the phone.

"Sheriff Parker."

"Sheriff, this is Mac—that is, Sarah Mackenzie. I need to report—I found—there's a dead body in Cornplanter Cemetery."

Chapter 2

This some kind of sick joke?" Sheriff Parker snapped out the words.

"No! I mean, of course not. There's a body, a man with a hole in his chest. I think—that is, I'd *guess* he's not been there long," I stammered, thinking I must sound like a loon.

"Cornplanter's, you say?"

"Yes, sir. Near the back row after you enter the cemetery, along the line of trees on the east side." I paused to consider what else to mention. "There's a stone, I'd say a marker of sorts? It has something engraved on it, the words 'sins of the soul.'"

"I see. You need to stay put for a while, Miss Mackenzie. I'll drive up as soon as I get in touch with the coroner's office. Be about an hour?"

I detected the timbre of his voice had softened somewhat. How could I blame him or Uncle Chaz for their initial reaction? A body in a graveyard? I pressed my lips together. The urge to laugh was strong, but nerves kept my teeth chattering. I bit down hard on my tongue to stop. A little too hard. "Ouch! I mean, you might find me in my truck. I think I'll wait there."

With a grunt of approval, Sheriff Parker ended the call. The silence on the phone left me with a sense of abandonment. At once, I grabbed my tool bag, pivoted on my heel, and moved forward. There was no need to worry. Nothing here but tombstones and trees and the flock of crows, which, from where I stood, still guarded the open grave. My pace grew faster, and my gaze darted side to side. Rational or not, an ominous sense of fear shimmied its way through me. Dead bodies in open graves. Of course, I had a right to be irrational.

My breathing quickened and my heart pounded, an internal beating so loud I nearly missed the crackling snap, the sound like steps on fallen tree branches. I paused. Long enough to regain the use of my weak, wobbly legs, and while I was at it, give myself a chance to search the woods. At once, a deer bounded into view and stood in a small clearing formed by the rotten decay of dead trees. The animal stared with a narrow-eyed gaze locked on me and its tail twitching. Then it raised two front legs and leaped into the dense brush.

My shoulders dropped. I forced air into my lungs and took deep, even breaths. My legs were threatening to collapse, and I forced them to finish my walk to the truck. Tired and hungry, I settled comfortably into the front seat. Despite the avalanche of worry, my eyelids grew leaded and heavy, weighted down until they closed. I'd earned my keep today and then some. I force-fed my brain with jumbled bits of this morning's research, anything to distract me from the bizarre predicament I found myself in. Those rambling images of the deceased, buried with only markers to sum up their lives left me uneasy. Just two dates and a name, and seldom an epitaph to describe them.

Restless, I squirmed in my seat. This wasn't working.

Impatient, I set the air conditioner on max and

moved closer to a vent. The cool air relaxed me somewhat. Closing my eyes, I reclined once more. Soon, my
breathing evened and slowed while I slipped into a dream.
The hum of chanting and the beating of drums seemed to
resonate with its hypnotic rhythm inside me. Hum. Beat.
A relaxing rhythm my conscious mind couldn't fight.

A staccato rap on the window broke my reverie and
startled me awake. "What?" I mumbled before I straightened and turned toward the noise. The tan and brown uniform of an officer and the label across the chest with the
name Parker embroidered on it shadowed the window. I
opened the door and stepped out on wobbly legs that resisted the posture.

He tipped his hat and greeted me without a smile.
"Miss Mackenzie."

"Please, call me Mac. And thank you for coming," I
said, but my words sounded lame. "I mean, you got here
so quickly." Of course, how fast that was, I had no idea.
How long had I slept? The way Parker raised his brows
for a brief second told me it was long enough. "It's been
an exhausting morning. Seems I was more tired than I
thought." I shrugged with a careless gesture.

Parker removed a notepad from his pocket and a pen
from behind his ear. "All right, Mac. Exhausting how?"

"Well, I've spent the past several hours recording
birth and death records from those grave markers. My
uncle needs the research. He writes historical books and
documents, you see." The scowl on Parker's face implied
he didn't see at all. I sighed. "I'm his assistant, a fact
finder of sorts. My uncle can't get around anymore because of his diabetes, so I do the leg work and research
for him. Anyway, he needs to trace a local ancestry line, a
Seneca family, to help write his latest work. It's for the
Pennsylvania historical society." Hopefully, the last part
gave my story more credibility.

"And while you collected this data, you found the body of a man with a hole in his chest, lying in an open grave?" Parker raised his chin to gaze at me and waited, his pen poised above the notepad.

I slowly nodded. To hear him say it aloud made it sound preposterous. Who has something like that happen to him? Nobody I knew. Yep. I sounded more like a loony tune every second. And right at this minute, as uncomfortable as it was, I wanted to get my part in it over with and go home. "If you're ready, I'll show you."

"Coroner and his team should be here shortly. As a favor, I promised we'd wait," he said and then shrugged. "Joe Smuthers is somewhat finicky when it comes to crime scenes. Besides, he's had lots more experience with this than I have."

The conversation lulled. I shifted my weight from one leg to the other, twitching with impatience. Silence was torture to me. I'd heard from folks how stoic Sheriff Parker tended to be. All business and little talk. Or, at least on his job, that's how it was. However, this quiet moment would go in another direction if I failed to stop it. My mouth would take up the slack. Before he'd see it coming, I'd begin to chatter and jabber about anything and everything, mostly facts and useless nonsense to everyone but me. I crossed my arms and hugged my chest. The urge got to me.

"Did you know there are over eight-hundred square miles to the Allegheny Forest? And that comes out to five-hundred and thirteen acres of which the Kinzua reservoir is just a small portion, approximately twenty-four miles long." Inwardly I groaned. If the coroner and team didn't arrive soon, Parker would get a full-blown report on the history of the Seneca and construction of the Kinzua Dam.

Though it was faint, a smile surfaced to curl the corners of his mouth ever so slightly. "No, can't say I was aware of the exact number, but that is fascinating."

"Well, it's what I do. Fact finding. And all those bits of information I gather? They manage to take up residence in my brain. Every single one. I'm like an entire set of encyclopedias." I shrugged. "I'd say it takes up too much of my time, but Uncle Chaz tends to be particular and fanatical when it comes to research. So…" My words trailed off until the silence was back, broken only by the cheerful tune of two whippoorwills calling to one another somewhere above.

"Sounds like a useful pastime."

"I guess you could say that." I nodded and drummed my fingers on the hood of the truck.

Parker nodded. "Yep. I suppose you know how the dam came to be built?"

I relaxed a bit. "Built in the early to mid-sixties, but, in truth, there was talk about it decades before that. Some say the debate between the government and the Seneca Nation took up plenty of courtroom time."

"I imagine that's true. Ah, I do believe I hear them approaching. Sorry for making you wait, but we'll get to that crime scene now."

I flinched hearing the words "crime scene." Given the fact I'd avoided to mention the body's resemblance to Reese Logan troubled me. For one, I didn't want such an idea to be remotely possible. To suggest it out loud made it so. Not such a rational train of thought, but how to dismiss it? And second was the memory my discovery dug up, no pun intended. I'd cared about Reese. My body shivered as queasiness filled my insides. Truth was, I'd never meant to hurt him. Never that. To imagine for a second that the body lying a mere one hundred yards away was Reese? It was a cruel joke to play.

In any case, that discovery, whatever it turned out to

be, was Sheriff Parker's job to find, not mine.

"Sheriff." Coroner Joe Smuthers nodded curtly before turning to me as he approached. "You're Mac, Chaz Mackenzie's niece, aren't you?" Before I answered, he snapped his head around and waved an arm to the men who had followed in their van. As soon as they grabbed equipment from the back, they hurried their steps toward Smuthers. "Lead the way. We need to get started before we lose too much daylight."

I waited until Parker nodded at me. I clenched my fists and kept both arms close to my sides. I'd experienced plenty of heartache in my young life, but none of the violence. Definitely not murder. It took a lot of time, but I'd found peace and a new purpose when I'd committed to caring for Uncle Chaz. I managed to forget certain parts of my childhood since those memories were not the happy kind. However, this was different, intimate in a disturbing sort of way, like the death in that grave touched me and groped at me, like I'd been violated. And that made it personal.

The crescendo of squawking crows grew louder when we approached, as if the birds protested the intrusion. I imagined they claimed the body as their personal discovery and were willing to defend it. It was a ridiculous notion, but maybe not, given the circumstances. Panicked, I picked up the pace and suppressed the urge to chatter about the percentages of murders committed in Warren County each year.

I raised an unsteady arm to point. "There, in the far-right corner, next to the tree line."

Sheriff Parker, Joe Smuthers, and his assistants stopped for a moment. The coroner was the first to speak. "Saul, you and Emery cordon off the site ten feet each side. No less. Understood?" He barked the order with a sourness in his voice then turned to me. "What time exactly would you say you found the body?" He pulled out an overly large black ledger and clicked open his ballpoint pen.

"I already got what you need, Joe," Parker said.

Smuthers held up his hand. "I'd like to take my own notes, if you don't mind." His mouth formed a stiff smile while Parker nodded in silence.

"Ah…" I took out my phone to pull up my recent calls. I noted the one to the sheriff's office. "I'd say it was nearly one-thirty, give or take a few minutes."

Smuthers nodded as he scribbled in his ledger. He clipped the pen to the cover and marched off toward the gravesite.

"Don't mind him. Irritable as he might be, he's good at his job, more dedicated than any I've known. Leaves little time for the pleasantries of conversation," Parker said.

I gave a slight nod. *Takes one to know one.* I crossed my arms and hugged them tightly to my chest. A cool breeze rushed through and moved in dark clouds overhead to shade the sun briefly. "Might rain soon."

"Yep. It might." He chuckled. "And it would certainly rile Smuthers. Talk about messing with his crime scene."

I studied Parker's face for a moment. When he smiled, tiny crinkles feathered out from the corners of cornflower blue eyes. They seemed more pronounced because of his deeply tanned, rugged skin. I estimated his age to be no more than late thirties, but he'd become sheriff almost eight years ago, only a year after he moved to Warren. That would've made him twenty-something when he started, rather young to be promoted to such a position of authority. He was tall and his build was noticeably trim and firm—in contrast to my curvy, five-foot-five frame. He most likely kept active. At once, the image of Parker working out at the gym made me queasy.

"Oh, boy." I placed an arm tightly over my stomach. No surprise. It finally hit me, the horrifying experience of it all. "You think this will take much longer?" My lips pressed together and I stifled a groan while waiting for him to answer.

"I imagine Joe will take quite a while to examine the body." Parker tilted his head and frowned. "I must say you look a bit peaked. If you like, we can finish your account of this tomorrow." He stuffed the notepad back in his shirt pocket, as if that ended the matter.

I certainly wasn't about to argue. I squinted my eyes to shade them as the clouds vanished and intense sunlight returned. I'd left my sunglasses on the dashboard and now a headache threatened to take over. Nausea and headache. A deadly combo. "Tomorrow morning? I'm free until one."

"I have a meeting with my deputies scheduled at nine. Let's say ten-thirty. You know your way? My office is on the first floor. Just ask at the front desk."

I nodded. "I've been there before." Several times. I shuddered at the unpleasant childhood memories. "I'll see you tomorrow, then. Good luck." I tipped my chin upward and let my gaze travel past the rows of gravestones to settle on Joe Smuthers as he squatted down next to the open grave.

"Never count on luck, Miss Mackenzie. It's hard work with a lot of sweat most times. Especially when a murder case comes along," Parker said.

"Handled many of those, have you?" I tried being polite, even though all I wanted was to leave the cemetery and the gruesome scene, and soon, before I hurled all over Parker's shiny black shoes.

"Ah, no. I assisted on one at my previous post. First year as a deputy." Parker shook his head. "Finally closed the case after a couple years. Never got any answers."

I swallowed hard and held out my hand to shake his. "Maybe this one will turn out better. Until tomorrow?"

Quickly, I set my legs in motion to leave Parker and the crime scene. Every nerve in my body sparked and triggered emotions better left alone. The body, the one whose features reminded me of Reese Logan, and all those memories I didn't much like to recall, got the best of me. I'd have to get myself together before tomorrow morning's visit with the sheriff. Nearly all murder suspects indicated their guilt through nervous behavior while being interrogated. I forgot the exact percentage, and that lack of recall reaffirmed how distraught I must be.

"A hot meal, warm bath, and a full night's sleep. That's what I need. Then I can start to figure this out," I mumbled and griped until I reached the truck. I threw open the door, and with swift moves slid behind the wheel and turned on the ignition. In seconds, I sped down the dirt drive and steered around all three authority vehicles like a pro. Once I reached the highway, my pulse slowed, my stomach settled, and the muscles in my back eased to relax my shoulders. With one free hand, I dug inside the bag until I grabbed hold of my phone. Uncle Chaz had to be either steaming mad or fraught with worry by this point.

"Call Chaz," I commanded and waited for the call to open.

"Saints be blessed. What took you so long? I don't know whether to scold you or say a prayer you're alive," Chaz snarled.

I swallowed a chuckle and cleared my throat. Behind his thick armor rested a soft and gentle heart. He hid it well from most everyone, but not from me. "Well, thank you, I think. And yes, I'm simply peachy, or almost as much."

"Maybe you could explain? I don't like playin' twenty questions."

"To sum it up, all short and sweet as you like it, there's a dead man with a hole in his chest back at Cornplanter's. I stumbled, almost literally, onto his open grave." I paused to take a deep breath. My nerves threatened to frazzle and break me again.

"You called Sheriff Parker, and I assume he came tearin' up there, salivatin' over the possibility of investigatin' a real crime for once," Chaz added.

I detected his bitter tone. Chaz had no praise for Warren authorities. Not after a few personal altercations, which he claimed were handled unprofessionally. Quite the opposite, I didn't slight the men in uniform. And never would I make excuses for my family.

"He came, but hardly seemed excited over the fact. I'd say he even looked sad."

"If you say so. How about Joe Smuthers and his entourage of monkeys? I'm sure they added to the fun. You can't argue that he must've been pleased as a preacher on Sunday to see a dead body, in an open grave no less."

"I can't say one way or another. He's as dead pan with his emotions as I've ever witnessed."

It was true. No one could possibly discern what that man was feeling—and I was a fair expert at reading people's emotions. There was a fact about the percentages of those who easily read facial expressions, but that detail evaded me, as well.

I was definitely off my game today. My mind ventured onto other topics when a deer leaped out from the wooded edge and landed on the road. I swerved and missed clipping its rear end. "All right. Focus, Mackenzie," I muttered and gripped the wheel.

"Focus? I am focused. I'm as focused as this crippled body can be."

"Not you. Anyway, I'm ready to switch topics. This one has me seeing things."

"What things? Now you got me askin' those questions, anyway. Try explainin' better, like what are you seein' that you shouldn't?"

"If I told you, you'd insist I take a long vacation. Let's say I'm overloaded with the sight of dead people and grave markers of, yes, dead people. I'd like to focus on the living for a bit, if you don't mind," I argued.

"Right. Am I to be expectin' you soon?"

"Soon as I make it back around the reservoir and a quick stop at Big Joe's. I'll bring home a jar of those pickles you love."

"About an hour, then. And thank you much for the pickles. I already started supper. Slow cookin' our meal today. Venison stew."

"Thanks, Uncle Chaz. Love you." I tossed my phone on the seat and concentrated on the drive once more. Getting through this day was all I wanted. Tomorrow brought a new start, and with any luck, it might turn out a whole heap better.

Chapter 3

I passed up Wolf Run Marina and the café. Yellow, blue, and red patio flags flapped in the wind, and patrons sat at tables with a view of the reservoir and its flock of pontoon boats floating in the harbor. Stopping for a drink at Docksiders Café was tempting but getting home seemed more urgent. Besides, relaxing was out of the question. My mind wrestled with all those thoughts about the dead, despite my claim to Chaz that I needed to concentrate on the living. Some things, like my emotions, never worked the way I wanted.

On impulse, I picked up the phone once more. "Call Nash." I'd avoided him all morning, since we'd left our conversation last night on a sour note. Talk about avoidance issues.

"Hey, boss."

The deep tenor of his voice managed to waken those warm places inside me and create heart-racing moments I'd rather sidestep and forget. However, I winced at the word *boss* and the needling emphasis he gave it. "Hi, Nash. Thought I'd check to see if the delivery from the beer distributor came in this morning." I skated around last evening's argument. It frustrated me to admit he'd do the same. It was the dance we stepped to on occasion when we disagreed.

"Early morning. Nearly didn't make it here to meet and greet him. How are you today? Better, I hope."

How about that? He did try to stir up the issue, though in a roundabout way. "It's been quite a day, so far. I'll say that much. The rest will have to wait until later. I'm heading home, but I promise to be in by seven or thereabouts. You think you can handle things until then?"

"Don't I always?"

I grimaced at the likely dig at me for not tending to the bar as much as I should. I deserved it. Uncle Chaz and his project swallowed up too many hours for too many days. I needed to correct that and balance my obligations. That included the bar.

"I promise things will change. I'm sorry about last night. I expect this particular research has taken a toll on me emotionally, as well as physically. Forgive me?" There. I took the higher road and hoped he would accept it.

Nash was my best friend. At least it was how our relationship played out most of the time. Though, as of late, I'd begun to question what we had. He acted differently, and, for the life of me, I didn't know how to define it. We'd been friends since high school when he'd come to live in Priest Hollow. The building had housed all grades, K through twelve, and a ninth-grade class of no more than twenty-five. Nash Redwing couldn't have hidden from all the curious eyes if he'd tried. He'd remained an enigma with his quiet, somewhat stoic nature. The only time he'd allowed anyone in was when he'd played his guitar and sang. And those moments had been beautiful. It was like his voice had showered people with magic. At least he'd made me feel that way. Still did.

"Nothing to forgive. Hey, before you go, if Chaz

cooks this afternoon, please bring me a doggie bag."

The pleading in his voice made me grin. "What if I told you I'm in charge of supper this evening?"

"I can always fry up a mess of trout. There's some in the freezer."

"Relax. The cook of the family is making his venison stew. You don't have to worry about offending me."

"Oh, that's not what worries me. I'd like to live another day without my stomach finding unpleasant ways to protest the contents of your cooking."

"Ha! That's harsh," I teased, but my insides warmed up to his humor. Truth was, I avoided most tasks done in the kitchen other than washing dishes or mopping the floor.

"Nothing you haven't heard before. I'll see you later this evening. I still have to clean the bar and set up the stage," Nash said before ending the call.

I stuck the phone back in my bag while spotting the Penn Avenue Bridge a few yards ahead. Slowing down, I made the right turn and crossed over the river. The Allegheny's surface remained several inches low. It had been a hot June with little rain. July wasn't promising to be any different. Not the usual for the northwest corner of Pennsylvania. Even in the mountainous town of Priest Hollow where cooler nights and comfortable days were common, the grass showed signs of browning out.

As I maneuvered the streets through town, I let my mind linger on Nash. Complicated was the first word I'd use to describe him. Always had been. Brooding, sentimental, intelligent. He had a lot to say, but seldom did.

In some ways, Nash Redwing saved me when he showed up in Priest Hollow fifteen years ago. My mother had abandoned the family and then died a year later. Nash's friendship provided solace that I've always cherished, even when he moved away.

After a quick stop at Big Joe's for pickles, I was back on Hatch Run Road heading for home. In twenty minutes, I'd pull into my drive. Another ten, we'd sit down to supper, and at last, I'd chew on Uncle Chaz's ear about the mystery man lying in Cornplanter Cemetery. I wondered what he'd have to say about the body's resemblance to Reese Logan. With a forward and cantankerous manner, he'd most likely tell me whatever he thought. No matter if I wanted to hear it, good or bad, complimentary or condescending, he'd dish it out. But I had to tell someone, because I was bursting with the juicy news.

The dry weeks of summer had left most of the back roads covered with a powdery layer of dust. The truck tires stirred it up, and a cloud of brown trailed behind me as I sped down Roper Hollow Road. The path twisted and wound at least a mile beyond the turnoff and led far back into the woods. Peepers croaked, chickadees whistled, but, otherwise, the surroundings offered a quiet, peaceful retreat without the sounds of traffic and other man-made noises to distract or annoy folks.

Once I rounded the last bend, I spotted the familiar white patch of siding with its fresh coat of paint. It stood out against the dense greenery, and a hundred or so yards to the right sat the cottage belonging to Uncle Chaz. He'd insisted on his own space, and I was more than willing, even relieved, to give it to him. At twenty-nine, I deserved my own space, too. Not that I had much of a social life. Occasional, though infrequent, visits from Nash, most of the time to talk business, and my get-togethers with Callie, which had dwindled to almost never in the past few years, about summed it up.

In recent years, thinking of Callie saddened me. Callie was Reese's sister. We used to be the closest of friends and shared everything. I wanted to talk with her about my experience at the cemetery, but it was selfish to consider. For now, I'd put it aside. Most likely, my mind was playing tricks, which had to be the logical answer, and the John Doe resting in that grave was some stranger I'd never met. And wouldn't it be nice to avoid stirring up old ghosts?

The truck bumped and dipped on the crude gravel drive as I pulled up to the house. The deep, throaty bark of Opal greeted me as I stepped onto the porch. Once I opened the door, two huge forepaws pressed against my chest, followed by some warm, slobbery kisses. I scratched Opal's chest with its patch of white on an otherwise coal black body of fur. "You're such a good girl. Yes, you are." With a free hand, I dug into the box of treats sitting on the counter and tossed her a couple. This gave me the needed moment to set my things down.

Opal was in fact Chaz's guide dog, but he refused to have her stay with him. I knew his protest was nothing more than denying he needed help. Sort of like his last bit of independence. I didn't argue much about it since it would do no good. Besides, I enjoyed Opal's company. And the sad reality was that Uncle Chaz's eyes would eventually lose what sight he still possessed. Opal would be a godsend then, and I knew he knew it.

"You ready to go visit Uncle Chaz? I bet you've been smelling that stew all afternoon, haven't you?" I grinned and bent down to touch her, nose to nose. "Maybe if you smile pretty and wag that flirty tale, he'll give you some." Opal let out a hearty bark and I laughed. "You are such a charmer, you are. Come on. I'm starved."

We trotted across the yard until we reached the thicket of trees and brush. With careful steps, I skirted around the prickly bushes until I arrived on Chaz's doorstep. Opal had found her own way and sat on the porch with tail wagging. I didn't bother to knock since a few loud barks had already announced our presence.

"Door's open. Stew's ready." Chaz always came to the point with his words. I guessed that was one reason he and Nash got on so well. Low-maintenance, no-fuss conversation. It was a perk for both of them.

I patted Opal's head as we stepped inside. "Smells good, and we're starving."

I did a quick scan of the room. Books and papers filled the top of his desk. Dirty plates, one with a half-eaten sandwich and chips and the other with a puddle of melted ice cream rested on the counter. I zigzagged across the floor to avoid any food particles that may have dropped. I suppressed the nose-crinkling response bent on showing my disgust. It never changed his behavior, anyway.

Chaz remained quiet as he set bowls and glasses on the table along with the pot and serving spoon. Silverware clinked against china while his hands shook a bit to finish the place setting.

I waited for it, and it came.

"No reason to waste my stew on a dog. She has her own food, don't she?"

I patted Opal on the head without a word. After pouring drinks and dishing out a healthy portion of stew for both of us, I sat down and waited for Chaz to roll in and take his place.

He folded his hands and I followed suit. "Come, dear Lord, be our guest. Let this food be blessed," he mumbled and then passed the bread. "Tell me more about this body you found."

I swallowed a bite of stew. "I swear, Uncle Chaz, it had me shivering and shaking for a moment. Maybe because, well, after all, it's in a cemetery. But that's not the half of it." I pointed my fork at him.

Opal rested her chin on my leg. With the next bite of

stew, I put a napkin to my mouth and coughed. "Excuse me. Got a tickle in my throat." I laid the napkin in my lap. Opal nosed into it and retrieved the piece of meat.

"Might this have to do with your words about seein' things?" Chaz worked his jaw as he waited.

I shrugged. "Somewhat. You see, when I first glanced into that hole, I had a strange feeling come over me. When I looked again, the feeling became clearer."

"How so?"

"This will sound crazy, but the face staring up at me looked a lot like Reese Logan." The last few words came out barely above a whisper. I held my breath and waited for Chaz's response. Loony loon, right? Why should he think any different?

"Reese Logan, huh?" Chaz nodded as he chewed. After a long pause, he added. "Well, they say everyone has a twin. Maybe this'n is his."

"Oh, good gravy. Is that the best you can give me?" I sat back in my chair. This was worse than calling me a crazy person. "I'm surprised you don't have a stronger opinion on the matter." This time, I didn't try to hide it. I plucked out another chunk of venison from the bowl and dropped it on the floor. Opal snatched it up and gulped it down in seconds.

"Good as it gets. I can't say what you should think, one way or another. If you tell me he looks like Reese, then he must. Sayin' he looks like don't mean everythin', does it? And, missy, if you are hell-bent on feedin' that dog my stew, set out a bowl instead of moppin' my floor with it."

My cheeks burned as I mumbled an apology. In a few quick moves, I pulled a bowl off the cupboard shelf, scooped a spoonful of stew into it, and set it on the floor. Opal devoured the tasty meal before I sat down.

"You're right. Even if he looks like Reese, doesn't

mean it's him. Anyway, it can't be him. He's been dead for ten years," I reasoned aloud and finished my meal.

It didn't erase the image of his face, though. His *dead* face. I shivered as I cradled the bowls and glasses in my arms and carried them to the sink. Chaz wheeled close behind with the pot and silverware.

"True enough. I expect Jeb Parker will figure it out. Most likely, sooner than the uppity-nosed Coroner Smuthers can manage." Chaz snorted.

I raised my brow to form a wide arch. "Before, you argued that the sheriff didn't have the skills. And I'll admit, after this afternoon's encounter, I found him somewhat lacking in ability to take charge. Now, you say he can outsmart Joe Smuthers? Make up your mind." I scraped the leftover sandwich and chips into the trash and added plates to the cleanup. A combination of irritable, frustrating, and panicky emotions set my energy into overdrive. Within minutes, I'd dried the last of the dishes and closed the cupboard doors.

"Don't matter to me who does what. Not my affair." He scooped a healthy portion of stew into a plastic container for Nash and slid it across the counter in my direction. His hand paused a second before he pulled out a large chunk of meat and held it above Opal's head. She sat up on two hind legs and whimpered before Chaz dropped it into her mouth.

"Ha! Since when is anything not your affair? Around here, you are known as the go-to man. Most folks who want details on past or present events point their fingers at you and come running." I leaned sideways and dipped down to whisper in his ear. "You are dying to know the name of our John Doe. No pun intended."

Chaz raised and lowered his shoulders. "I'm curious, but not about to spend one minute dwellin' on it or helpin' if they come runnin', as you put it. I got too much on my plate. Speakin' of plates, let's take a listen to those names and dates you recorded."

"Left my recorder at home. I'll bring it round tomorrow sometime, after my visit with Sheriff Parker."

My stomach churned at the reminder of our appointed rendezvous. I didn't have much to tell him, but I hoped he'd have something interesting to share with me. Like maybe the identity of the body. Odds were, he wouldn't know yet. Smuthers would have to do his thing, and that took time.

"Don't expect him to tell you much. He's tight-lipped, that one."

"I know. Maybe since I found the body, he might make an exception."

"Don't. I see that look in your eyes, all full of bright and shiny optimism. Whenever will you learn, Sarah Blue Mackenzie? Life don't carry on that way." Chaz wheeled slowly over to the picture window in the living room and stared out across the front yard.

I studied his back with sadness. "Please stop torturing yourself."

"I miss her each and every day. After leavin' the mines to come here, I'll admit I had plenty of doubt about my decision. That all disappeared the moment I saw my Grace. I screwed up, Mac." His voice cracked. "And I can't blame her none for leavin'. My ugly meanness drove her from our home. Plain and simple."

I sighed. The conversation was far from new, yet it never changed things. The diabetes had taken a cruel toll on Chaz's body, both physically and emotionally. In due course, he lost the use of both legs, and his sight dimmed more and more each year. His bright, refreshing outlook on life shriveled away. No wonder he lashed out and hurt all those around him, even the one he loved most.

It was hardly worth the effort, but I always made an

attempt. "You've done a lot of good, too. What about your degree? How many folks would go back to school that late in life? You earned it. Nobody can argue that."

"I'm just an old fool who wouldn't listen. Not to doctors about this cruel disease. Not to my wife about our marriage. And here I am." His shoulders shook.

Anger surged through me. I smacked my hand on the table. "Yes. And here you are. Writing all those books and articles, making a name for yourself. Plenty of folks appreciate that."

"Alone and miserable. That's what I am."

"You've got me, dammit. Whether you accept it or not," I snapped. His words, or lack of them, hurt. Did he think I couldn't understand? I'd lost both parents by the age of eighteen. I had no siblings. Why didn't he consider that? "And you've had plenty of family to help you along the way. Including your brother and my dad. Remember?"

When he didn't answer, I crossed the room to stand behind him. My heart skipped a beat, and while hot tears stung my cheeks, I choked on the cry wanting to escape my lips. "I know life hasn't played fair, Uncle Chaz. But we live with our choices, good and bad. You're strong in so many ways. You have to push on. I need you, even if you don't recognize it."

Chaz reached up with one arm and patted my hand. "I recognize that, Sarah Blue. I recognize." After clearing his throat, he turned to face me just as I dried my eyes. "Now, as for Reese Logan. He made his own fate. If he hadn't gone to the warehouse that evenin', gettin' all fired up over money, he'd most likely be alive today. Not charred to crispy bits in that fire."

"We don't know that for sure. Authorities never closed the case." I shivered hearing his description. The memory of Dillard Hopewell came to mind. How he'd come forward to tell authorities Reese wanted to arrange a meeting and straighten out a business deal they'd shared.

According to the *Warren Gazette* article, Dillard explained the deal had gone sour, and the two of them had argued over money when Reese claimed Dillard owed him. Dillard told the authorities there was absolutely no truth to Reese's claim. He'd only agreed to meet with him because Reese wouldn't let the matter go. They were to talk about a new arrangement, another business deal. The agreed upon location was the warehouse, but at the last minute, Dillard had a family emergency and didn't go. His story sounded reasonable, since I'd heard Reese complain about Dillard a couple days before the fire.

"Only because they couldn't identify any of the remains. You know what Miss Birdie said," Chaz argued.

Miss Birdie. I recalled her words like it was yesterday. This came a day or two after the fire, after authorities had sifted through the remains and found the charred bits Uncle Chaz referred to, but, mostly, it was powdery dust. However, they discovered some valuable evidence lying close by. Once the lab team in Philadelphia had given it a strong cleaning to remove the black residue, they were able to identify a watch and a belt buckle, both made of silver and carved with Reese Logan's initials. The fire marshal commented how if the fire had burned much longer, they might not have salvaged those items. Thank goodness for the durability of silver.

On the other hand, the human remains told them nothing. Not even the teeth were salvageable to ID dental records. Only one particular fact seemed to sway them in Reese's direction. A bystander, Miss Birdie, who was out walking her dog, witnessed the fiery explosion and claimed someone fitting Reese's description entered the warehouse only minutes before the fire.

Furthermore, Coroner Smuthers determined there was enough alcohol in and on the victim to cause him to burn in much quicker time than was typical. I puzzled over his claim. Reese seldom drank liquor, and certainly not enough to do what Smuthers evidenced. Still, the physical description the witness gave described Reese in some respect. Tall, dark-skinned. But wearing a ball cap and ragged army jacket? At the time, I argued with the authorities about it. None of it mattered. The final report labeled it as an unsolved case of arson and with an unknown victim.

Still today, it remained in the cold case files. Most everyone had their doubts. Gossip was gossip. In Warren, Priest Hollow, or any other town, it was that way. Reese was gone, disappeared, never to be seen again. I'd heard the story so often, I'd begun to believe it myself. Whatever the true story, Reese Logan may as well have perished in the fire.

Dillard was found in the clear. He had a solid alibi. He came home the next day after receiving the call about Reese and the fire then went straight to the authorities to tell his story.

"Despite your gloomy outlook on things, I believe life tends to rule with a balance. Positive experiences come along when needed to level the playing field. You should try a little bit of optimism." I smiled, despite the mood Chaz brought down on us. Even Opal lay in a corner with one paw covering her head.

"Think what you will. And I prefer my glass half empty, thank you kindly." Chaz turned back to stare out the window.

"Fine. Everything's cleaned up and put away. I'm heading over to the bar before Nash throws a fit. Do you mind if I leave Opal here?" I waited for the affirmative response. He may love Opal's company, but it had to look like he was doing me the favor, not the other way around.

After hearing the grunt of approval, I slipped out the door with keys and plastic container in hand. I skirted through the woods and sprinted across the grassy lawn. Within minutes, I was fueling down Scandia Road, south toward Priest Hollow and Moe's Deja Blue. I sparked with energy and grew more anxious by the second to see Nash and tell him all about the morning's traumatic event.

Chapter 4

oe's Deja Blue was nothing fancy. The bar counter, several tables, a stage to showcase the entertainment, and a kitchen where Cisco prepared no-fuss meals, like his famous deer burger with taco fries on the side. Patrons were enticed by the rustic ambiance. Antler chandeliers hung from the ceiling while antique weapons adorned the walls, along with objects of Seneca Native American art. Musk-scented candles burned and mixed with the odors of whatever was cooking in the kitchen.

The sweet music played by Nash and his band entertained the crowd every evening. Moe's was inviting and provided a homelike refuge to many.

Nash garbled his words while he scarfed down the venison stew: "Reese Logan rises from the dead. That's *my* kind of story."

"But it's not him." I reached across a nearby table to light the candle centerpiece before moving on to the next. An urge to protest made me add, "He *looks* like Reese."

"Seems you're the one who needs convinced of that particular detail." Nash scraped out the last remnants of stew from the plastic container before shoving it in the trash.

"Pretty important detail. And, no, I'm being logical, is all." I extinguished the match after lighting the last centerpiece and returned to the bar. I'd settled and re-solved my grief over him—as much as I could—a long time ago. How was I to handle facing this all over again?

"Uh huh. You want my opinion or not?"

I narrowed my eyes into slits. "Since when do you ever wait for an invitation?"

"I don't think you should rule it out. That it's Reese, I mean."

"Why? And don't bring up Miss Birdie."

"Burned beyond recognition. No viable means to identify the corpse. Sound familiar? With only a couple of personal items to persuade authorities to claim it was Reese Logan who died in that fire, sort of leaves it open to discussion." Nash kept his gaze level with mine, like he dared me to argue the point. "Admit it, Sarah. You had your doubts at the time, and still do."

"I know. I thought the same thing, which added to the spine-tingling moment back at the cemetery. I wish it was tomorrow morning and time for my meeting with Sheriff Parker. I have so many questions."

"He won't answer them. I'd say not to expect much. He goes by the book."

I sighed. "You and Uncle Chaz. What's with you two? All the time negative. No matter, I have other ways to find out." Nash's cousin, Deena, worked the front desk at the sheriff's department. Deena loved to gossip, even if the conversation dipped into that unprofessional gray area. Deena would talk.

"Don't go asking Deena. She's already on probation after a two-week suspension for leaking info about the burglaries last month." Nash wagged a finger at me. "If there's a next time, Parker promises he'll fire her."

A scowl crossed my face. Did he read minds, too? I raised a hand and crisscrossed my chest. "I promise I won't ask Deena about the body's ID." Of course, that didn't include questions as to whether or not Deena overheard any conversation between Parker and Smuthers about the case.

"They wouldn't have that yet, anyway."

My shoulders slumped. "I know. They need to wait for forensic lab results to verify who it is—or isn't." All at once my mind lit up. "Death's mailing."

"What was that?" Nash raised a brow in question.

"It has nothing to do with forensics, but all this talk about mysterious graves reminds me of the common practice used by medical students back in nineteenth century England. They'd rob graves of freshly buried cadavers and use them for their anatomy classes. And it became quite a lucrative business for criminals. Death's mailing."

"Pleasant thoughts. But back to our current problem. Opens a big can of worms if the body turns out to be Reese," Nash said.

"You mean with questions like whose remains are buried in Reese Logan's grave?"

"Like that, and where has Reese been all these years if he didn't die in the warehouse fire?"

"Hmm." I stared out the window. Dusk painted the sky a pinkish hue. I shifted to the left when the tinkle of the bell announced a few more customers coming through the door. Within an hour, all the tables and barstools would be filled.

"You talk to Callie about this?"

I shrugged. "I think I'll wait until tomorrow after my meeting with Parker."

"Wise move." Nash slid off the barstool. He walked

around to the other side, as he grabbed a rubber band from one pocket and tied his hair back before mopping the bar counter. Never one to conform to conventional style, he'd let his mane grow down to the middle of his back since he'd returned home. Though only half Seneca, he favored that part of his heritage more than the French side.

"Give me a sign when it's time for me to take over. Okay?" I smiled. "What's on for tonight? Blues or country?" His music was a gift. Nearly three years ago, I'd made the decision to hire Nash when he returned to Priest Hollow after a long stay in Baton Rouge, broke, and homeless. Though he helped to manage Moe's Deja Blue Bar and Grill, it was his music that drew the customers. One only had to listen when Nash played and sang to know why.

He gave a casual shrug of his shoulders. "A mix of both, I think. Depends on how the crowd acts."

"They love it all." I hesitated then rested my hand on his, but for only a second. Though I tried to suppress it, the touch sparked my emotional wiring. At once, I turned to face the stage and squeezed my eyes shut as the image of Reese forced its way into my mind.

"All right then. Talk later?" Nash said.

I nodded without turning and waved my arm as I walked away to mingle with customers. The conversation kept a lively pace, and I contributed my fair share to it. However, thoughts of the murder mystery and its disturbing details interrupted my concentration more than once. No surprise, a few of Priest Hollow's residents kept me on that train of thought.

"I heard from Reed Gentry over in Warren that you discovered a body in Cornplanter Cemetery today."

I groaned while Carl Mackey chuckled and jabbed his younger friend in the side. "Ha. Good one. And, yes, I did. Now, would you like me to start a tab for you? Carl, you're Genesee, and it's Yuengling for Steve. Right?" I pulled an order pad out of my pocket while I studied the woman who sat in silence, next to Steve. Her black hair was cropped short, buzzed on the sides. She wore long earrings, silver feathers with turquoise studs. Most striking were the doe eyes, deep brown and soulful with sharply defined brows, the sort of eyes one expected easy to read, but not in this case. Hers barely stayed focused in one place long enough. They darted from side to side, like she wanted to take in every detail of the bar. I cleared my throat. "And how about you?"

Steve wrapped an arm around the woman and squeezed. "This here's Jemma Bluehawk. She moved to the area from New York, up near Ellicottville. A month or so ago?" He glanced sideways. "Jemma, Sarah Mackenzie, but we call her Mac. She owns Moe's Deja Blue."

I reached across the table to extend a hand. "Glad to meet you, Jemma. Welcome to Priest Hollow. Of course, I'd watch the company you keep. This one's full of mischief and will drag you into trouble if you're not careful," I teased, and Jemma laughed.

"Oh, don't worry. I have him figured out. Besides, I'm too busy trying to settle in and find a job. You wouldn't happen to know of anyone who's hiring?"

I scratched my nose and ticked off local businesses in my head. "Maybe Ludlow's over in Russell? It's a grocery store. Drew always seems to need help. Other than that, I can't think of any. Sorry."

"So, who do you think it is?" Carl interrupted.

"Think who is?"

My eyebrows arched into half circles and I tipped my head to the side. Why did people have to be such vultures about murder? Always speculating. Always needing the gory details. I refused to comment on it, especially with a stranger sitting at the table. Besides, Carl and Steve were locals and would find out plenty, maybe before I did. Carl's nephew was the janitor at the city building. Janitors heard everything.

"Oh, for Petey's sake. Come on. You can't give up one detail?" Carl exclaimed while he threw his arms up in the air.

I covered my lips to stifle a laugh at the sight of his desperate expression and turned back to Jemma. "Would you like something to drink?"

Jemma shrugged. "I'll have a water. I need to get up early tomorrow." She leaned forward then. "So, that sounds exciting. You finding a body."

I gripped my order pad hard enough to bend it in two. "I'd hardly call it exciting. More like frightening, but, yes, I did."

"And in a cemetery no less. That part sounds thrilling. I mean, you come to a place like that and think you'll find it peaceful, but then discover a murder victim?" Jemma placed her elbows on the table. A rigid smile formed, and she fixed her doe eyes on me. "Maybe it's both. Frightening and exciting."

I slowly gave her a nod. Jemma had no idea. "If you'll excuse me, I'll get your drinks." I hurried away before any of them said another word.

"When's Emmie coming in?" I asked, handing Nash the order.

"You should know." He let a dramatic pause go by with a feeble attempt to hide the grin behind his sternly set mouth. "Seven-thirty. Or maybe a few minutes after. Depends if the sitter comes on time."

I sighed. "I give that woman too much wiggle room. This is a business, and customers don't give a hoot if she finds it hard to get a sitter for Benny. I'll have to let her go if this keeps up."

"Don't strain yourself. That forced expression of meanness on your face doesn't come off the least bit genuine. You know Emmie is a worker." Nash set the beers and water on the counter.

It was easy enough for me to vent on the wrong person when I got flustered. Like now. All those questions and the new girl's morbid fascination with murder. Nash knew me too well. I'd never fire anyone. Especially not Emmie Wyatt. She was a hard-working employee who didn't deserve any criticism. Overnight, she had become a single mom left with a five-year-old to raise when her husband had died in Iraq, serving his country. Soon after, she'd come into the bar during a busy evening and had begged me for a job. On the spot, I'd handed her an apron and motioned her behind the counter to tend bar, no questions asked. Everybody needed a friend to help them along when tragedy touched them.

Nash leaned closer to whisper. "Tell you what, you get behind the bar and I'll deliver these to the table. It looked like you weren't having much fun with Carl, Steve, and...who is the looker sitting with them?"

I snorted, but then my lips slid into a smile. "Deal. And thank you. A word of warning though. Don't talk about death. The looker's name is Jemma Bluehawk. She's a bit on the dark side." I shook my head. "Just saying."

I fixed my gaze on Nash as he wove through the tables. Let him deal with Carl's nosiness and Jemma's gloomy nature. He would have no problem putting them in their place.

"You're Sarah Mackenzie, right?"

I twisted around at the mention of my name to see a somewhat familiar face with a tall, muscular frame to match. I frowned. "Right. And who might be asking?"

"I'm Emery Gantz, one of the coroner's assistants.

We were at the cemetery earlier this afternoon?"

My eyes widened. "Oh! Yeah, sorry. I was pretty rattled and—"

"No apology needed. I get it. It rattled me, too. And I'm supposed to deal with that stuff." He chuckled.

My mind raced. This was a rare opportunity, but if I was going to do it right, I needed to ask questions without stepping over the line. Taking a deep breath and a few seconds to relax, I gave him my most flirtatious smile. "It was nerve racking, wasn't it? I mean, the guy looked like he'd taken a bullet to the chest. Not long ago, either. Of course, I suppose Joe Smuthers had a lot to say." I lowered my head slightly and waited.

"Hmm. He keeps most of what he's thinking to himself. Not a big talker. You think I could have a boiler maker?" The muscles in Emery's face tightened.

At once, I picked up on the shift in mood. Too much, I thought and cursed myself, figuring I'd lost him. That left Deena. She was my best chance. It frustrated me how everyone else belonging to the Warren County Sheriff's department most likely would keep a firm lock on their opinions. Emery was giving me a taste of that.

"Draft beer okay?" I cooled my smile and stopped batting my eyelashes.

"Perfect. And, yes, it was a shot to the chest. And, yes, again, it's a recent wound. Maybe a day or two ago."

I stifled a gasp. Obviously, I'd read Emery wrong. Forcing my hands to keep steady, I wrapped both around the mug and set his beer on the counter, followed by the shot glass filled with Wild Turkey. "On the house."

He nodded and tilted his head back as he downed the whiskey then sipped at his beer. "I shouldn't be talking about this, but you seem like someone who'd keep it quiet." His smile grew warmer. He leaned in and his voice lowered to speak. "I know this might be too forward of me, but what the heck. Spontaneity keeps things interesting, right? I was just thinking maybe we can get together sometime, catch a movie or dinner?"

"Ah, yeah, maybe so. And of course I won't tell anyone about the case. Don't want to be the cause of trouble for you." I smiled and resumed the flirtation. Might as well play along. *Be subtle*, I warned myself and lowered my head while mopping the counter. "Any guesses as to who the victim is?"

"Nah. Joe's got his work to do. Once the lab comes back, I'm sure we'll get an ID."

"A murder investigation. Boy, I bet that's got the department all in a tizzy." With a casual gesture, I raised my eyes to meet Emery's. He stared at me, unblinking, over the tip of his beer mug. I shuddered.

"First one in almost fifteen years, I hear," he said.

"Before Sheriff Parker's term."

"Yep. Sheriff Billings was in charge back then."

"I expect Parker has his plate full. Solving a murder can be such a tall order." I folded my arms and rested them on the counter. My brain worked at a rabbit's pace as I thought about all the trivia on murder. "It's a real shame. Did you know the number of solved murder cases in the US has dropped in the past twenty years from ninety to sixty-five percent?" A sudden rush of adrenaline kicked my wheels into high gear. I was back on my game. "And in Mexico, ninety-eight percent of murders go unsolved."

Emery's eyebrows arched. "How about that? I wasn't aware."

I bit down on my lip to suppress the giggle bubbling to the surface. Emery Gantz might be having second thoughts about a date night, I figured.

"Of course, it's worse in big cities, but still," I continued, now on a roll, "six thousand murders every year with a mere sixty-five percent solved. It's a scary thought."

Emery leaned back and laughed. His eyes grew wide as he shook his head. "How—"

"She likes to read a lot." Nash came up behind Emery, who straightened his back and scowled then turned to face Nash.

I stiffened as Nash gave him a cool stare in return. "Emery, this is my close friend and business manager, Nash Redwing. Nash, Emery Gantz. He works for the coroner."

It was an alpha male meets alpha male kind of moment. Most likely, Emery would measure Nash up and cut his losses. I let go of a smile. No dating in the foreseeable future.

"I enjoy reading, too. There's no way my brain can carry that much information around all the time," Emery said but kept a guarded look on Nash.

"It's a gift she has," Nash said and turned to me. "I'm almost ready to go on. Emmie should be here any minute. You need anything else, boss?"

"I'm good. And here she comes through the door now." I waved to Emmie as Nash headed for the stage. Turning back to Emery, I added, "I hope all my babbling about murder didn't alarm you. I do research for my uncle. He writes history books and articles which need a lot of facts and figures. For some odd reason, most of it sticks in my head. I can't help it." I shrugged, letting a lopsided grin express my apology. His eyes were so easy to read. The alarm had gone off in his head with the words "weirdo alert" screaming, loud and clear. I wouldn't be running into Emery Gantz anytime soon.

"Everyone's got their thing." He set the mug on the counter. "I should go. I have an early shift tomorrow and need to rest up. Besides, if I oversleep...well, let's just say the coroner doesn't take kindly to tardiness."

I chuckled and nodded at Emmie as she slid behind the counter. "I'm not surprised. Tell Smuthers I wish him the best of luck on the case."

"Oh, no. He doesn't believe in luck." Emery pointed a finger to the side of his head. "Brains and careful detail to one's work, that's what solves cases. And I'm quoting the master."

"Sounds like he and Parker make a great team." I recalled the sheriff's similar remark, though my hunch was Smuthers, not Parker, was the real deal.

"I'd say it's where Joe Smuthers runs the show most of the time." He stood up. "It was nice talking to you. Thanks for the drink."

My gaze followed him until he disappeared. The bar and the crowd of customers who all focused their attention on the stage drifted away as Emery's news infused me with more questions. A man died in a violent way and, odds were, within the past forty-eight hours. Then he'd been dropped into an open grave, waiting for someone to discover him. That someone unfortunately was me. Was it intentional? Then again, what murderer does that? Hiding the crime seemed the logical move.

"Glad you folks decided to come out this evening. I see some familiar faces, new ones, too. Here's hoping we put on a great show for you. A little blues, rock, and if the mood hits, we'll throw in some kick-ass country to get you on the dance floor. All right, let's hit it." Nash nodded at his backup players, and they started in with a Muddy Waters tune as the stage lights dimmed to a mellow glow.

While Emmie took over the bar, I sat down on a stool to watch Nash play and sing. His fingers rolled over and picked at the strings of his Gibson. How would those smooth moves and controlled hands be when making love?

I squirmed to adjust my rear on the seat. Thoughts like that made relationships complicated. Our friendship was comfortable. Easy and familiar. Of course, I wasn't fooling anyone. The excuse I gave anybody who asked why I didn't date was a lie. I didn't have time for love. I had a business to run and a sick uncle to care for. The truth was, if I admitted it? I was afraid. Pure and simple. After my miserable life and who I'd lost, no one should blame me. Sure, Nash teased with flirty words, touched the small of my back, placed his hand over mine for long, lingering moments, and even gave me an affectionate peck on the cheek occasionally. Yet, he'd never said words like *I love you, Sarah*, or asked me if I wanted to date. His behavior up to now wasn't enough to convince my reluctant-for-love attitude that he wanted more. Besides, a really genuine friend was hard to come by. My shoulders drooped as I shifted more deliberately on the stool. "One excuse is as good as another," I muttered.

"I am singin' you the blues. My woman left me and the whole world's got me down…"

At once, my back straightened as I remembered where my reasoning had been headed. "What if the killer was interrupted? What if he was ready to cover the body, but something or someone scared him off?" I whispered.

"What did you say? Something about a killer?" Emmie frowned at me as she topped off a tall boy and handed it to the customer.

I brought a finger to my lips then tilted my head toward the other end of the counter. I stepped sideways, along the bar, and Emmie followed.

"What's up?" Emmie asked.

I leaned forward and kept my voice lowered. "Okay. This will sound like a crazy question, but play along." I paused, rethinking the idea, but after a second or two I moved forward. "Let's say you murdered somebody. I mean, I know you wouldn't, but for the sake of this discussion, if you did, what would you want to do with the body?" I gave Emmie an eager nod and waited.

Emmie straightened, her mouth formed into a circle, and her eyes looked as if they'd pop out and roll across the counter.

"I know, I know. This is crazy, but please don't spaz out and faint or something. Just answer the question." I clenched my jaw and my hands gripped the counter. I should have remembered Emmie tended to overreact. What was I thinking?

Emmie took a deep breath and whispered, "You are insane, Sarah Mackenzie, but I'd say if I murdered someone, I'd get rid of that body. Hide it where nobody would find it for years or ever."

I smacked my hand on the counter so hard that Emmie jumped. "Exactly what I thought." Without explaining, I turned to walk back to my stool. Emmie stepped along to keep up with me.

"This is about that body you found in Cornplanter Cemetery, isn't it?" she hissed.

I nodded but avoided further comment. "Good evening, Clint David. It's nice to see you out and about."

He saddled up to the bar while Emmie poured his usual beverage. "I was ready to climb the walls along with the cat. I wanted out of my house worse than anything I can recall. Tonight's my grand escape." He slapped his thigh and added, "Leg's doing fine now."

"Well, thanks for choosing Moe's as your first stop," I said. "I'm sure you being one of Dad's best friends makes him smile down on us right now, pleased to see you."

I patted his shoulder before heading toward the stage. A quick glance at Emmie showed me she wasn't ready to drop the subject of murder and bodies left in cemeteries.

Fair enough, but the discussion had to wait until curious ears weren't listening. I shimmied sideways between two crowded tables but kept my eyes on Nash. Whenever I found the time to watch the show, a table up front waited for me, off to the left of the stage. The sign with "reserved for proprietor" remained on display to claim the spot, even when the bar grew crowded. Nash insisted.

As I reached the stage, a vibration tickled my thigh. I shoved a hand into my pocket and pulled out the phone. I frowned at the unfamiliar number displayed with its message but stiffened in wild-eyed surprise as I read the words. Dropping into the chair with a thud, I reread the message slowly.

Wise people say it's best to leave matters alone that don't concern you. Consider this a warning. ~ Spirit Talker.

Chapter 5

The time slipped past one as the remaining handful of customers waved before disappearing out the door. I locked the entrance and flipped the switch to turn up the lights. Lingering odors of leftover fries and taco burgers wafted across the room. Passing from one table and onto the next, I loaded a cart with plates and glasses. Cisco came out of the kitchen to take the cart off my hands.

"Thanks, Cisco. You can leave once the dishwasher gets started. I know it's been a long evening."

"Nice for business, though." Cisco nodded before wheeling the cart away.

I returned to the bar counter, untied my apron, and tossed it into the laundry hamper.

Emmie shoved glasses into the tub of sudsy water. "It makes no sense. Why would someone who calls himself Spirit Talker, which is pretty darn odd, send you a warning? All's you did was stumble on the body. It's not your fault," she argued.

"I know, but it would be stupid to ignore it, right?" I chewed on a fingernail while my foot tapped on the floor.

"Listen. Don't say anything to Nash when he comes out."

Emmie frowned. "Why not? He'd have your back in a second. If this is for real, you need all the protection you can get."

I shook my head with deliberate force. "No. I don't want him following me around like some guard dog. And that's precisely what he'd do. Leave it be, Emmie. Like you said, it makes no sense. Besides, I have to get home before Uncle Chaz has a cow. He kept Opal at his place this evening. No telling what he might do if she starts in with one of her barking fits. That man has little tolerance."

"Why would she have a barking fit?"

"Raccoons love to raid our trash late at night. Opal hates raccoons. One sniff and she's all geared up, barking and scratching at the door. I can't listen to Chaz complain on end. I have to get some sleep. Got my meeting with the sheriff tomorrow morning..." I trailed off as I stared out the window with its view of the parking lot. The full moon cast a yellow glow across the ground, leaving no place for shadows. It would be an easier ride back home.

"Why don't you go on? I can lock up," Emmie offered.

I raised my eyebrows. "You sure?"

"Yep. Nash is still here, and I personally don't mind his protection." Emmie flashed an impish grin.

"Ha. All right, then. Tell Nash I'll call him tomorrow after my meeting with Sheriff Parker." I snatched my handbag and jacket from behind the bar and hastened to make an exit before Nash appeared. Without a doubt, one look at my face, and he'd read the troubling thought currently occupying my brain. I needed time to sort this out and stop worrying. The message from Spirit Talker left me a bit frightened, definitely unnerved, yet somehow curious. Which emotion would take the lead and dictate my next move, I wondered? Hopefully by tomorrow morning I'd have my answer.

The cool chill of night air rejuvenated my energy levels. I drove down the road and lowered the window to breathe in fresh scents of pine, mulch and dampened field grass, and the sweet fragrance of Pink Lady Slipper orchids budding in the shadows of trees. The resonating chirp of night peepers calmed my nerves and chased away every anxiety about bodies and warnings and murder.

At the last bend in the road, I eased up on the gas pedal to creep into the drive but heaved a loud moan when gravel popped and crackled, most assuredly loud enough to wake Chaz from his light sleep. And that would cause a whole different stream of complaints. As it was, the shrill bark of Opal managed its own alarm. I winced as I reached the end of the drive and exited the truck.

Cautiously, I stepped up to the porch. On the other side of the door, Chaz snapped his command to quiet Opal. His next words, however, caused me to chuckle. My hand closed over the door knob as I waited for him to finish.

"Good dog. Here's a treat for you. You just keep lettin' me know when there's company. Good dog." Chaz softened his tone.

"I told you she'd eventually wear on you in a good way," I said, entering the house.

"Wear on me is one way of puttin' it. Late night, heh?" Chaz rolled over to the sink and dropped his glass into it.

A half empty bottle of Wild Turkey rested on the table. I frowned. "You in much pain?" Reaching down, I scratched Opal's head.

"This weren't for medicinal reasons, missy."

"I see." I bit down on my tongue. It was a well-worn

argument not worth repeating. "Nash drew a decent crowd this evening. I kept the place open an hour longer since business was good. And then I got to talking with Emmie." I shrugged.

"The bar draws the customers. Nash is an added attraction," Chaz said, his tone argumentative as he lay both hands in his lap. "Next time, give me a call when you're plannin' on a late one."

I glanced once more at the whiskey bottle. "It doesn't matter what draws them. We made good money. Enough to pay the bills this month and next. I think I'll buy steaks for dinner tomorrow evening to celebrate." Common sense warned me not to argue with a cranky old man. "And you don't need to worry if I'm later than usual."

"Fine by me. Now, I'd like to get some proper shut-eye, so how 'bout you take this mutt with you," Chaz grumped before turning his chair around to face the bedroom hallway.

"Good night, Uncle Chaz. Pleasant dreams." I smiled and motioned for Opal to follow me out the door.

⌘⌘⌘

By morning, a troubled mix of emotions still left their mark. Of course, I'd never been threatened before in such a way. The messenger's name alone—Spirit Talker—puzzled me and caused some concern. This, on top of my discovery in Cornplanter Cemetery? It was enough to unsettle anyone. What direction was I supposed to take?

"Go meet with Sheriff Parker, for one." I sighed. While Opal chowed down on kibble, I occupied myself by mulling over Emery Gantz's disclosure about the body. New shivers waved their way through my body. Our tiny community, tucked deep inside the Allegheny forest, had a murderer in its midst. And I had the misfortune to be the one who stumbled upon his victim. Literally. Well, almost. And, by the hand of fate, I'd become a major player—like it or not.

"You be a good girl and guard the fort. I think maybe you should stick around here this morning. Uncle Chaz in small doses is the most we should subject any lady to, right, girl?" I gave her a hug before I headed out the door.

Taking the direct route down Scandia Road made the ride into Warren a quick one. With a final left turn, I drove into the city parking lot. I stayed in my seat and gripped the door handle for a moment. Taking one deep breath followed by a few more, I calmed somewhat. My legs wobbled a bit as I stepped out of the truck, but, with a determined gate, I walked into the building. This wouldn't be hard. I refused to allow Parker's questions to unnerve me any further. My mind was frazzled enough. I'd done nothing wrong. My nails dug into closed fists. It was a crazy notion, believing the body was none other than Reese Logan's. Even if I convinced myself, telling anyone, especially Parker, opened me up to a Pandora's Box of ugly questions. "Oh, boy. Aren't you a mess?" I mumbled and walked through the doorway.

As I reached the front desk, my decision had been made to tell Sheriff Parker about the warning message, but only if he gave me some news in return. News about Reese Logan. If the body was his, they'd suspect it by now.

Heck, Joe Smuthers had been the Warren County coroner for over three decades, and he knew plenty about the folks who lived around these parts. And how about the others who worked here? The older employees who were related to or acquainted with the Logan family and what happened ten years ago? One of them would recognize the body's face, see the uncanny resemblance, and make a comment. Without concrete proof, of course, it wouldn't be official. But that wouldn't stop people from talking.

I stood at the counter and smiled at Deena Redwing, who gave me a big grin in return. Her round face dimpled with the pleasant gesture and her almond-shaped eyes twinkled.

"Hey, Deena. How are you?"

"Sweet and saucy, as usual. How's my cousin? He keeping out of trouble?"

I shrugged. "Only what he can manage. You know Nash and his mischief."

Deena snorted. "Sure do. You here to see the sheriff?"

"Yep." I leaned over the counter and lowered my voice to whisper. "Anything newsy about the body?"

Deena rubbed her hands together. "Oh, boy. You bet there is, but I can't talk about it here. Nosey people with jumbo ears. I take no chances. Anyway, I'm on this silly probation thing, you might know."

I frowned. "Yeah, that's a shame. Nice person like you shouldn't be punished."

"I'll say. Why don't we meet for lunch? I still get that privilege. Stingy bums. I can't take no breaks in the coffee room, and I have to go out for lunch, too."

"Why?" I didn't see the logic in that.

"I guess I upset some folks. Always talking and laughing, they say. Too much talk sours their digestive systems. Hogwash. Stupid, stupid people. It don't matter. Looking at them upsets *my* digestive system." Deena let go of a deep belly laugh.

I smiled. "How about Woody's? It's close by, and today's lunch special is rainbow trout."

"Sounds perfect. We can go after your meeting. I'll break for an early lunch."

I glanced at my watch. "You think this will take long?"

"Fifteen minutes tops. We go at around eleven? I think Woody's starts serving lunch then."

"Deal. So, where do I find Parker?" I listened to Deena's directions then made my way down to the end of the hall and rapped lightly on his door.

"Come in."

I eased the door open and peeked around the corner. "Sheriff Parker?"

Parker swiped papers into his desk drawer and rose from the chair. He shimmied his way through the tightly packed space of stacked boxes and file cabinets. "Miss Mackenzie, right on time." He extended his hand. "You must excuse the mess. I'm still settling into my new office. They tell me it's roomier." He shrugged then gripped my hand to give it a firm shake.

I followed his gesture to a nearby chair and sat down. "I'm not sure what more I can add to my story," I began. It took extreme effort to keep my voice from squeaking with nerves and anxiety.

Parker shook his head. "This is protocol for every case. I need to get details for the report, make sure it's exactly as you experienced it, you see." He quickly leaned over the desk and pressed the button on the recorder in front of him. "My writing is horrible." He shrugged with a smile. "You don't mind, do you?"

"No. Of course not." I stared at the machine and chewed on my lip. "Where do you want to start?"

"Let's go back to the morning when you first arrived at Cornplanter Cemetery. Did you notice anything out of the ordinary? Any sounds, movement, anyone come out when you drove in?"

I pushed my memory into reverse to picture yesterday's venture. The images flashed like movie frames, one

by one, right up to the second I found the open grave. I
shuddered at the thought of it and smiled nervously.
"Okay, well, I arrived there at around ten, maybe ten-
thirty. No other visitors were around. I parked my truck,
opened the passenger door to grab my bag, and headed
down the path. Nothing strange about that. I—No. Wait."
I frowned as I remembered something. A noise that didn't
belong? I struggled for a few seconds but shook my head
as the detail disappeared. "Sorry, I can't remember."

"No problem. Just move on. It may come back to
you." Parker smiled with his eyes.

I stared at them in silence for a few seconds. They
seemed to change color, bluer than yesterday and much
brighter. "All right. After I reached the first grave, I
brushed away the dirt and recorded the dates. I use a
voice recorder, too, you see." I tipped my head at the
black box sitting between us. "It helps Uncle Chaz when
he needs to go over the details. Anyhow, that's what I
kept doing, moving from one stone to the next, brushing
off dirt, reading the dates, recording the dates, it's pretty
tedious." I shifted in my seat. We were getting closer to
the moment I discovered the open grave.

"Think carefully. There was nothing different about
your routine? I mean, you say at each gravestone you
came to you used the same procedure?" Parker leaned
forward, his hands gripping the edge of his desk.

I forced myself to picture the markers, walking the
path, passing by them, from one to the next. All the
women, men, and even children like Jacob Bluehawk. At
once, I gasped. My eyes widened while I connected with
Parker's. "I think there was one tiny difference." A smile
spread my lips.

"No matter how small, it might be important," Parker
urged.

"One of the markers was clean when I got to it. No

dirt to wipe away. Not like the others." Parker seemed to deflate, and my smile flattened. "I mean, that is unusual, isn't it? All, and I'm saying nearly a hundred stones, covered with dust, dirt, leaves, and other debris, except for one?"

Parker let go of the desk and leaned back in his chair. He remained quiet for a minute before commenting. "Do you remember which stone?"

I nodded. "Joseph Bluehawk, father to Jacob and Joseph Junior Bluehawk, wife to Etta Bluehawk. He died in 1904, one year after Joseph Junior was born, and five years after his first born son, Jacob, died..." My voice trailed off into a subdued whisper.

Parker cleared his throat. "It might be of some importance, but I won't know that until we have more answers."

"Do you have any answers yet?" I said, willing my voice not to sound too eager.

Parker shook his head. "Coroner Smuthers won't have results from the lab until later this week. They're jammed full of cases from all around the county. Seems crime has heated up as much as the weather."

My shoulders dropped. "I see. Well, should I finish my account of yesterday?"

Parker nodded. "Might as well. Maybe there's another tiny detail you've yet to remember."

I hesitated. Was he being sarcastic or sincere? His tone didn't give anything away. And his face was as impossible to read as Joe Smuthers's. They could be twins. I went on to relate details of the remainder of my visit at the cemetery, minus any references to thoughts about Reese Logan or the dream with its strange music. Why share those crazy details? I relaxed when I got up to leave Parker's office. Not one slip of the tongue.

"Thank you for coming in. If you think of anything

else, let me know." Parker stood and shook my hand once more, this time less firmly.

"I will. And perhaps you'll let me know when you have an ID?" I raised a questioning gaze. Perhaps he'd see the fairness in my request.

"As soon as I can." The guarded look in his eyes implied otherwise. I knew what it meant. I'd find out when the whole town found out, and not a second before.

Covering the disappointment on my face, I said goodbye. My claim of optimism was slowly fading. Chaz and Nash had been right. I approached the front desk. The clock overhead read ten fifty-eight. Exactly fifteen minutes. Deena was good. If only she was as accurate with department gossip.

"See. What did I tell you?" Deena smiled and tapped her watch. She snatched her bag from behind the counter and shouted. "Leaving for lunch, Paula. It's all yours."

Deena grabbed my arm and hustled me out the revolving door. "Boy oh, boy oh. Do I have juicy news for you?" She threw back her head, tossed the thick, dark mane of hair over one shoulder, and laughed.

I hoped she was right. In fact, I was counting on it.

Chapter 6

Woody's restaurant was actually a diner. In 1948, the owner and decorated war hero, Woodrow Wilson—his parents adored the twenty-eighth president—bought one of the last trolley cars in Warren County and converted it into his restaurant. Though many others followed suit to build diners with newer, streamlined technology, none survived for long. Woody's did. Loyalty among town folks had never wavered, especially for a town hero.

Down to the smallest detail—even the toothpick holders and sugar dispensers, Woody's post WWII décor made customers think they'd stepped back in time. Servers were still called waitresses, and they dressed in red-checkered skirts with aprons to match.

We had settled into a booth near the door, and within minutes, a waitress named Stella delivered plates filled with generous portions.

"I tell you, tongues are wagging and ears burning from all this mess," Deena said between generous bites of pan-fried rainbow trout, fries, and slaw.

I moved my food around on the plate with a fork.

Half my meal remained and grew cold. Excitement about what Deena had to say took over my appetite. "Those were the exact words you heard?"

"Yep. Rudy's words. 'Boy, don't he look like Reese Logan? Only older.' He said it, all right. I was at the copy machine on the other side of the divider wall. I heard him plainly." Deena wiped her mouth with the napkin. "But that's not all. Like I said, tongues keep wagging, been that way since last evening and all this morning."

My stomach did another flip flop. Speculation didn't make it so, but more than one person who thought the same as me must count for something. It had been all I truly expected to learn at this point.

Deena's brows drew together. "You okay?"

"Sure. Just a lot to think about." I shrugged.

"Well, open your arms, because I'm ready to toss you the big one."

"From who?"

"How 'bout Joe Smuthers? He big enough?" Deena smiled. Her hand slid across the table and snatched a couple of fries off of my plate.

My heart raced. "What did he say?"

Deena's lips curled into a devious smile. She leaned forward as far as her stout middle would let her, squeezing in the last few inches. "I happened to be passing by the general area of the morgue this morning on my way to the little girl's room, of course." Deena nodded with a forced look of childlike innocence.

"Don't you have restrooms by the front entrance?" I tilted my head to one side.

"I needed a little exercise to work off breakfast. Rudy brought in donuts. I figured the basement restroom would do the trick."

"Especially since that's where the morgue is located." I choked down the laugh struggling to escape.

Deena scowled. "This end justifies any sort of means. And if you stop nitpicking, I'll get on with my story. Now, I happened to catch a few words of their conversation when I stopped to tie my shoe. Eh, eh! No judging." Deena wagged a finger. "Anyway, after Emery asked him what he thought, Joe answered by telling Emery to look up Callie Logan's address, because they might be needing to pay her a visit after results came in from the lab."

I leaned back in my chair. It was really happening. From the moment I'd laid eyes on the body yesterday, I had that first suspicion things may become personal, here it was, delivered to me on a platter with all the gruesome trimmings.

"When the coroner thinks it, I'd say you've got your ID." Deena pulled away from the table and released a deep breath.

"Seems so." My mind returned to Callie. She'd go through the pain of losing her brother all over again. I searched Deena's face and found common ground.

"It's gonna hurt like hell," Deena said. "When she finds out."

I lifted one hand to wipe my eyes in one swift move. I pulled out a ten and shoved it at Deena. "I should go talk to her."

"Before we have positive ID? Might be putting her through this for nothing," Deena suggested.

"I don't know. Maybe you're right. I guess I'll decide what to say when I get there." I lifted my chin. "I know this much. If or when the time comes, I won't let some cold fish like Coroner Smuthers or Sheriff Parker be the one to deliver this kind of news."

"Good point. Give my cousin a hug, and I'll call if I hear any more news from those wagging tongues." Deena wore a toothy grin as she pulled my plate of half-eaten fries across the table.

I hurried toward the exit, silently playing with the words needed to let Callie know what happened yesterday at the cemetery. I'd ease into it, suggest how strange it was. But maybe everyone was right. What if the body merely held an uncanny resemblance to Reese? Would it be fair to unload on her just to ease my own stress? Nope. I couldn't do that, wouldn't do that. At least it would be nice to visit and sit a spell. I sighed. Selfish or not, the truth was I needed this visit. I missed Callie.

My stride lengthened to rush across the street and enter the parking lot. Tripping on an uneven spot in the pavement, I nearly toppled into someone coming around the corner. Strong arms reached out instantly to catch me.

"You must not be in such a hurry."

I looked up, ready to argue that I was *not* in a hurry, only preoccupied. Instead, my breath drew in sharply as I recognized Plum Steelwater. Close up, the harsh lines of his chiseled face were well-defined, and his eyes, dark as Pennsylvania coal, bore through me. He smiled as if his lips struggled against the kind gesture. A faint scar trailed along his right cheek in a thin, crooked line. As often as I'd spent time in his company, never once had I felt comfortable. I found it odd how Chaz respected and admired him, and when I drove us into town, he'd spend evenings at the bar with him. Many others, especially the older folks, liked him, too. Some even claimed he was a chosen one, able to read thoughts from the beyond. I thought it was all hogwash. However, no matter what anyone said in Plum Steelwater's defense, none of it helped to calm my nerves when in his presence.

Slowly, he let go of my arms and nodded. He backed away and to the side, leaving room for me to pass.

"Sorry. I should watch where I'm going, I guess," I muttered and quickly passed.

My leg muscles flexed to steady my gait, and I

weaved through the rows of cars to reach my truck. Safely away, I brooded over why I let Plum Steelwater get to me. Whether his looks with that scar or his lack of social amenities caused it, I couldn't say.

With a casual shrug, I hopped into the seat. "Stop being ridiculous, Mackenzie." I turned my head as I shifted into reverse and spotted a folded sheet of paper tucked in the top corner of the rear window. "What now?" I sighed and popped open the door.

Reaching across, I grabbed the folded paper. I glanced cautiously back and forth, scanning the parking lot, but found no one in sight. Carefully, I unfolded the sheet to see it was a flier: *Seneca Pow-Wow, Saturday, July twelfth.*

I headed for the truck door with the flier clutched in my hand then froze.

A scowl shadowed my bright mood. Not one other window had a flier attached to it. I slid back into my seat and smoothed the paper out on the steering wheel. What was this supposed to mean? Whoever left it for me to see must've done it for a reason. I stared, as if the information would magically reveal some code to explain why this was left only for me. Nothing. I noticed the time and tossed the flier on the seat. Later on, a second look might tell me more.

I motored out of the parking lot, heading east on Route 6. It was a short distance to Callie's. She lived just beyond the outskirts of Warren on Cobham Park Road. If I picked up speed, I would catch her before she left to visit her mother in the nursing home. *Every afternoon between one and two*, Callie said, and Martha Logan counted on it. At least that had been Callie's routine several months ago, the last time I'd spoken to her. My shoulders slumped. The reminder of Martha brought tears to my eyes.

I drew closer to the turnoff at Park Avenue and slowed down. Ten minutes of my drive left. My mind hadn't settled on exactly what to say. Instead, it tossed and juggled words around until they became a jumbled mess. "You're trying too hard," I scolded.

As my foot tromped on the gas and the truck sped out of town, my phone began to ring. With one finger press, I had the call on speaker. "Hello."

"Blessed saints. I caught you on the first try. Must be my lucky day," Chaz answered.

"And good afternoon to you, too. Tell me you didn't just wake up," I chided.

"And what if I did? Sleep is sleep, day or night. I'm old and get it when I can. But I didn't call to gab about sleep, missy."

I steered the truck right when I came to the fork. Five minutes. I came close to figuring out what to say, but not close enough. After such a long time, every word that came to me sounded awkward or lame. "Uncle Chaz, maybe we can talk later? I'm about to visit Callie and need all my concentration focused on her."

"Heavens. Have you lost your mind? Callie don't need to hear what you suspect. Wait 'til you know for sure."

"Don't worry. I won't tell her about Reese." I gripped the wheel.

"Well, it don't matter. You have to wait, because there's somethin' I need you to do."

I gauged the amount of determination in his voice and groaned. I was in for an argument, and it felt like I'd already lost. "What is it?"

"I got a call from Papa Birdsong. He's found a copy of Clearwater family history. Documented birth and death records, land ownership, court battles, military records...you name it, it's in there. This could be the news

I'm needin' to put this project to bed. And I can't wait another day."

"But…"

"You need to keep headin' north to Salamanca," Chaz ordered.

My fingers tapped the steering wheel. "Sure, Uncle Chaz. Will he be at the museum?"

"Says he's stayin' there to meet you. He squawked some, tellin' me he needs time to get ready for a hot date." Chaz snorted. "At eighty-five, he can't handle more than a lukewarm one. You should get there by two. I'll call and let him know."

In the next minute I passed by Callie's place. My breath hitched as I caught sight of her inside, passing by the living room window. Later would be a better time to visit. I pressed the gas pedal and powered down the windows. My heartbeat grew regular once more.

Chapter 7

Salamanca sat just beyond the New York border. I took West Bank Perimeter Road, which trailed along the west side of the Allegheny with Onoville Marina on the right, and a short distance later, the Horseshoe Inn on the left. I made good time. When the sign announcing Route 80 came into view, I steered my way northeast.

I focused my attention on the visit with Papa Birdsong. His warm smile and earthy brown eyes that twinkled when he let go of a belly laugh placed a warm glow inside me. To spend time with Papa was like holidays and family gatherings with simple, nurturing goodness. Of course, I was well aware the flip side to him was one I'd never dare cross. News of his reputation spread all across New York and Pennsylvania during his first year of practicing law. He was a ruthless litigator.

After years of success in the courtroom, his line of potential clients grew and grew. They sought his help on a regular basis. His career had some Oscar winning moments. Like the case of Stan Redfellow. Stan had been charged with murder based solely on circumstantial evidence. Papa managed to break the case and find the real killer. It made national front-page news.

At present, Papa spent most of his days as the sole curator of the Seneca-Iroquois Museum. It's where he felt at home, more than the courtroom. He claimed old age had left him unable to argue any case effectively. Most locals learned soon enough that didn't stop him outside the halls of justice. If anyone walked the streets of Salamanca, it was no surprise to catch Papa arguing with a jaywalker or someone cutting in line at the movie theater. He always had a defense ready.

At last, I reached downtown Salamanca. The town bustled and buzzed with traffic and shoppers. Signs were hung on street posts, telephone poles, and empty walls of buildings to announce the July pow-wow. The busy streets would become all the more so on the weekend. Though most of the festivities, like the dance competition and ceremonial drum roll, would be held in the casino. Many vendors in town had put up their annual clearance signs. Saturday morning, they'd pull tables outside and load them with items tagged at dirt-cheap prices. People reconnected and socialized. It was great community fun.

My attendance was mandatory since I couldn't miss Nash do his smoke dance. I'd bring Uncle Chaz, who would complain how the campground trails made for a bumpy, uncomfortable ride and gripe about the heat sweating his handgrips. Some days, nothing satisfied his sour mood when it came down to it.

The lot offered no empty spaces, so I parked in front of the museum. My spirit deflated. There'd be little chance for a chat with Papa. He'd be too busy curating. I stepped onto the sidewalk and found another pow-wow poster tagged to the parking meter. This time, I paused to study the details. My finger traced each line as I read the description and upward to the logo representing the event.

At once, I frowned. Something didn't add up. I pointed my arm at the truck and clicked the remote, then retrieved the flier off the seat. I absently scratched my cheek while glancing from the flier to the poster.

"Well, I'll be," I exclaimed. Flier in hand, I directed my steps up the museum walkway and through the entrance.

"Hey, Little Mac's come to retrieve my valuable find," Papa said, greeting me from behind his counter.

"Shouldn't you be with all those curious guests instead of here, waiting for me?" I teased as my smile widened.

Papa raised his palms. "I get breaks, too. Besides, I hired a new assistant curator. Real sharp lady. Knows loads about Seneca history. Maybe more than me. Anyway, she will be coming up front with her group in a few minutes. Can't wait for you to meet her."

I hesitated, but figured it was worth a shot. Extending my arm, I handed Papa the flier.

"What's this?" He pushed his glasses into place and read. After a minute, he looked up. "It's a pow-wow flier."

"I know *that* much." I came around the other side of the counter.

"It's not from this year," he added.

"I figured that, too." I pointed at the description of events. "I hoped you might be able to tell me what I haven't figured out yet. See? The events include these names I don't recognize. I've come to suspect this is from a previous pow-wow, maybe years ago?"

Papa's brow furrowed into deep creases and he remained silent. A minute later, he swiveled around to grab a thick binder from the wall shelf and flipped through the laminated pages. He finally stopped at one labeled 2003.

My eyes grew wide as I laid my flier next to the

binder. "What do you know? It's a match." I shook my head at Papa. "Why do you keep these?"

"This part of history appeals to me. I keep them as mementos of my past. Been attending pow-wows since I was three and filling this binder for more years than I'd care to admit." He slid a finger over to the margin. "See here? I kept notes of each festival. Anything I found interesting."

I leaned closer to read Papa's scribbles. "Sam Waters performed the smoke dance while—Wait. Does that say what I think it does?" My heartbeat raced.

"Hmm. Let me see. Reese Logan, Toby Clearwater, and Elias Jamison played the drums. I remember it seemed odd."

"Why odd?" I stared at the page notes once more.

"Unusual for anyone but Seneca to perform, but there he was, alongside the other two. In fact, I recall running into them quite often. I used to have a pretty wild nightlife, you know. It was no surprise to find them spending evenings at Salty Sal's bar, jamming or just hanging. Of course, they did work together. Polson's Delivery—Say! Wasn't it their warehouse that burned down when Reese Logan died?"

I tensed and my breathing became shallow. I reeled as all of it hit me. The body, the warning message, and a flier from the 2003 pow-wow—the year before Reese supposedly died in the warehouse fire?

"You okay?" Papa lightly touched my arm.

"Oh, sure." I scratched my ear and nodded firmly. I waved the flier at him. "Someone left this on my windshield. I think it's meant as some kind of message."

Wrinkles knitted Papa's brow and creased his leathery face. "You're worried? Must be serious."

"Maybe." I really didn't want to burden him with all the details of my past twenty-four hours, though it might help to have a legal mind's perspective. "Actually, I'm pretty sure it's serious." I pulled up a stool and explained my story. What I got from Papa were many nods and utterances of "um hmm." It was as if his mind took the time to process and waited to hear all the details before commenting.

"You're sure it's Reese?"

"Ninety-nine-point-nine percent sure. I mean, at first, I really thought it was one of those weird moments playing with my imagination. Like I saw things that weren't there, you know? But…" I threw up my hands. "I get the text message warning me to stay clear and now this flier." My shoulders sagged. "I don't want to think it was him in that grave."

Papa nodded. "Hmm."

"What? You don't agree?"

"Maybe it's not a warning." Papa sat back in his chair. Palms and fingers drew together to rest underneath his chin. "If both of these are from the same person, this Spirit Talker, you must consider another possible motive. The flier is much like a clue to point you in one particular direction. Perhaps the message only warned you to be careful, but with the hope you will continue to search for answers."

I frowned and absently scratched my cheek. "I guess, but I'd rather err on the side of caution. Wouldn't you?"

"Do you plan to let the message stop you?" Papa asked.

"I don't think…" I paused. After a second, a sheepish grin formed. "I guess not."

"So, good or bad, it doesn't matter. You know, when you were a little girl, grown-ups would often warn you, 'You can't do this, Sarah Blue. No, you'll never do that.' And what would happen?"

I laughed. "I'd be determined to prove them wrong

and then go do it. Or sometimes fail, but be proud I tried."

"Exactly. Looking forward, I am filled with vision. Looking upward, I am filled with strength. At least that's part of it, but wise to remember. Have you spoken to Callie?"

"I started there, but then I got Chaz's call about your discovery."

"Hmm. I think maybe you should wait. No need to have her upset if the body turns out to be someone else," Papa advised.

"That's exactly what Chaz said." I sighed and slid off the stool. "I suppose you're both right. It's strange. I mean, we haven't spoken much lately. Yet, she's the one I want to talk to about this, more than anyone."

"Maybe there is another reason you want to talk? Something you haven't admitted? None of my business, I guess. In any case, if the body turns out to be Reese, someone she knows should break the news to her." Papa nodded and reached under the counter to pull out a leather bound book, worn and frayed at the edges, nearly three inches thick. "Here's what you came for. It's a ton of reading, but interesting stuff."

"Yay for me." I cradled the book in my arms and managed a thin smile. I hadn't really gotten anything much out of Papa. At least I learned about Reese's party pals and fellow employees. "Say, do you know if Polson's is still in business?"

"Nope, not since 2005. A few months after the warehouse fire, I think."

"What about Toby Clearwater? Do you know what happened to him?" I thought I might dig a little and find out, but an answer from Papa saved time.

"He moved down to Pittsburgh is what I hear. Got a

job in one of the mills. And Elias followed Nash to Baton Rouge, but you probably know that."

I did. Nash spoke of the band they played in while living there. They'd performed in lots of night clubs before Nash called it quits. Elias remained while Nash moved back to Priest Hollow. Nash seldom talked about those days, but he shared memories when his mood softened and he became melancholy.

"Okay. Thanks, Papa. I should scoot. You know how impatient Uncle Chaz can be." I lowered my chin until it touched the cover of the heavy tome resting in my arms. "Much thanks for this. I'm sure I'll have loads of fun going through...hmm...I'd guess around five-hundred pages of Clearwater history?"

Papa threw back his head and erupted with one of his deep belly laughs. "Sarcasm becomes you."

The sound of multiple footsteps and the voice of a woman echoed up the hall. Words about Seneca and Iroquois history broadcasted in a deep voice announced the group's arrival.

Papa smiled. "Ah, here she comes. I want you two to meet."

I kept my gaze on the hallway and waited for whoever would come around the corner. As the group appeared, a small gasp escaped me. In the lead was a tall, willowy woman with short-cropped dark hair and dangly earrings.

Papa walked around the counter and toward the group. He grabbed hold of his assistant's hand and nodded at the visitors. "If you'll please excuse us for a moment? Jemma, you must come and meet a good friend of mine."

Jemma walked forward and smiled. "Hello, Sarah Mackenzie. It's good to see you again."

Papa's eyebrows shifted upward. "You know each other?"

"We spoke briefly at the bar. Please, call me Mac." I tried not to appear too surprised. "I see you found work. In record time, at that."

Jemma patted Papa's arm. "Mr. Birdsong was kind to hire me. I'm a lucky girl."

"I'm the lucky one," Papa said before he turned to me. "It's not often someone like this walks into my museum."

"Well, I'm happy for you both. Congratulations, Jemma. And on that note, I better get going. Uncle Chaz will be anxious to see this." I held up the book.

"See you on Saturday? Looks to be a generous crowd coming," Papa said.

"We'll be there. Thanks for your wise words. I'll keep looking forward and upward." I hugged him and planted an affectionate kiss on his cheek before adding, "Bye, Jemma."

I swiftly exited. I could be home by three and spend a couple hours poring over the contents of our latest collection before suppertime. If nothing else, the task would pull me away from my worries and pondering the weird coincidence that brought Papa and Jemma together. I needed a time out.

On the highway, I powered down the windows and breathed in fresh air to clear my head. Cooler winds and grey clouds promised thunderstorms and much needed rain. A fitting atmosphere to go with gloomy events. "I'm looking upward, Papa."

I sighed and tromped down on the gas pedal.

Chapter 8

The rain drummed a steady rhythm on the roof and against the window panes for nearly an hour, like fingers persistently tapping on my head. I was annoyed. Even though the downpour lightened to a mere sprinkle several minutes ago, my head ached. And the cool drink did nothing to help. I tightened my grip on the glass and squeezed my eyes shut as I sat at the table.

"I don't see your point," Uncle Chaz said, his jaw clenched.

"I'm telling you, this is the generation we want to focus on," I argued. Frustration overflowed to sour my mood. It left my wiring frayed and impatient. I knew his impatience wouldn't stand for any postponement. So, after returning from Salamanca, I had planned to sneak into my house, relax a while, soak in the tub, and then take a snooze. I was exhausted and in need of a reprieve. However, Uncle Chaz was not to be underestimated.

"I want you to go further back. If this one has any credibility, the others will show it." Chaz leaned closer to the page, leaving little room for me to see.

"Maybe we should take a break." My voice cracked.

I ran my tongue over dry lips and reached for the glass of water. "Get some food in our bellies?" I suggested, thinking that chugging down a beer or three wouldn't hurt, either.

"You're quittin' on me already," Chaz grumped before he wheeled toward the kitchen.

I narrowed my eyes as I watched the back of him. My devotion and love for him pained me at times. At nearly every turn, he managed to challenge my usually calm self and provoke a torrid tantrum of words, which I always regretted later. This time, he'd waited on his porch until I pulled into my drive. He insisted I come to his place. We could examine the book together, he argued. No amount of words, persuasive or threatening, swayed his opinion. I finally stomped off across the yard and slammed his door behind me, leaving him and Opal outside. He waited a minute before making a dramatic entrance, flaunting his well-practiced, dignified air of superiority. His chair reached the table where he sat in silence until I set the book in front of him. I tried to persuade Opal to join us, but she had the good sense to remain outside until the volatile mood diffused.

Within minutes, Chaz brought the leftover pot of stew to the table, along with bowls and silverware. "There's a pan of biscuits sittin' on the stove if you'd be so kind." He motioned behind him with the tilt of his chin while he ladled stew into the bowls.

As I returned to the table, I asked, "Did you know Toby Clearwater well?"

"Not as much as I did his daddy. Greer was headstrong, with plenty of temper to throw around." Chaz raised his eyebrow at that comment. "Anyway, we used to play a game or two of poker with the gang over at your daddy's bar. That was a real long time ago, before he, well, passed on."

I stirred the bowl to cool my meal. "What did you think of Toby?"

"Like I said. Didn't know him well. He got into his fair share of mischief. Most boys do. Nothin' unusual there." Chaz frowned. "You gonna play with that stew or eat it?"

I took a bite and slowly chewed. I shifted between thoughts of Elias and Toby. "What about Elias? Did you know him?"

Chaz dropped his spoon into the bowl and leveled his gaze at me. "Why you askin' about folks we ain't seen for years?" He leaned forward and pointed a finger. "This have somethin' to do with that body you found in the graveyard?"

I gave my shoulders a slight shrug. "Just curious." I didn't want to let him know about the warning—which is exactly what he'd call it—and the flier. His reaction would match Nash's, worrying until I'd end up locked in my bedroom with one of them standing guard at all hours.

"Well, I never met the man and barely knew his daddy or mama other than to say hello in passin'. Makes more sense you'd ask Nash since I sure don't know much." He stabbed his finger at the book resting in the middle of the table. "That's why we need to keep lookin' through this monstrosity. Saints almighty, there's got to be near six hundred pages," he groaned.

"Six hundred and fifty-three to be exact." I smirked.

"Be glad to wipe my hands of this. I swear my darnedest, I'm never takin' another call from the historical society." He shoved stew into his mouth and chewed vigorously.

"Amen to that." I finished the meal in silence while checking off a mental list of errands to cover tomorrow. First would be to stop by the sheriff's office and see if Deena had any news. Most assured, Parker and Smuthers would keep their lips buttoned, at least in front of me. Who else did I have? The bar crowd, perhaps. Locals in a small town like Priest Hollow heard things. Locals like Clint David Sanger. His nephew worked as a clerk at the station. Clint David would be at the Deja Blue. He never missed a happy hour or free appetizers. This evening provided both.

I stood and stretched to relieve the kinks in my neck and back. "I have to go. Nash needs me at the bar this evening." In truth, I did want to make an appearance. I promised to come around more often.

Chaz threw up his hands. "What about our research?"

"Tomorrow morning, early. At first light. I promise." I gave him a quick peck on the cheek and grabbed Opal by the collar. No point in pushing my luck. Or Chaz's buttons. One or two nights a week with the dog was near all he could tolerate.

"I'll be wakin' you when the sun first peeks her pretty head. Don't you worry," Chaz called out.

"Oh, I would be disappointed if you didn't." I chuckled and Opal woofed in agreement while we made our way back to the house.

I grabbed the car keys off the hook and a biscuit from the jar. With a quick toss, Opal caught it in midair. "Be good, and don't invite any strangers inside," I teased before shutting the door.

On the drive to Priest Hollow, I let my mind drift. The conversation with Papa gave me little doubt. Whoever placed the flier on my windshield meant for me to focus on Reese Logan. He was the only one associated with that particular pow-wow I actually knew. Besides that, I couldn't dismiss Papa's suggestion how both the message and the flier might be from Spirit Talker, intending to give me some sort of helpful clues.

But what did that tell me about Reese?

I approached the familiar sharp bend in the road and gave it my full attention. This blind spot was noted for collisions, which occurred most often when some young hotrod drove too fast and veered into the other lane. I knew well enough to play it cautious. Easing my foot off the gas, I took the curve but, in seconds, slammed on the brake. My breath hitched at the sight of a coyote. It stood there in one spot on the road, hovering over some bloody carnage.

Slowly, it raised its head and stared. I leaned forward over the wheel while the truck idled still. Patiently, I waited as my pulse slowed to normal. I wanted to move forward, but my foot remained steady on the brake. The coyote appeared determined to hold its ground, for it hadn't budged one muscle. I debated on turning back, to take another road. Finally, it bent down. Teeth bit into the carnage and took hold. It carried the prey off the road and into the woods, leaving a trail of blood.

I released my breath and let off the brake. The truck moved slowly forward to resume the trip down Hatch Run Road. After a bit, I returned to thinking about Reese. The one conclusion, which seemed to be the only sure thing I had, led me to where it all started—the grave in Cornplanter Cemetery. My hands gripped the steering wheel more tightly. "Reese Logan, what did you do to get yourself murdered?" I whispered.

The bar finally came into view. I spotted Nash's vehicle, a dated and somewhat battered Ford Mustang he claimed to have won in a card game while living in Baton Rouge. It sat alone in the parking lot. I pulled my truck alongside and hurried to the back entrance. I hoped to carry on a private conversation with him before Emmie or any early bird customers arrived.

With all the news I had from this morning's events to

share, this might take a while. "Nash? Where are you? We need to talk," I called out, entering the building.

A brief glance showed no sign of him at the bar or the lounge area. That left the kitchen or storage room and pantry. As I wove my way through the tables, a loud ping reached my ears. Or the stage. I smiled and turned with hands on hips to spot Nash tucked away in a far corner. His guitar rested in his arms while his upper body leaned over, inches away from the fret board.

"Koko T giving you grief?" I said, approaching the stage.

"Not as much as her namesake, but yeah. Simple fix, only need to replace the E string. Figured I'd get a few more sets played beforehand. Don't think that will happen, though."

I took the stairs and sat on the stage floor's edge, letting my legs dangle. Koko T was the nickname for his Gibson. He'd listened to the Chicago Blues singer for years and was lucky enough to meet her in concert. "Wang Dang Doodle" was one of his favorite songs. Koko Taylor died several years ago, and Nash travelled to Chicago for her memorial.

"So…What do we need to talk about?" He looked up to study my face while he propped Koko T next to his chair.

I swiveled around on my rear and tucked my knees in close to my chest. "Let me start with my visit to Sheriff Parker's office." I went on to explain my sudden recall, how unusual it was to find Joseph Bluehawk's grave marker swiped clean, then proceeded to describe the luncheon conversation with Deena.

Nash shook his head and threw out a tsk-tsk. "I told you to leave her out of it. Gossip is like a drug to Deena. She knows it will mean trouble at work, but the woman can't help herself. If she gets fired it's on you, boss."

"Don't worry. We devised a cover story in case one or both of us get questioned. Besides, from all appearances, it looked like a friendly, innocent get-together. Two girls who wanted to share time. That's all." I shrugged.

Nash strummed on Koko T. "After your day, I suspect you need some cheering up."

"Don't think you'll mesmerize me with your music. I need to keep my mind focused on this mess." I wagged a finger at him. Still, the notes he played lulled me into a calmer state of mind. "Stevie Ray," I murmured.

"Now tell me, what in the world can be wrong. Hmm, hmm. Oh yeah, my sweet Sarah, let me help you move along. Hmm. Hmm."

Warmth flushed my face, and I scooted off the stage. At the last second, I turned and caught Nash's eyes following me. Heat radiated from the spark in them. Things had shifted. I didn't know exactly when it started to show, but somehow it had. I should admit that much at least. A mix of relief and regret washed over me when he suddenly ended the tune. Setting his guitar down, he jumped off the stage to walk toward the bar counter.

"Wait." I shook off the emotional buzz resonating through me and motioned him to sit back down. "After lunch, I had an errand to run for Uncle Chaz. He wanted me to visit Papa Birdsong and retrieve some research materials."

"Ah, Papa always has an interesting story or two he wants to share. What was it this time? The one about how he saved the black bear from becoming a local zoo resident?" Nash laughed as he lifted up to sit on the stage floor next to me.

"No, but that is an entertaining one. This time it was about past Seneca pow-wows. In fact, *this* one involved Reese Logan." I formed a knowing grin.

"What do Reese Logan and pow-wows have in

common? And what makes it important enough to mention?"

"Did you know Reese played drums during the dances? Maybe for more than one year. I'm not sure. He, Toby Clearwater, and Elias Jamison played and worked together. Real buddies, I hear."

Nash scratched behind one ear. "I remember Toby and Elias, but I don't recall Reese playing with them in the pow-wows."

"Didn't you tell me Elias still lives in Baton Rouge?" I conjured up an image in my head of Reese pounding the drums while Toby or Elias chanted.

"Not sure. I haven't spoken to him since last year." Nash frowned. "In fact, one of the band members, Trey, called me a month or so ago."

"Why?"

"He wanted to know if I was interested in returning to the band. Of course, I said no." Nash wrinkled his nose. "Funny thing. He claimed Elias was slipping."

"In his performance, you mean?" According to Nash, Elias never played a bad set. In fact, he taught Nash how to play. Being ten years older, Elias was like his big brother.

"I guess. I didn't pursue it because I was in a hurry to end the conversation. Now, I wonder. Maybe I should give him a call." Nash stood up once more.

"Now?" There was more to discuss. I hoped to get Nash's opinion on Papa's theory.

"No, not now. It's close to seven. Time to get the bar ready. Emmie should be here soon and I'm hoping Cisco is in the kitchen."

"Oh. Yeah, shoot. I didn't realize." I held out a hand and pressed it against his chest before he walked away. "One more thing. Someone left a pow-wow flier on my windshield. It's an old one, several years old as a matter of fact. That's why I brought up Reese and them performing together. Anyway, I showed it to Papa. He seems to think it was left for me as a clue. Like it was meant to point at Reese and give me a way to explain things." I chewed on my bottom lip for several seconds before going on. "And he suggested it might even be from Spirit Talker."

Nash's eyebrow shot up. "Who is Spirit Talker?"

I winced. Time to fess up and face whatever his reaction might be. I sighed and took a deep breath before continuing. "Yes, well, here's the thing. I received a text message on my phone last night. The message encouraged me to continue my search for answers but to be careful. That's really all it was. And it was signed from someone calling himself Spirit Talker."

"Do you still have the text?" Nash clenched his jaw muscles and worked them back and forth.

My stomach flip-flopped. I promptly led our talk in another direction. "The real point is that Papa suggested the two pieces, message and flier, are from the same person who means to help me."

"Help you with what? You don't even know for certain the body is Reese's. And if indeed it is, so what? Let Parker handle it." He reached out to grab my shoulders. "I'm worried, Mac. The message might be a threat. Don't do anything careless. Your uncle would say the same."

Of course he would, I thought. "I'm not five. I had to take care of myself and the broken shell of a man my dad became for quite a while. You know that. I think I can handle plenty on my own." I shook loose from his grip as my temper rose.

"And you did an outstanding job. Not many young folks lose a mother, only to have the other parent die a few years later. A father who, by the way, was supposed to take care of *you*."

I nodded. "Exactly. So, stop worrying about me."

"This is different, and you know it. This is murder we're talking about." His voice lowered to a whisper while his fingers stroked my arms. "I couldn't handle losing you."

He stood close enough for me to smell the sweetness of his breath. Now, my heart raced for more than one reason. What was I so afraid of?

I smiled. "I promise you, I won't do anything reckless or dangerous. I'll send you out there instead."

"That's my girl. Harsh, but wise." Nash stood up straight and patted me hard on the back. "Now, we have a bar to get ready."

Relieved, I followed him away from the stage. Not a chance I'd mention Papa's theory or the text message again. Honestly, I didn't know which one of us worried about the other the most. Me, Nash, or Chaz. Protecting people's well-being was exhausting, especially when murder was involved.

"I'll check on Cisco in the kitchen. You take care of the front." I reached the back doorway when my phone buzzed. Fishing it out of my pocket, I read the number displayed and smiled. "Hey, Deena."

"Thank goodness you answered."

I hooked my arm around the nearest chair and pulled it toward me. I eased into it before asking, "What's wrong?" I remembered Nash's warning that Deena's fate was on me.

"If you're at the bar, you want to leave soon, real soon. Like right this minute," Deena said, keeping her voice soft and low.

I grew exasperated. "Why, Deena?"

"Sheriff and his deputy are coming to arrest you," she hissed.

"What?" I shouted and popped out of my chair. Nash

stopped wiping the counter to frown at me while Cisco peeked around the doorway. I waved my arm at both men to go on about their business. Turning my back to them I whispered into the phone. "What are you talking about?"

"I can't say much because somebody might come in the bathroom and hear me. I'm on probation, you know."

I sensed my composure falling apart, and my patience. "Yeah, I do. But, Deena, can we get back to the part about me getting arrested?"

"I heard Parker tell the deputy there was evidence about the case and how it tied to you, something on the body. It's probably physical evidence linking you to the crime, you know?"

My heart raced. What could they have found? I hadn't touched the body. Right? I shuddered. Not possible. Then what was this about? And what was I supposed to do? Run away? "I'm not going anywhere, Deena. I didn't do anything wrong."

"Suit yourself. But in case you change your mind, I have a friend who owns a cabin up near the New York border. It's deep in the woods where nobody's gonna find you."

"Thanks, Deena, but no. I'm staying put." I ended the call before turning back around. Nash stood a few feet away. "I suppose you heard."

"Why are you getting arrested?" He chuckled. "I told you to pay those parking tickets." When I didn't laugh, he immediately sobered up.

"Seems they found some evidence on the body that ties to me, which gives Parker a solid reason to put me behind bars, according to Deena." I grinned sheepishly. "Looks like I'll continue the family tradition. Maybe I should buy clothes in shades of orange. What do you think?" I quipped.

Inside, though, my chest tightened as twinges of fear

pushed their way inside me. How did things get this messed up in such a short time?

Chapter 9

Nash scowled as he reached for his phone. "What do *I* think? I think I should call Papa, that's what. Hopefully, he can get you out of this mess."

"Geesh. Lighten up. You realize this has to be some kind of mistake." What I didn't comment on were the numbers running through my head, like how many people are arrested each year and sometimes sentenced for a crime they didn't commit. And what about all those who'd been framed? I sighed. It was time to give my encyclopedia brain a rest. I was scaring myself.

Arguing with him didn't matter, anyway. By now, Nash would be on the phone talking to Papa, my soon-to-be lawyer, if I needed one. Before he had a chance to finish, the front door chimes jingled, and Parker entered with Deputy Severus on his heels. The grim looks on their faces didn't help my churning stomach, which threatened to send me rushing to the restroom.

"Miss Mackenzie." Parker tipped his hat.

I searched for a smile to put on a pleasant front. Formal greetings were never a good sign. "Good evening, Sheriff. What brings you out to our little burg?"

Parker cleared his throat. "Yes, well there's been a development in the case involving your body."

I winced at the possessive attached to it. That gave me too much of a personal connection. And it was about to get much more so. "Oh?"

"We took inventory of everything found in the grave with the body, and after studying it all...well, we found a particular object that places matters in a different light." He nodded firmly without adding more.

"Oh?" That appeared to be the only word my voice would utter, although what carried on inside my head could fill a dictionary.

Parker nodded at Severus, who reached out to hand over the clear plastic evidence bag. He kept it close to his side as he opened his mouth to speak again. "I needed to show you because of what's engraved on it." He raised his arm and extended the bag. "Does this look familiar?"

My heartbeat hiccupped. I studied the pitted wooden handle of the brush tool with the initials S.M. etched across it. I nodded. "It's mine. I must've dropped it when I looked into the grave?" It was a question because, at the moment, I failed to remember. My mind raced over the actions of yesterday afternoon, then slowed down to contemplate each in careful detail. It didn't help.

Parker shook his head. "That would be a trick if you did. See, this tool of yours was found underneath the body. How did it find its way there if you dropped it from above?"

I remained quiet. I didn't have an answer, only more questions. Like, if it wasn't me who put it there, who did? My eyes suddenly brightened. "Did you check it for fingerprints? Other than mine, that is?"

"We found only yours." Parker shifted to one side. He handed the evidence bag back to Severus. "You understand how this looks, don't you? You discovered the body. You made the call. You were the only person in the cemetery when I arrived." He coughed to clear his throat. "Then Smuthers and his crew find this brush belonging to you?"

I struggled for a response as Nash walked forward to stand close to my side. "Yes, but I'm sure I didn't place my brush in the grave. Just as I'm sure you'll find nothing else on the body that implicates me as a suspect."

Nash wrapped an arm around my waist. "Mac would never kill someone."

"Regardless, I have to ask her to come down to the station. We need to take a DNA sample. It's procedure, you understand."

I glanced nervously at Nash. "Yeah, sure. Let me get my handbag."

"We'll wait outside by the cruiser." Parker tipped his hat and motioned for his deputy to follow.

"Whatever you do, don't say anything until you've talked to Papa," Nash advised as he gave my hand a hard squeeze. "It's gonna be fine, Sweet Sarah."

"Ha. Yeah." I playfully slugged his arm. My mind refused to quit wondering about who placed the brush in the grave. And when. "I don't get it. Now that I think about it, I had my tools put away before I discovered the body. What did the brush do? Hop out of the tool bag and fly over to the grave and shove itself underneath the body? Makes no sense."

"Don't worry about that. You didn't do anything wrong. Papa will take care of it."

I had grabbed my handbag and already started walking away when Nash pulled me close to him. He lifted my chin and kissed me on the lips. It was warm and passionate. And it surprised me. I stayed there for several seconds, inches from his face, and then stepped back.

Embarrassment and confusion flushed over my body.

"I...Thanks for calling Papa. I'll stop by later on my way home from the station."

"Sounds good." Nash nodded, his face inexpressive once again. Without another word, he took long, quick strides to the bar.

I turned and somehow steered my way out the door. "What just happened?" I mumbled aloud before reaching Parker, Severus, and their cruiser.

If I had ever been sure of what sort of relationship we had, that kiss had definitely changed things. New script. Start over. Redefine. I couldn't hide behind my emotional baggage much longer. I sighed and, without a word, climbed into the backseat of the vehicle. In the meantime, I'd concentrate on what was about to happen. Sarah Mackenzie, murder suspect. It didn't get much worse than that.

სთსთ

I followed Deputy Severus down the hall to the department's examination room.

"Just take a seat. Someone will be coming in shortly to take the DNA sample," he said before leaving.

I stared at the four walls, one by one. Shiny white paint covered them, with no ornamental decorations to add color. Polished silver drawers layered the cabinet, along with glass cylinders of Q-tips, gloves, and cotton balls that lined up across the counter. As sterile as the exam rooms in a doctor's office.

My foot tapped against the table leg as it picked up the rhythm of Stevie Ray's "Double Trouble" tune that played in my head. "Help me move along, why don't you?" I sang, making up my own words to the verse in a low whisper, until the creaking of the door sounded. It opened wider. The foot tapping and the song playing inside my head slowed to a halt. I stifled a gasp as Plum Steelwater walked into the room. "Good evening, miss." Plum nodded. He walked to the counter, opened a few drawers, and pulled out some items.

"Hello, Mr. Steelwater. How are you?" I croaked out the social greeting while my pulse quickened. "I didn't know you worked here."

"Been nearly a year since I left the department. I thought retirement would suit me, but..." He shrugged. "And you?"

"Me? Me what?" My face drew a look of confusion.

"How are you doing?" A smile separated his lips and displayed two gold-capped teeth.

"Oh! Yeah, I'm great. I mean, other than the obvious." A nervous twitter managed to escape.

"Understandable. This won't take long. Normally swabbing the inside of the mouth is enough, but Sheriff Parker wants a hair sample, too." He motioned with his hand for me to open wide. In the next instant, he placed the cotton swab in a plastic container. With another quick move, he tweezed a strand of hair from my head and added that to my DNA sample. "You know, I remember your father." Plum laughed. "Moe was a wild one in his younger days. Sad when your mother...He never was the same. Used to see him regular at the station. I think Sheriff Billings had a jail cell reserved for such occasions."

I winced. "Uncle Chaz used to gripe, but he'd bail him out every time."

"You did, too, once or twice." Plum turned to study my face. "I see this memory pains you, but there was plenty of good in your father. I was grateful for it, too." He pointed to the scar on his face. "If it wasn't for his help, this could have been a lot worse. He fought right alongside me and scared away the thugs who seemed to believe the old saying."

"What saying?" I grew curious.

"Only good Indian is a dead Indian." Plum continued to smile, but it was stiff. "And he took care of my family while I was in the hospital. Brought them food and even stood guard the first night in case the thugs came after my wife and kids. He was a kind and generous man, your dad was."

It suddenly occurred to me how I never really knew Moe. Or may have but forgot that side to him. I watched as Plum gathered the samples and walked to the door.

His hand reached up but paused on the handle. "You know, every family has skeletons, but it is wise to remember the good qualities in them, and to defend them so you carry on your heritage proudly. Otherwise, the chain of suffering will never be broken."

Emotion lodged in my throat. Memories of my parents tended to be clouded with miserable images. I wasn't exactly helping to break that chain. Yet how different life would have been if Kate Mackenzie hadn't left home, if the couple shared their remaining days in bliss, along with me, their only child? Still, somewhere in that dark portrait I knew there was some good, as Plum suggested.

I reached over to grab my things and walked out of the tiny, sterile cubical. A question came to me as I entered the hallway and caught sight of Plum, his slow shuffle taking him toward the elevator. Yeah, I was curious to know. How many skeletons haunted his family tree?

"Miss Mackenzie? I believe your lawyer is waiting at the front desk."

I turned to see Sheriff Parker behind me. I conveyed the question my mind pondered. "Do I need one?"

His voice carried no variation in tone. "As of yet, I'd say no. After we examine all the DNA samples, I might have an answer for you. But you should go on up front. Mr. Birdsong isn't a patient man from what I gather."

I tried not to sound surly. "Actually, he's extraordinarily patient when it's called for. You'll be in touch?"

"Of course. Soon as we know, but it'll take a few days. Like I said, the lab has more jobs than usual. Happens every year after the holiday."

"Right. Until later." I took several steps, but then my keen defense trigger stopped me. I wanted to discover the truth just as much as anybody. I pivoted on my heel. "You know, maybe if you focused on the victim's time of death and whatever else Smuthers found, tool brush or not, you'd know I'm innocent."

Parker frowned. "Who told you about Smuthers?"

"That's not important. Think about it. If I murdered him, why would I place evidence there to incriminate myself?"

"Unless you killed him earlier and decided to wait until yesterday to notify authorities, hoping to throw us off."

I clenched my fists and pressed them against my sides. "All the more reason not to place evidence with the body. Sheriff Parker, I didn't murder anyone. Please don't stop looking for the real killer just because you have a hunch it might be me." I twirled around and with determined strides marched down the hall. Relieved to hear no further comments from him, I forced air into my lungs to calm myself.

The idea that I was a murder suspect? It was so preposterous I failed to wrap my mind around it, but it certainly frightened and disturbed me. Whoever placed the brush underneath the body wanted to point a finger at me. The question was how to stop the oncoming train wreck? My shoulders slumped. I hadn't a clue.

Chapter 10

Turning the corner, I found Papa Birdsong. He stretched his arms out to give me a firm hug.

"Boy, am I glad to see you," I mumbled into his chest.

"What's this?" He rubbed my back. "You're trembling. What happened? Maybe I need to speak to the sheriff."

His arms straightened to pull me away, and he didn't hide the worry in his eyes. I patted his shoulder and forced a smile to my face. "It's nothing. Just an awfully long day. And I don't care for this place. You know that."

"Ah, but it's been a long while since those times. Near twelve years? Besides, I'm here. I won't let anyone or anything get to you, okay?"

I squeezed his hand. "Okay. Let's go. I want nothing more than to be on the other side of these walls. Let's stop at Woody's for a drink. I sure need one."

Papa tipped his chin toward the front desk. "You're done?"

"No more to do. I gave them my DNA. No questions asked. Now we wait for the results." I tugged at his arm to hurry him along.

"Fine. But we will discuss this at Woody's. Something doesn't add up."

"You don't have to tell me. In fact, nothing has added up since I found the body yesterday." My gaze shifted from side to side to check the road, and then I crossed with Papa alongside me.

"Murder never adds up or makes sense. It's not natural."

We entered Woody's to find the bar seating and most tables in front filled. The buzz of conversation filtered and echoed throughout the diner. Pungent odors of onions, ground beef, and Woody's famous salsa wafted from the kitchen and tantalized my taste buds. Home fried chicken and burgers, the main attractions at the local eatery, brought in customers from all across the county. I simply enjoyed the people. Coming here on any given day, morning, afternoon or evening, I'd find at least one familiar person to chat with and hopefully help me unwind.

"Let's take that one near the back," I suggested and led the way. The challenge was to make it there without stopping every few seconds. Folks wanted to say hello or ask Papa for some free legal advice. In my case, the topic of choice wasn't a surprise.

"Hey there, Mac. I hear you're in the business of tracking down dead bodies." Kip Monroe laughed and slapped his knee. "Sorry, couldn't resist. Hope your uncle is feeling better."

I let go of a snort. "He's always complaining, but that's a good sign. When he stops, then I'll start worrying."

"Tell him I said hi. Any news on who the dead guy is?" His smile flattened and his brows knitted together as he leaned forward. His wife did the same.

"Ah, no, not that I've heard. If you'll excuse us?" I pushed forward and past a server with a tray of dishes.

Stopping here might have been a mistake. People were bound to ask questions, and I didn't want to talk. Not about dead bodies found in cemeteries.

"If you want to leave and go somewhere quiet?" Papa whispered close to my ear.

I shook my head. "Nope. This is fine." I slid into the seat and waited for Papa to situate himself. "I might as well get used to it. Right?"

With a shrug, he set his elbow on the table and rested his chin in one palm. "Tell me. What happened? The only detail I got from Nash—and, by the way, he's worried to pieces about you. The only detail he gave me was how the authorities found a tool belonging to you in the grave. Did you drop it, perhaps?"

I looked up as the server approached our table. "I'll have a Yuengling Light."

"The same for me." Papa nodded before returning his attention to me.

"I've thought about it. A lot. And, no, I'm sure I didn't. I packed up my tools before I called Uncle Chaz. It was afterward I found the body. So, no."

"Any idea of how, then?" The server set coasters on the table with the beers. Papa sipped at his but didn't take his eyes off me.

"I've thought about that, too. Especially how the person or persons had the opportunity to remove it from my tool bag."

"And?"

Clutching my beer, I used my free hand to rub my upper arm. I turned away from Papa to view the neighboring tables.

No one seemed to be watching us. Still, I lowered my voice. "I took a nap, probably for a half hour or thereabouts, while I waited for Parker. It was strange." I stared intently at Papa. "I think it was a dream, but I heard chanting and drums beating."

Papa leaned back. His lips tightened into a thin line. "That is nothing to joke about."

"I'm well aware, Papa." I reached out to touch his arm. "What I'm trying to say is that the more I think about it...I may not have been alone in the cemetery. And while I slept, someone went through my bag, took the brush, and planted it in the grave."

"Why?" Papa threw up his arms.

"To frame me. Why else?"

"Little one." He shook his head.

"I know." My hands dropped to my lap. The story sounded far-fetched, even to me.

"If someone took the brush while you slept..." He tipped his head and emptied the glass. "I guess we need to figure out who."

"Yeah. Who." I was surprised, but pleased, to hear his support. Maybe not so crazy after all. I held the glass to my lips, but I didn't drink. "I want to believe it will help when they decide on the identity of the body. I don't know. I'm well beyond frustrated and tired of trying to figure things out." I set the glass down with a thud and beer sloshed over the sides.

"Wisdom comes only when you stop looking for it. Or something like that." Papa pointed a finger upward.

"I doubt if your Indian spirit words about wisdom will help me, but thanks." A sigh drew out my breath slowly.

"I mean, stop trying so hard. You'll only give yourself indigestion or a headache. And be patient. I have some words on that subject, too. Can't think of them right at the moment." Papa tapped his fingers on the table.

"No matter. I'm heading back to Deja Blue. I promised Nash I'd check in to let him know all about my wonderful experience." I chuckled. "You're welcome to come visit."

"It's a tempting offer, but I need to rise early tomorrow. Somebody is stopping by to talk about his legal rights to keep a tiger on his property," Papa explained.

"A tiger, huh? Have fun with that. Come on. I'll walk with you to—Oh, wait!" I smacked my forehead. "I didn't drive to town." A sheepish grin formed. "Would you mind? It's on your way."

"I should charge you triple for my services," he growled. However, a hearty laugh escaped in the next second while his large belly shook. "No criticizing my driving, though. My ex-wife used to dish it out to the point I wanted to wreck the car to spite her."

"Papa," I scolded. "For such a smart man who likes to quote all those words of wisdom, you certainly act like a child."

"A child lives in all of us. It's an eternal spirit which keeps us happy."

I stepped aside while he pushed open the door. "Another Indian proverb?"

"No. Simply me attempting to sound smart."

"Figures." I snorted. "Like I said. A child."

Within twenty minutes, we reached the Deja Blue. The pounding *thump, thump* rhythm of bass guitar and drums resonated from inside. A full moon gave the building an eerie, haunted glow. I opened the car door to get out then leaned across to give Papa a brief peck on the cheek.

"Thank you. The ride, the company, the advice, and support…for everything you do, oh Wise One," I teased.

"Takes one to know one, or so I've heard." He reached out to grip my shoulder. "Be watchful and weary. I can't have anything happen to my goddaughter."

I laughed. "Goddaughter? Since when?"

"Since this morning. My guiding spirit warned me you would need protected. He was right. He's always right. So, I claim myself your godfather and protector."

"Hmm. How do you know your spirit is a he?" My mind sparked with mischief. I quickly hopped out of the car before he howled a protest. Above all, Papa Birdsong was set in his old ways. No true regard for the concept of feminists. That part of history never happened, he continually argued. Not in his world.

He beeped his horn as he sped down the road. I waved and took quick steps toward the front entrance. My watch showed two hours remained until closing. Enough time to relax, unwind, and have a beer or two. I'd barely had a sip of my drink at Woody's. Besides, Nash was performing, and it gave me a reprieve. Talk about murder was off the agenda. Not to mention that kiss. Not yet, anyway. I sighed deeply and opened the door to a chorus of laughter and chatter accompanied by the narcotic harmony of blues music. Conversing with customers about trivial stuff sounded more fun. A lot more.

"Let's liven it up a bit with a little country and get you folks out on the dance floor," Nash announced. He turned to nod at the band members. The guitars picked up the tempo.

"Hey there, Mac. Haven't seen you in a long while."

I shifted my attention toward the voice calling to me. A couple tables over sat three familiar faces. I grinned and shimmied my way around until I stood next to them. "It has been a long while. How've you been?" I took turns shaking hands with Glenda, Shawn, and Trish. "Five-year class reunion, right?"

"That's right. We all rode into town and agreed this would be our first stop. How've you been?" Glenda leaned back in her chair and lifted her bottle to take a swig.

"Well enough. Nothing much goes on around here, you know." My smile struggled to win a fight with the dark thoughts in my head.

"Yeah, I do. One of the first reasons I put on my senior year list of why to move far away from Priest Hollow."

"Oh, I don't know. I miss the peace and quiet. Pittsburg is sometimes too much," Trish commented.

"Peaceful is nice," I agreed. "We should plan a night out before you leave, if you don't get too bored and hurry back to all that noise and traffic." I shot Glenda an impish grin.

"Ha. Funny. I guess it depends on what Callie wants to do. We're staying with her and—Oh! Here she comes, now." Glenda and everyone at the table turned to look back as Callie walked toward us.

My chest tightened and my breath became short. The one thing I'd avoided was about to take place. I wasn't prepared. No clue what to say or how to pretend nothing happened. My face would be transparent, hardly able to contain the panic growing inside. And Callie would recognize it instantly.

"Sorry. There's a line at the restroom." Callie slipped back into her seat before she looked up. "It's been a while. How are you?"

"Ha! That's what we said," Glenda exclaimed. Everyone managed to smile and nod, except for Callie.

"Oh, you know. Same old routine." I tried for casual, but sensed it failed miserably.

"Not routine from what I hear." Callie's face remained solemn. The mood shifted, which generated around the table, as the smiles and laughs stopped. Trisha cleared her throat while Shawn pushed buttons on his phone. Only Glenda seemed to be unaffected.

"Why not? What's going on?" she said. Her gaze

held steady, first on Callie and then over to me.

"I hear Mac discovered a body in an open grave. Somebody was murdered. I can't imagine how shaken you must have been. Why didn't you call me?"

I instantly recognized the look. Callie's eyes always reflected her mood. This time, they stated concern and worry. She'd gone into nurture mode. It was the role she played best when we were kids. "I planned to. It's been crazy since yesterday. Sheriff report, running the bar, taking care of Uncle Chaz. But I did want to call you or stop by." I willed myself to relax. This wasn't too uncomfortable. If I managed to get away in the next minute, there'd be no mention of who the body was or any other details.

"How exciting. Whose body is it? And I said nothing ever happens in this town. Ha! Leave it to you, Mackenzie, to bring a little action to Priest Hollow." Glenda laughed and swigged on her beer some more.

"Yeah, do they have any leads?" Callie leaned forward and gave me her full attention.

I shifted my weight from one foot to the other and tried to shake off the edgy tension starting to build again. "Guess not. At least I haven't heard any news. Say, I should get over to the bar. Looks like Emmie has her hands full. We should get together. Tomorrow maybe? Or whenever you have some free time. Call me. Good to see all of you." I rambled on at warp speed as I stepped backward and ran straight into a customer. "Oops, sorry." I smiled and turned to hurry away from Callie's table.

Only when I reached the safety of the bar did my pulse return to normal. In one swift move, I poured a shot of whiskey and downed it in the second it took to catch the scowl on Emmie's face. "What? Don't judge. Not this." I scowled back.

"Hey, bartender, what you servin' them tonight?" Nash's voice carried over the bar. Folks near the stage clapped while people on the dance floor swayed and circled to the beat.

"I'm not judging. I'm not." Emmie squirted triple sec into a glass. "Glad you made it over my way, though. The crowd is surly and demanding this evening."

"Oh, right. Sorry." I wiped my lips with a napkin. I needed to decompress this anxiety and act normal. With a steadier hand, I poured a glass of water and took a long sip.

"So, what's this news Cisco tells me? You and Nash kissed?"

Water sprayed out of my lips and showered the front of my shirt. Grabbing a bar towel, I blotted the wet spots while trying to regain my dignity. A couple of snickers from bar patrons didn't help. Neither did the grin on Emmie's face.

"I had to ask. It's too juicy not to," she whispered close to my ear.

"Not going to talk about it." I spat the words out. "Not to you. Not to him. Not to anybody. Not now."

"Fine. Don't have a fit. You don't want to talk, we won't talk. Whose table did you stop at on your way in?"

I groaned. "Friends from high school. We haven't seen one another since our last class reunion."

Emmie frowned. "But isn't Callie Logan sitting with them?"

"Yes. She is." My lips stretched to form a rigid line. "I think Clive is waving at you. Probably wants a refill." Once Emmie turned away, I busied myself with customers at the other end of the bar. This was not how to relax. The urge to leave before Nash's set was over tempted me, but dumping all this business on Emmie wouldn't be fair. I lectured myself to buck up and manage the uncomfortable moment I feared was coming. It didn't help any being cornered into speaking with Callie. To avoid any further contact with her this evening was the challenge I had to meet.

Otherwise, I'd be spilling my heart out with the confession about Reese, and me being a murder suspect. It was bound to happen. Most everyone knew, including me, I never could keep secrets from Callie.

The next hour flew by while I served drinks and meals from the kitchen. The register dinged like a never-ending church bell on Sunday morning. After a bar fight or two, which Nash and his guitar buddy, Vince, brought to a halt before any blood was shed, the place vacated with its last visitor stumbling out to the cab they had called for him.

I cleaned and polished the tables while Emmie wiped down the bar and washed dishes. Nash helped put equipment back into cases and turned off the stage lights before walking my way. Somehow closing the distance between us intimidated me. I kept my gaze fixed on the table and scrubbed.

"Everything all right?" Nash said while he turned a chair around to sit down and then rested his arms on the back. He stared up at me. I trembled, but slight enough I didn't think he noticed. The childlike innocence in his eyes rattled me even more.

"Yep. No jail. Pain-free DNA sampling. Oh, and guess who works there?" I waited until he shrugged. "Plum Steelwater."

"Is that supposed to mean something?"

I frowned. "Well, no. I guess. It's what he said that might. Mean something, that is." I sat down in the chair to concentrate and played back the words. "'All families have skeletons, but you need to remember what's good about them so you can be proud of your heritage and not repeat the bad stuff.' *And* he told me that my dad helped him and his family at one time. He was grateful for it."

"Sounds like an old man who wants to share his wisdom. That's all."

"I suppose. Anyway, I had my own words of wisdom for Sheriff Parker before I left the station."

Nash grinned. "Good for you. What'd you tell him?"

"I said he better keep looking for the real murderer, because I'm not it." I grunted and went back to polishing the table.

"Just like that, huh?"

I glanced up to catch the sparkle of mischief in his eyes. When my attention moved to his lips, I suddenly thought of the kiss. A red blush must've painted my face, as I grew warmer and my skin tingled. If he didn't bring it up, I sure wouldn't. This was more than awkward. Of course, we'd have to talk about it eventually, *after* he suggested it. I was a coward for sure.

Nash tilted his head. "Mac? You zoning out on me?"

"Oh. Sorry. I was thinking of the brush. It was in my bag. I know I put it away. Somebody removed it from there. Why didn't Parker ask to see it?"

"Your tool bag? Good question." He nodded while his fingernail scraped at a piece of wax stuck to the table. "I saw you talking to Callie."

"Yeah," I sighed. "She mentioned the body. I wimped out and didn't say much. Definitely not about Reese or how I'd become a person of interest."

"I'd guess she's worried about you. She's a friend, after all."

"Not like we used to be." Not after Reese disappeared. Both of us were left with emotional bruises and scars that refused to go away, still after ten years. Whenever I'd see Callie, it sent me into a guilty funk. Somehow Callie blamed me for breaking her brother's heart. I sensed it, which sounded crazy since she'd never said as much. But I knew in my heart it was true. Because of guilt and blame, we'd pulled further apart. That's how it'd been for many years.

"I think she's reaching out. Maybe you should try to make amends." Nash moved his arm across the table to touch my hand with his fingertips.

"There's nothing to amend. We've just been too busy to get together." I shut down my emotions rather than admit the truth. Ironic, I thought. If the body turned out to be Reese, Callie and I would be forced to deal with one another. My stomach twisted into a tight ball. The heart-break, the tension, the emptiness it left us, all of it could've been avoided if Reese hadn't been the victim in the warehouse fire. It was selfish, but in a certain way, I wasn't ready to learn the truth about the body. Not yet, maybe never. I'd grown comfortable with the way things were.

I flinched at the firm touch of Nash's fingers caressing my hand and blinked as I stared at him. My tongue ran over dry lips. His warm touch, his fiercely intense look. What was he doing to me?

"Mac, we should talk." His voice lowered and his smile softened.

"Sure. How about tomorrow? Right now, I should go home and check on Uncle Chaz before bedtime." I shot up from my seat. "But tomorrow for sure, okay?" Without waiting for a response, I took long strides to the bar where I grabbed my handbag and keys. Emmie gave me a scowl and headshake, which I ignored. Nothing like turning into a human iceberg when it came to romantic relationships, especially since this was about Nash. Each day his behavior became more apparent. He made no attempt to hide it. Any naïve fool would notice. However, I'd always thought of him and treated him like a close friend. He did the same. Until lately, my mind hadn't explored the idea of more. Why did he have to push me?

"See you guys tomorrow," I shouted and rushed out of the bar, but not before catching a glimpse of Nash's face. My heart sank, lower than low. His eyes had lost their shine.

A moan escaped me as I threw open the truck door. Pathetic. It was sad to admit I didn't deserve whatever he wanted to offer. Of course, now, I'd have plenty of time to dwell on it—all the way home and all night. With a louder moan, I shifted the truck into gear and tore down the road, leaving a trail of dust and Moe's Deja Blue behind.

Chapter 11

With a quick good-night, I headed to my place, leaving Chaz to wonder why I refused to answer any of his questions about my day. A mix of emotions had brought on my exhaustion and lack of patience. I knew Chaz too well. He'd gripe and groan when I disclosed the story of my adventure down at the sheriff's station. I'd wait until tomorrow.

Opal came home with me, and, for once, I let her cuddle in bed. I sniffed her fur while burying my face into her side and whispered a few affectionate names. The bitter irony of the situation hit hard and made me cry. Pillow talk with a dog, my one companion, in bed.

A cozy warmth surrounded me. Soon, my eyelids drooped and my breathing fell into a soft, even rhythm. I pictured Nash, his long, black hair hanging over the side when he leaned down to kiss me...

The wet slurp of a tongue on my face woke me with a jolt. I opened my eyes to stare at the close up of Opal with mouth wide as she panted. A loud bark erupted as she threw back her head. I giggled and scratched her chin.

"Good morning to you, too, silly pooch. Ready for

breakfast?" I sprang out of bed. Opal leaped to the floor and galloped to the kitchen. "I'll take that as a yes," I said.

Looking in the mirror, I found myself blushing. The memory of the dream replayed in Technicolor with panoramic images big enough to cover my bedroom wall. "Stop!" I smacked the mirror frame, and my reflection wobbled. Opal came running back into the bedroom with a whimper. "Not you. *Me*." I pointed to my chest while Opal cocked her head to one side.

I grabbed my robe and shoved my arms into it, shuffling out to the kitchen. My place was the right size for one person. A kitchen slash dinette area with walls of planked knotty pine took up most of the eight hundred square feet. In front, there was a small sitting room with a sofa at one end and a Lazy Boy recliner next to the picture window. The hardwood floor was bare except for an oval, braided rug placed in the center. It once belonged to my paternal grandmother, and I was exceptionally proud of it. That left my bedroom, which was quite spacious, and a small bath adjoining it. Indoor plumbing. It was the one luxury besides electricity I'd insisted on when having the place built. It was fortunate that Moe not only left me the bar, but a sizable insurance policy, too. It was enough to hire a contractor to build the house. The property sat on a century-old cellar once part of an Amish farmhouse. I seldom went down there. It was damp, dark, and full of spiders, cobwebs, and critters I'd rather avoid. A coal furnace remained below, but I didn't use it. Instead, a wood burning stove made of cast iron, which sat in the kitchen on a firebrick base, provided heat. I'd chosen one painted bright red to give the room color.

I poured some kibble into Opal's bowl and filled the other with water. "I guess we shouldn't put off the inevitable for too long, right?" Opal glanced up for a second to stare before she pushed her nose back into the bowl.

"Yeah, I knew you'd agree. But we won't fight it. We'll be brave and take on whatever the old man dishes out." I poured a mug full of coffee, strong and black, a much needed fortitude.

Within a half hour, I was ready. With keys and bag in hand, I walked toward the door. At the last second, I ran back to the bedroom and snatched the recorder from my dresser. Papa's book, along with all the other research materials, were at Chaz's place. He insisted on keeping them. Poring over books and papers for his latest project helped to pass those restless nights when he got little sleep. And to help forget the pain, I guessed, though he'd never admit it.

"Come on, girl. We have lots of work to do," I said as I opened the door.

The morning fog delivered a thick and heavy mugginess to the air. The mosquitos buzzed and hovered, eager for a chance to get their first meal of the day. I picked up the pace and sprinted across the yard toward the road, refusing to take the buggier shortcut through the tree grove separating our houses.

"Good mornin', missy. Had breakfast yet? Got bacon fryin' and fresh brown eggs if you're hungry any," Chaz said from the front porch with a smile that stretched ear to ear.

I frowned. His happy expression looked genuine, but unfamiliar at this early hour. "What's with the smile? You win the lottery or something?" I climbed up the stairs and placed my handbag on the floor.

"Wouldn't be sittin' here if I had." He kept the grin on his face.

"What?" My arm circled. "Please don't keep me in suspense. This is a rare occasion to see that goofy grin on you."

"I got a call from the uppity biddy over to the historical society. She says my work is goin' to appear in some national magazine, a cover issue no less. I'm burstin' with pride and tryin' not to let the other side of me ruin it."

"What other side?"

"The side tellin' me I still don't have the proof I need. That side." His voice edged up. The grin became an evil looking grimace.

I rubbed my forehead to smooth out the wrinkles of confusion. "Congratulations?"

"Don't matter, because we're gonna find that proof right this mornin'. Or else." He pivoted his wheels in a one-eighty and rolled back into the house.

I let out a lengthy sigh, picked up my handbag, and followed him inside with Opal trotting behind me. My breath hitched as I took in the sight. Scattered papers, many with blotches of coffee stains, covered the table. Sticky notes pasted to walls, counters, windows, where ever he found free space, he stuck one on it. Bacon sizzled in the frying pan and a brown cloud of smoke trailed up from the toaster. "Ah, Uncle Chaz?" I pointed at the kitchen counter and choked on my laughter while he spewed out expletives and wheeled across the floor.

"Maybe you should take a break. I'll finish breakfast and you..." I tipped my chin at the table. "Why don't you clear some space on that for our plates? Hmm?"

"Sarcasm duly noted," he grumbled. Within seconds, he tidied up the mess like it had never been there.

I was *duly* impressed.

"Ready to tell me how yesterday went?" He leaned back in his chair and sipped coffee from his mug, his attention on me.

My heart skipped. "Ah, well, lots of business at the bar. That was good." With my fork, I shifted the bacon strips from side to side.

"Nice to hear. What else?"

I tossed ideas in my head on how to start.

"Dad burn it! I already know about your visit to Warren and how Parker, the squat for brains, thinks you're a murder suspect." He smacked the arm of his chair.

I set the fork down and turned to scowl at him. "How? How did you know?" Nash deserved a proper scolding, if he was the squealer.

"Clive called me. He found out from Benson who works the nightshift at the station. What's gotten into that place? I'd say a bunch of Mickey Mouse morons are run-nin' it." He wheeled around the table and to the counter, then swung open a cupboard. With unsteady hands he pulled plates out of it. "Are they at least lookin' for other suspects?"

"I told Parker as much. I said I'm not his man, or woman, and that he'd better search for who is."

Chaz grunted as he placed silverware alongside the plates. He settled back into a pensive mood while I fin-ished the bacon, eggs, and toast. The meal kept our mouths busy, which was a relief to me. I didn't want to discuss the issue any longer. It upset both of us, especial-ly Chaz. His unhealthy condition, whether he'd admit to the description or not, worried me. I feared any emotional upset would push him over the edge. No matter how our relationship played out with its thunderstorm and light-ning theatrics, my heart ached at the thought of losing him. He was the only close family member I had in my life.

I rummaged through my bag to find the recorder. Once I set it on the table, my finger pressed play. Might as well have some kind of noise while we ate in silence, I thought.

Chaz kept his attention on the information emanating

from the recorder. Once or twice, he stopped chewing or drew his brows together and grunted.

I wasn't sure if that meant he was satisfied or displeased.

"Well, what do you think?" I said, pushing a button to stop the recorder. "Anything catch your attention as meaningful?"

"The young Bluehawk who died a young infant, and maybe how many in that family died around the same time." He scraped his fork across the plate to pick up the last bits of egg.

"Hmm. Maybe an epidemic of some kind? Cholera, influenza, smallpox?" I suggested. "Or how about tuberculosis? The late nineteenth century outbreak affected seventy to eighty percent of people living in urban areas, though twenty percent of those who were infected did survive. And then cholera wiped out—"

"I know the statistics, missy. I did a paper on epidemic diseases of the nineteenth century. Remember?" He sighed. "But what about the other families like the Corydons? Didn't hear any similar reports on them."

"I'm not finished. I was interrupted by an unexpected occupant in the cemetery, remember? There are two-thirds of those graves left to cover." I picked up the plates and carried them to the sink. I pushed aside the facts about diseases and concentrated on the current data.

"And not finishin' up anytime soon, I imagine."

"Sheriff Parker has cordoned off the cemetery until they are done with the investigation. He made that clearly known to me, more than once." I laughed. "I guess he's heard about our family's notorious past and is worried I'll sneak into Cornplanter's."

"But you won't." He narrowed his eyes. "You're already on his mind in a bad way. No use pushin' it. How 'bout we start goin' over this monstrosity instead?"

I groaned. The Clearwater tome. "Sure hope it has some kind of index or other method to organize the information. Otherwise, it will be that needle in the haystack to look through and find what we need." At once, a thought came to me. "You know, there is one resource we can tap into, and it's conveniently close by."

Chaz raised his eyes, giving me a questioning stare.

I smiled. "Jemma Bluehawk."

"Who's Jemma Bluehawk?"

"She's Papa's new assistant curator who moved to our area from New York a month or two ago. According to Papa, she has a sharp mind when it comes to local Native American history. And she's offered to help with our research more than once. Anyway, she might fill in any blanks we run up against."

"Let's wait. You know I don't like too many cooks in the kitchen, as they say. We'll see what we can figure out on our own."

I nodded and leafed through the pages while Chaz sorted out his notes.

One item caught my attention enough to make me pause. "Listen to this. 'During the late nineteenth century, the Bluehawks and Clearwaters had some sort of feud that lasted for some years.' You think this is the cause of those deaths?" I looked at Chaz when he didn't answer and found him bent over a paper clutched in his hands. "What's that?"

After a moment, he glanced up. Deep creases furrowed his forehead. "Found this document tucked in the back of the Clearwater book last night but didn't take the time to study it until now." He slid it across the table.

I scratched my chin while reading the contents. A second later I glanced up. "A property deed for land located in…" I bent down closer to study the document. "Nope. I can't read it. The print is too faded. But there's a name." I hitched my breath when I read the words. "Jacob Bluehawk?"

Chaz nodded.

"But it doesn't make sense. Why deed property to an infant?" I read the date. It fit within the time the young boy was alive.

Chaz shrugged. "Maybe it was a gift from a relative or friend? You know, for his future like when your daddy set up a trust fund for you."

"Oh, you mean the trust fund that he cashed in to cover his personal debts? That trust fund?" I tapped my fingernail on the table then went back to studying the deed. "Your suggestion makes sense. Too bad we don't know who owned it before this."

"Easy enough to find out. Go down to the Warren courthouse and check with the department of Deeds and Records." He winked. "But you knew that already."

"I practically lived there last year thanks to you, huh?" I pointed at the Clearwater book. "Maybe the two pieces of information connect somehow." I explained how the feud continued from 1885 to 1902. The diary-like entry described how most often one person, maybe two, shot at whichever enemy trespassed on the other's property. Once or twice it mentioned dozens of Bluehawks and Clearwaters doing battle with each other. That was all.

Chaz shook his head. "We'd still have to prove as many Clearwaters perished during that time, if this is the reason for those deaths. I'm sayin' it can't be the Bluehawks had that bad of aim."

"Another thing that puzzles me. If the feud was such a big deal, why didn't the government intervene? By that time in history, they seemed to stick their noses into everything the Native Americans did. Good or bad."

"True. It could be the Indians hid it well. Most lived

far enough out where civilization didn't care what went on. And if it was on the reservation, local authorities let the Indians handle most criminal matters themselves. As long as the Indian trouble didn't leave their land, the whites would turn a blind eye."

"You think this gift to Jacob might have been a peace offering of sorts?" I held up the deed.

"Anything's possible. You need to visit the court-house. Find out who owned this land before Jacob."

"While I'm at it, I'll visit the library. We've got one connection to the Clearwaters, which is a start, but I want to see if I can find any more information on the feud." I stood to gather my handbag and keys. What I didn't share was my plan to search through archives of the *Warren Gazette* to read the articles surrounding Reese's death and the warehouse fire. Though I'd been around at the time, emotional forces left my memory sketchy by erasing the unpleasant and personal details. I needed to face them. It was the one way to figure out the truth and clear my name.

Chapter 12

I approached the stairs of the Warren Public Library. Its whitewashed stone façade was in stark contrast to the centuries-old homes on Market Street. Though founded in 1873, it had been given a facelift or two in the nineteen hundreds, complete with an automatic sliding glass entrance door.

Passing through to the inside, though, was like a journey in a time capsule. The musky odor of aged wood drifted and permeated the air. Antique brass fixtures and decorative carvings adorned the walls and shelves at every turn.

Paintings of historical figures were scattered and hung all around the library, as well as artistically woven tapestries made by local artisans. Huge walnut-trimmed wing chairs in every corner provided a place to get comfy and read. I spent many days wandering through row upon row of books stacked on shelves from floor to ceiling. Much of my encyclopedic brain had absorbed its knowledge from this library.

"Good afternoon, Miss Mackenzie," a gravelly but kind voice called out.

I offered a warm smile to the woman behind the desk. "How are you, Mrs. Quintero?"

As head librarian for nearly seventy years, she approached the century mark of birthdays. She was my go-to person.

"Is there something in particular you're looking for today?" she asked with eager eyes.

I nodded. "I need to search through the newspaper archives."

"Year?"

"Two thousand and four." I fidgeted with my keys. I hoped she wouldn't comment or remember how that year was significant. No such luck.

"Ah, the year of that warehouse fire when poor Reese Logan perished." She studied me with curious eyes. "Wasn't he a friend of yours?"

I tensed but remained polite. "Yes, he was. The truth is, I'm doing some research for Uncle Chaz, and I'm sort of in a hurry."

"Oh! Of course, how rude of me." Mrs. Quintero blushed. "If you'll go up to the second floor, Kenneth will help direct you. Good luck with your research." She managed an awkward grin before returning to her computer.

Relieved to get away, I hurried to the stairs. Kenneth was able to set me up at one of the carrels. I scowled. Articles from that year hadn't been converted to computer files, which meant I had to view microfiche. It would give me eyestrain, to say the least. With a shoulder heave, I leaned forward to place my forehead against the view finder.

I soon relaxed. It didn't take much time to find the articles I wanted. Two on the fire and three on Reese's death, along with a biography of him and his family. To recall how much we all lost that day left a hollow feeling inside me. I went on to read anything that might be unusual or puzzling which happened around that time.

I jotted down several details and tucked the information away in my handbag. "Thanks Kenneth." I waved and traveled down the stairs. My research wasn't finished. Traveling to the rear section of the library, I found materials on local history. A quick scan of the titles led to one on Seneca tribes during the post-Civil War period. That was the closest match. Leafing through the pages and the index gave me nothing on a Bluehawk-Clearwater feud.

I shoved the volume back on the shelf and with determined steps made my way to the front desk once more and searched for Mrs. Quintero. "Ah, there you are."

"Oh my! I didn't hear you." She held a hand to her throat. "Is there more I can help with?"

"I know this is a longshot, but since you've lived in the area for...a while, did you ever hear of a feud between the Bluehawk and Clearwater families during, say, the late eighteen hundreds?"

Her face scrunched up in deep thought. After a minute or two, she shook her head. "Sorry, but can't say I have. I do remember some of the Clearwater clan got into a heap of trouble with the law a few years back, but nothing about the Bluehawks." Suddenly, her eyes lit up. "Maybe you should talk to Grandma Sage Bluehawk. She's the sole living relative around these parts since her grandson died." Mrs. Quintero frowned. "Well over a hundred, no doubt. She hasn't been to one of our Women's Auxiliary meetings—that's where I met her, you see—in well over a year. Anyway, that's who you should speak to. She lives in Kane on Laurel Falls Drive. I can't recall the address, but she showed me pictures. Bright purple two-story. It should stand out plenty."

I felt a glimmer of hope. "Thanks, Mrs. Quintero."

"Sorry I couldn't give you more information. Perhaps the museum in Salamanca has more on it?"

I had thought of Papa this morning but hoped to avoid a trip north. As it was, it seemed I would be making a long drive in another direction. Kane was forty minutes from Warren. And by now it was past three. It didn't matter. My impatience and Chaz's desire to get the project finished didn't allow for procrastination.

As I exited the library, I pulled out my phone to call Chaz with the new agenda. While it rang, I glanced across the street to see an older man sitting on the front porch of a brick and stone century home. He smoked a cigar as he rocked in his chair. After I reached the sidewalk, the sight of him became clearer. However, it was not until I'd crossed the street that I was certain. The details of his dark hair streaked with silver and his tan, leathered skin, which had hardened his face, belonged to only one man I knew. Plum Steelwater. His expression dared you to read what he thought, however frightening it might be. I trembled as a cold uneasiness traveled throughout my body. With a quick nod, I hurried down the walk, but not before I caught the slight wave of an arm. At once, I dismissed the notion that he smiled, flashing those gold-capped teeth. That would be out of character. Right?

"Hello?" Chaz called out through the phone.

"Oh. Sorry, Uncle Chaz. I was…preoccupied. Okay, anyway, change of plans. I'm going to Kane. There's a chance I may get to speak with Sage Bluehawk. According to Mrs. Quintero, Sage is the only living Bluehawk relative in the area. Let's hope she can add to our research."

"It's worth a try. What did you find at the library?"

I held my breath for a second. I didn't want to talk about what I'd read in the gazette, not to Chaz. He'd scold me, warn me to leave it alone. No matter. It was not the way I worked. A curious mind and the desire to find out the truth was what drove me. He should remember that.

This afternoon's search pushed me still further. There were a couple of eyebrow-raising details in the articles that I questioned. Like all the vandalism which happened in cemeteries around the area. Ground turfed, gravestones cracked and smashed, a sizable amount of damage that left residents to wonder why. However, after a couple of months, it stopped. No one had been charged with the crime. It had nothing to do with the warehouse fire, but it was curious, all the same.

The second point which troubled me was the evidence found on the fire victim. The article listed the items. A silver watch and belt buckle with Reese's initials. After the case was closed, those items were given to Callie. What bothered me was how there'd been no mention of the ring I gave him for his last birthday, a silver band with a single turquoise stone. I bought it at the pow-wow held near Export a few months earlier while visiting Mackenzie relatives. Reese loved Indian jewelry and he loved that ring. He promised never to take it off. What happened to it, then?

"Are you still there?"

Chaz's voice brought me back. "Sorry. No. I didn't find anything about the feud. That's why I want to visit Sage Bluehawk."

"What about the property deed?"

"I haven't gone to the courthouse yet. I figured I'll wait until tomorrow. I really want to speak with this Bluehawk woman today. According to Mrs. Quintero, Sage is older than dirt. Who knows? She could be dead by tomorrow." I winced at my callous remark. Not like me, but circumstances challenged any ability to stay rational.

"Fine. You stoppin' back for supper? Or will you head straight to the bar?"

"The bar." Images of Nash and our kiss left their imprint. My brain did the tango with my heart, full of steps and pauses, to argue the point. I couldn't change things between us overnight, no matter how much he wanted. It didn't work like that. Not for me. Not while ghosts from the past haunted my soul.

"See you later on this evenin'? I'd like to hear what the Bluehawk woman has to say. Give me somethin' to think about tonight."

I ended the call and reached for the door handle. Once on the road, I let GPS guide my way to Laurel Falls Drive, and I prayed the woman hadn't repainted her house. Going from door to door asking for Sage Bluehawk would not be my first choice, but if that was what it took, then I would.

The drive led me out to the right on Route 6, away from the dam. I approached the signs that warned of falling rock and kept an eye on the steep wall along that section of road. Once the sight of flat corn fields came into view, I relaxed.

Within half an hour. I reached the city of Kane and made a left turn at the main intersection. It led into an older neighborhood with streets named for various local attractions. I passed Niagara Falls Avenue, Jake Rocks Road, Rim Rock Road, and finally Laurel Falls. Slowing the vehicle, I made a right turn since the road only went in one direction. I studied each house, searching for the one painted purple. Hope faded. Every color in the spectrum adorned the faces of homes along the drive, from turquoise and canary yellow to more modest choices like white or gray. But no purple. Not until I reached a dead end and the last house on the left. It sat far from the road, behind a crowded line of maple and oak trees grown tall enough to obstruct the house's view from any approaching vehicle.

I steered to the curb and let the truck idle while I stared at Sage Bluehawk's home. Purple lived everywhere, on the house, window frames, porch, steps, door, even the picket fence skirting the yard. I puzzled over the color obsession and what sort of person Sage Bluehawk might be.

I took the path up the sidewalk and stepped around two felines napping in the sun to reach the front porch. I searched but found no doorbell. Instead, alongside the door hung a brass bell tied to a braided purple and white rope. I shrugged then wrapped my fingers around the rope. Giving it a tug, the bell chimed and clanged. At once, the thumping sound of footsteps approached. I readied myself with a smile to greet the elderly woman.

However, when the door opened, I let out a gasp. "Jemma?"

"Sarah Mackenzie?"

We stared at one another for a long, awkward moment before I finally spoke. "You live here?"

Jemma nodded with a puzzled frown. "I do, but whatever brought you here?"

"Sage Bluehawk? I was told she lived in this house and that she…" I sighed. "I wanted to speak with her about some research." Life didn't get more bizarre than this. Of course, Jemma was a Bluehawk, though not a blood relative. Why hadn't I thought of the connection sooner? Bricks for brains. It's what Uncle Chaz would've said, and I'd agree.

"I thought you were researching the Clearwater family." She stepped aside to wave me in. I was sure a slight scowl crossed her face, but in a second, it vanished.

"I was and still am, but something we found in the book Papa gave us is leading in another direction. A feud that went on between the Bluehawks and Clearwaters. I hoped Sage might shed some light on the subject. Is she here? Can I speak with her?"

Jemma's eyes grew dim as she shook her head. "Grandma Bluehawk died last month. That's what brought me to stay in Kane." She motioned for me to take a seat. "You see, my husband was her grandson. In fact, her only living relative. But he died last year. You already heard the details from Steve. Anyway, the family lawyer contacted me with the news. I have a legal claim to the house, which should have gone to Sonny. It's mine, if I want it." Her eyes moistened.

I looked around the parlor room. Framed photos decorated every wall. Beyond the hallway I peered into what looked like a library or den. Numerous artifacts hung on its walls.

I recognized medicine wheels, dream catchers, beaded wall hangings, cornhusk faces, and animal skins in brilliant colors, all of them artfully displayed. A variety of pottery items sat on a long table, painted with designs in vibrant colors of orange, blue and green. My heart raced at the sight. I could spend all day here, soaking up the rich Indian culture. Weeks even.

"If you would like to look around, it's fine," Jemma added.

Without responding, I took steps to circle the parlor slowly. I studied the details of each photo. A tall woman with silver gray hair which hung in a thick braid posed in many of them. She wore traditional Indian garb with a printed skirt flowing out to the sides and a long-sleeved blouse to match. Most were in black and white, but the newer ones in color revealed her love of purple.

I turned to Jemma. "Is this her? Your Grandma Sage?"

"Yes." Jemma's face softened. "She was a kind and

spiritual soul. Understanding and loyal to the family ways."

I scratched the back of my neck. "You know I have to ask...Why all the purple?"

Jemma laughed. "Purple was her favorite color, yes. However, there's more to it. To the Indians, purple can symbolize power, mystery, and magic."

"Did she ever tell you anything about that?" I reached inside my handbag and grabbed a notepad to jot down a few words.

"Not directly, but Sonny talked about it. He told me stories, those from his childhood when he'd visit Grandma Sage. Things he couldn't explain would happen. Wonderful experiences that only a child can appreciate without doubt or questions."

I watched her expression change. This was a different side to Jemma. She seemed kinder, gentler, and somewhat wistful. "Any you'd like to share with me?"

She fingered the feathers of the necklace resting against her chest. "One time he awoke during the night. A sound of laughter echoed through his open window. When he took a peek, he saw lights, twinkling lights in many colors, all over the backyard. They were in the trees, across the lawn, in the garden, just everywhere. And in the middle of it all, Grandma Sage twirled around in circles, arms spread wide, her face turned up to the sky. She danced and sang while all the lights twinkled and glittered around her. Sonny wanted to join her, but when he ran downstairs to open the backdoor, he found nothing. No lights, no grandma, only the yard and garden as it had always been.

"When he asked about it the next morning, his grandma smiled and told him he must have had a wonderful dream. He was a lucky boy to sleep with such imagination, she said. And that was it. He claimed there were other unusual moments, but none as great as that one."

"Hmm. She did sound unique." I mulled over thoughts about Sage for a brief moment. My gaze settled back on the room filled with artifacts. "Do you mind?" I nodded toward the hallway.

Jemma waved in that direction and I hurried across the hall before she changed her mind. My breath caught as shivers of excitement pulsed through me. All of it, the multitude of colors, textures, and history nearly over-whelmed me, yet my mind wanted to soak in every detail, every fiber of every item.

I touched the wall hanging closest to me with light fingertips. "How blessed to own such a piece. The beads...carved from wood, shells, bones..." I turned to Jemma, excitement sparkling in my mind. "This must be extremely old. I mean centuries old."

Jemma nodded. "Early to late seventeenth century."

"Maybe earlier. Indians didn't use glass beads before settlers brought them to America. In the fifteen and six-teen hundreds, wasn't it? After seventeen hundred, it be-came more and more common to sew them on clothing." My mind drifted off into its own world. I conjured up an image of a woman with dark hair wearing a buckskin dress. She sat with a purple cloth in her lap. With deft hands she threaded the beads and sewed them to the ma-terial.

"Grandma Sage claimed it was a Seneca ancestor, a grandmother—so many greats I can't count—who made it. It's been in the family all this time." Jemma stepped forward to stand next to me.

My gaze shifted to the side to study her face, and I frowned. The pain was evident. Jemma didn't try to hide it, either. "It's beautiful. You're lucky to have it," I whis-pered and, with swift steps, walked away to diffuse the uncomfortable moment. I stopped in front of the largest item in the room.

Jemma nodded. "It's mine. I brought it with me when I moved here last month."

Curiosity filled me. "You've danced in pow-wows?"

"Yes, once or twice. My father used to, but then…" Jemma gave her head a forceful shake and smiled. "I even won several ribbons. Those are in my room, somewhere in one of the boxes I haven't unpacked." She shrugged apologetically. "I want to place them next to the dress when I find time."

"It's incredibly nice. You should be proud," I said, not sure what else to say. All at once, my face brightened. "Speaking of history, did your grandma ever talk about a feud between the Bluehawks and Clearwaters, sometime during the late eighteen hundreds?"

Jemma's brows knitted together. "No, but there is an album of sorts. I found it upstairs in her room. I think it has photos and notations. Maybe you'd be interested in seeing it?"

There was an eager tone in her voice. I hid my disappointment. Odds were, this wouldn't give me what I needed. "Sure. Why not?"

Jemma took the lead up the creaking stairway and into a room, barely large enough to hold the single bed. Centered on top of the tall but narrow dresser was a thick album. I chuckled at the sight of a purple cover as Jemma placed it in my hands.

"I know. She was obsessed with the color." Jemma let a smile brighten her face as she rested on the bed. With a pat of her hand she motioned for me to sit next to her.

I laid the album on my lap and flipped through the pages. For most of an hour, I admired pages displaying the life of Sage Bluehawk, covering each decade, her face transposing from smooth, youthful innocence to the added lines and creases of experience and wisdom. Tiny notations scribbled underneath photos or in the margins of each page gave me a glimpse into the old woman's heart and soul.

I closed the album. "She seems like a special lady."

Jemma cleared her throat as she turned away to stare out the window. "She was, and enormously dear to me. After I married Sonny ten years ago, he brought me to visit Grandma every summer. We'd stay for a week or two. She'd always convince us to stick around longer. Sometimes a month, depending on Sonny's job." Suddenly Jemma stood. "Well, I hate to push, but I have someplace to be in an hour."

"Oh! Sure. I didn't mean to keep you. It's just so fascinating. All of it." I glowed with appreciation. "Thank you for sharing."

"No problem. I enjoy every bit of the family's history and love showing it to others. Maybe someday I will give the more valuable items to local museums, but..." She shrugged.

"Hard to part with, right? I understand." I walked to the stairs and descended with Jemma right behind me.

"Again, if you need help with your research, let me know," Jemma announced as she held the front door open.

"Thank you." I extended my hand. Jemma held it with a firm grip.

"You are blessed to have many who care about you," Jemma said then let the door close.

I frowned, staring at the closed door. Who did Jemma have, now that Sonny and Grandma Sage were gone? It didn't surprise me any longer why she seemed vehement, yet somehow needy. Embittered by life, maybe? She must hunger for someone to fill that empty place inside her. She needed to get out more. Later, after this mess I found myself in was over, I'd suggest a girl's get together. Maybe invite Deena, too. That would be fun.

Returning to the truck, I picked up my phone to call Chaz. I had little to tell him, nothing about the feud, but was anxious, all the same, to describe the colorful details of what remained inside those purple walls and the special person who once lived there.

Chapter 13

I busied myself thinking of the numerous details of my visit to Kane on the return trip. I breezed through Warren and continued on to Priest Hollow. By the time I reached the back roads and drove into the parking lot, a golden glow of light shown through the front windows of Moe's Deja Blue. Nash's car sat alongside Cisco's near the rear entrance. Emmie wasn't due in until eight when the bar opened. Of course, that didn't stop a few of the old timers from coming in at an earlier hour. They were used to the way Moe kept the business open from noon to closing, every day except Sunday. I refused to give up that much of my time or anyone else's. Still, if Nash was here, he'd invite them in for a quick drink and a bit of gossip.

My conversation with Uncle Chaz lasted a mere ten minutes. He cut it off when a knock at the door announced a visit from Zeke Dally, one of our neighbors—we had less than a handful—along Roper Hollow Road. They had a standing engagement to play checkers every Wednesday evening. It didn't matter if Zeke interrupted, since I had nothing newsy to share. And Chaz didn't seem much interested in my descriptive inventory of Sage Bluehawk's treasures.

I straightened my shoulders before entering the bar. My pulse revved like a high throttled engine when I stepped into the storage room and spotted Nash. His muscles flexed as he picked up a crate from the floor and placed it on the counter next to him. I traced the lines of those chiseled biceps with my eyes and how his shirt outlined his trim body. I swallowed hard before clearing my throat.

In an instant, he whipped around with a scowl creasing his face. "You shouldn't sneak up on a body like that."

"I wasn't sneaking. I came inside a second ago. What would you like me to do? Slam the door and shout?" As soon as the words escaped my lips, I regretted the snappy remark and how it sounded.

His eyebrow arched, but he smiled. "What brings you in this early? Boring day?"

My shoulders eased. He didn't raise the topic of our conversation from last evening. The relief it gave me came both as a surprise and a disappointment. *That* frustrated me. What did I want from him, really? "Not boring." I placed my arms behind me and on the back counter, lifted myself up, and sat.

"And I suppose you want to tell me all about it. Well, you'll have to follow me up to the bar. I need to stock these bottles before the customers start flooding in." He grabbed the crate and I followed him.

"You remember the woman who came in with Steve the other night?"

"Yeah, Jemma Bluehawk. We spoke." He set the crate behind the bar.

"Yeah. No, wait. You actually talked to her?" I stepped up to walk alongside him.

"Not much. Steve introduced us. She's a curious one. After a brief exchange of hi and how do you like living here, she kept quiet and stared at me while I talked with Steve, like her eyes could bore holes through me." He shrugged. "Why?"

I chewed on my bottom lip while I mulled over his observation. That had been exactly my take on Jemma, at first. But now...

"I ran into her today. We had a long visit. Did you know her husband was Sage Bluehawk's grandson?"

"Who's Sage Bluehawk?"

"I've learned she is—*was*—the last living blood relative from the Bluehawk clan. Anyway, Jemma lost her husband, Sonny, last year, and with both of them dead, she inherited the grandmother's house."

Nash set the last of the bottles underneath the bar. He braced both arms on the counter and leaned forward. "Is this going somewhere?"

"Oh, sorry." My face warmed. "I'm still giddy from the excitement of seeing all the Indian artifacts Sage had stored in her house. I mean, you wouldn't believe it. There's enough in there to fill Papa's museum and then some." I went on to describe what I'd seen, including all the photos. "Do you know Jemma has participated in pow-wow dances? Maybe in the Seneca pow-wow at one time. I forgot to ask."

"I don't recall seeing her there. But, then again, I don't pay much attention to the women's competition."

I caught the sly grin on his face and smacked his arm with a bar towel. "Yeah, right." When his eyes gleamed and his grin turned into a wider smile, I took hurried steps backward. "Oh, no you don't." I managed no more than turning around before I felt the snap of the towel on my rear. I squealed and hopped between tables to get out of reach.

"If I didn't have to get your bar ready, I'd catch up to you in a second," he shouted.

"Oh, sure. Like that will happen." With an impish grin, I disappeared into the kitchen to speak with Cisco. My skin tingled. The idea that Nash could make me feel so alive, so happy, so complete, so…everything my heart yearned for but my mind refused…made this evasive reaction to talking about it all the more frustrating.

The clock ticked on until it reached eight, which brought the first customers through the door. It felt strange to be there to greet them. Most evenings, I arrived when the bar was in full swing with the crowd filling every table. To see them trickle in, give each a nod, a handshake, and a warm greeting was how it used to be before I got caught up in Uncle Chaz's life. I didn't mind, though. Caring for him made my soul richer and my heart bigger. And, as his assistant, it gave me endless opportunities to learn more and add to the ever-growing knowledge cluttering my brain. Fact finding gave me another purpose: it was new and unique, and I loved it.

"Well, I'll be. Look what the cat dragged in. Never anything or anyone this pretty."

I stiffened at the heavy slap on my shoulder and struggled to release my breath as bearlike arms squeezed me in an embrace. "Good evening, Lonny," I croaked. "How've you been?"

Lonny Pewter leaned back but kept a tight grip on my arms. "Never been better. But I hear you've had enough to sink your day into a deep hole." He narrowed his eyes in concern. "Found a dead body, did you? Your uncle told me all about it this evenin' when I stopped by for a short visit to say hello."

I sighed while Lonny remained close, not moving a muscle. He expected some response when I didn't want to say a word about it. Of all times for me to promise

Nash I'd help out more around the place. Being here was like a rerun of high school cafeteria moments when everybody gabbed about everybody's business. It was exhausting and embarrassing.

I scratched the back of my neck. "Yep. Dead as dead can be. If you'll excuse me, Lonny, I should mingle."

Lonny let go his grip and backed away. "Of course! You've got a business to run." He smiled. The flush to his face hinted at his discomfort.

I felt badly. Still more, I was angry with Uncle Chaz for blabbing to everyone about the issue, *my* business, not his.

"Oh, and I'll try to put in a good word for you down at the station. Sheriff Parker and I have become fishin' buddies as of late." Lonny winked and then walked away.

I groaned. "This has to stop."

Tapping my foot, I focused on something other than Lonny. From the stage, the ping of guitar strings echoed. Nash stood next to Vince, both heads leaned in to listen as they harmonized their instruments. A twinge of irritation tickled my insides and left me exasperated. Not even soothing blues could relax me now. I stomped off toward the bar to find Emmie.

"You look in a great mood," Emmie retorted. She flipped the bar towel to rest on one shoulder.

"I'm fine, honestly." I shrugged. "As of late, too many nosy people come into this bar."

"Ha. You mean Lonny Pewter. Well, let me tell you, if you think he's bad, you should meet his grandson. I went out on a date with him last month." Emmie stuck a finger in her mouth and gagged. "He asked more questions about my past and personal history than a slew of news reporters scrambling to beat each other to the punch. As if that wasn't irritating enough, at the end of our evening, he expected more than a first date kiss, much more, if you know what I mean."

I picked up a glass from the dish pan and polished it dry. "I'm beyond tired from explaining all the unfortunate, miserable events of my life. I wish they'd leave it alone."

"Speaking of which, have you heard any more about the body ID? Seems like it's been long enough to get results."

I dropped my head and moaned. "Not you, too? I swear I will be the last to hear. Sheriff Parker doesn't seem to like me much. And I'm not trying to charm him." I explained what I'd told the sheriff before leaving the station the other night.

"Well, that shouldn't make him mad. You reminded him to do his job. Sounds reasonable to me." Emmie grinned and winked.

"Yeah, sure. It burns me to think he'd seriously consider me a suspect. I mean, why would I call him about the body in the first place? And leave incriminating evidence? If I'd done it, I sure wouldn't stick around."

"For someone who'd like to forget about it and not talk…" Emmie tipped her chin.

"You're right. I'm obsessing. It's what I do. Pathetic, huh?" I caught sight of Nash. He came down from the stage and stood close to a young woman. Extremely close. Her curly blonde mane bounced as she talked with one hand touching his shoulder. My breath caught for a second. Nash bent down to whisper in the blonde's ear. A deep, throaty laugh came from her mouth and Nash joined in. At once, I turned away. What did I care? I had no claim to him. After all, hadn't I given him that message by running out on him last night?

"You know, I feel a headache coming on. Maybe I'll take a break from all the noise and lights and go on home." I forced a pleasant look on my face and prayed it worked.

"Sure. I can handle the bar. It doesn't seem too busy tonight, anyway. You get some sleep. It's been rough the past few days, I imagine." Emmie patted my arm and turned when a customer called out for a drink.

I remained quiet as I gathered my things, and after a final glare in Nash's direction, I headed toward the front entrance. Moving fast, I avoided the questioning eyes and sympathetic stares. No way was I giving anyone an opportunity to slow me down to talk.

Once outside, I stopped to take a deep breath and then another. The moon shone brightly. It sent silver rays of light to the earth, which gave everything a ghost-like luminescence. I steered around rows of cars to reach my truck. My shoulders sagged as I settled into the seat. The weight of my tired self, both emotionally and physically, caught up to me. If I hadn't been in such a fired-up hurry to get out, I might have grabbed a cup of coffee to go. As it was, I put the windows down and let the cool breeze wash over my face.

Despite the moonlight's attempt to shine a path, the back roads remained shielded in a layer of black. I flipped on the high beams and slowed down to a crawl along Hatch Run Road. In another mile, I turned onto Scandia and pressed down on the gas pedal as the better surface and wider path gave me wiggle room, in case I needed to stop or swerve around deer or other critters. There'd been more than one collision with enough damage to send my vehicle to the repair shop.

The curve before Roper Hollow was up ahead. I slowed and turned the wheel. Another couple of miles left. I'd make a quick check on Uncle Chaz, grab Opal, and before long I'd be in bed.

I frowned as I reached Zeke's house. The windows

were completely dark. Unless he was still playing checkers with Chaz, it didn't make sense. His usual habit was to leave by nine so he'd settle in at home, watch his late-night program on television, and eat a bag of popcorn. A quick glance at the dash showed me it was after ten.

"That must be some game." I sped past. I knew this stretch of road enough to travel it blindfolded. One more bend and then a couple hundred yards to my drive. Getting out my phone, I glanced down for a second to slide it open to view the home screen. A quick call to Chaz would let me know when they'd be finished.

When I looked back to the road, I gasped and tromped down on the brake. My wheels skidded and sent the truck sideways, landing it at the edge of a ditch. My heart thudded with enough force to leap out of my chest. Frantic, I threw open the door and slid out. I searched back and forth.

I'd seen it, hadn't I? A woman in the road. She stood right in the middle of it, facing me, motionless and not as if a truck was about to run her over. But now? No one moved, not anyone or anything at all. It didn't make sense. I reached back inside the truck and opened the glove compartment to find my flashlight.

I lighted the path, and my legs wobbled as I walked to the spot. I squatted and searched the ground for footprints. Even hoof prints. I thought of a deer or other large animal roaming the woods for a late-night snack, but I really didn't believe that explanation for a second. It was a woman, older perhaps. A woman with long, silvery hair, and she wore a flowing skirt. I stood and walked back and forth from side to side, my gaze downward, my eyes still searching.

"There has to be something here because I'm not crazy," I muttered and wondered how tired a person needed to be before hallucinations occurred.

I nearly gave up. If I came back in the morning, day-light might reveal a print, any mark to convince me I did indeed see someone. I jumped at the sudden hoot of a night owl. "Okay. I'm done. This is insane. Nobody would be out walking alone in this dark. Especially not an old woman."

With long, quick strides to the truck, I reached out to open the door, but a glint of something colorful on the ground stopped me from getting inside. I steadied the flashlight and stared for a moment. My breath held as the object became clearer. Carefully, I picked it up, and with one finger I traced the edges of the woven fabric. The interior light from the truck shone on the piece. Bright purple thread mixed with a trace of white that wrapped around the circle frame. Inside the wheel, the webbing twisted and turned with one bead near its center. Feathers hung from the bottom, some brown and black but two of them were dyed to match the frame. I knew plenty about dream catchers. The Indian legends told of how one should hang it above the bed to have pleasant dreams. The web captured all the bad ones so you were always protected from anything evil.

I held the artifact in my hand and once more searched the area. For all my practical thinking and reasoning, this didn't make sense. I wasn't a person to fantasize or believe in superstitions or ghosts. In my research, I'd discovered plenty of believers, along with stacks of evidence, but I had never been convinced.

The muscles in my face tensed and probably formed a rigid scowl. I climbed into the truck and laid the dream catcher on the seat. Pulling away from the ditch, I moved forward at a crawl to reach my drive. I forgot all about calling Chaz.

In any case, this was something I didn't feel comfortable discussing with him. In fact, I didn't see how I could tell anyone. What would they think? That I went crazy and was seeing things?

"Yep. Exactly," I said and parked my truck.

With slow, methodical steps, I took the path to Chaz's house to tell him and Zeke a quick hello and goodbye. A sound night's sleep would give me better perspective. It was the least to hope for because none of this made sense. Not one bit.

Chapter 14

I raised one eyelid to peek at my dresser. On top lay the dream catcher. I had refused to buy into the superstition and hang it above my bed. Besides, I wasn't having any bad dreams, not that bad at least. Maybe if I did...

"Nope. No way." With both eyes opened now, I glared at the dream catcher as if it taunted and teased me, even begged me to believe. I shifted the other way as if to dismiss it.

Some trick of my imagination caused by extreme exhaustion fogged my brain and created the image. That's all. And the fact a dream catcher was in the road meant nothing. Someone, maybe a child hanging her arm out a car window as her parents drove down to the boat launch yesterday, dropped it on the road. That made logical sense. Better than the alternative. Even Nash, when he spoke of Indian spiritualism and folklore, tended to blow it off as mere superstition, the way the ancestors of previous centuries dealt with what they failed to explain any other way. It was before modern medicine came along. Nothing more than that. I rubbed my eyes and tried to concentrate on more important matters.

Pulling on my robe, I headed to the kitchen but stopped in the doorway. My shoulders slumped as I glanced at the dream catcher. With a sigh, I reached over to grab it and continued on to the kitchen. No more thoughts about dream catchers, I vowed.

Opal had spent the night with Chaz. It came as a surprise to me when he offered, but since Zeke had fallen asleep in the chair with his arm around the dog, Chaz didn't have the heart to disturb them. Despite all his gruffness and disdain for many, he had a real soft spot for his checker-player buddy.

I spent the morning acclimating at a snail's pace, like dipping one toe at a time in the chilly Allegheny waters. As I sipped my coffee, I contemplated events from the past week. Though three days had passed since discovering the body, my fatigued mental state tried to convince me it had been months.

Absently, I spread jam on toast and dipped it in the coffee. Though I didn't believe in the dream catcher's magic or other such folklore, I did believe in a certain amount of fate. Why had this happened? Why was I the one to discover the body? A hint of guilt about my past with Reese weighed heavily on me. As I downed the rest of my coffee, the phone rang.

I glanced at it with a weary gaze, as if I knew who was calling, all because I'd been thinking about Reese and the murder. The familiar number lit up the screen. I paused to take a breath and answered the call. "Hello?"

"Good morning, Miss Mackenzie. This is Sheriff Parker."

At once I sank down into the chair. My chest tightened. "Yes?"

"I have some news. Quite a bit of news, truth be told. You have a minute?"

"Yes. Of course." I frowned, and as if my insides wanted to explode, I struggled to stay seated. Instead, I got up to pace the room.

"First, there's been another murder. Same setup. Body found in a grave, but this time it was covered. Caretaker at Pleasant View Cemetery says he found it early this morning when he discovered the upturned ground and a marker on top, engraved with the words, 'sins of revenge.' And next to it, some burnt herbs. Real strange.

"The thing is, this time we got lucky. Soon as authorities up there uncovered it, one of the deputies recognized him. His name's Toby Clearwater. Ever hear of him?"

My breath hitched. There was no other way to go but the truth. "I have. In fact, my lawyer friend, Papa Birdsong, mentioned him to me the other day. Though he heard Toby moved to Pittsburg years ago." Unless he pressed for more, this was as close to the truth about Toby as I was willing to take it.

"Folks said he moved back home. Last month, I guess."

"Was he shot, too?"

"Shot, yes, but in the head." Parker sighed. "And there's the other bit of news."

My heartbeat pumped loud enough to resonate inside my head. "Yes?"

"We finally have an ID on your body. Dental records show he's Reese Logan. It seemed to shock everyone at the station. Can't manage to stop them from talking about him and this well-known story. Of course, it was before my time as sheriff. I didn't realize Logan, by all accounts, died in a fire back in 2004. I don't suppose you knew him, did you?"

I couldn't decide whether to laugh or cry. His tone of voice hinted that he already learned the answer. Anyone at the station who lived around the area long would know and eventually tell Parker. My relationship with Reese Logan wasn't a well-kept secret, except maybe the intimate details. Only Reese and I'd shared that.

Again, it did me no good to hide the truth. Either way, I looked guilty. I pictured the wheels in his head, and they came to an easy conclusion. No matter. His mind had already taken him there. "Yes. Reese and I were close. In fact, we grew up together. His sister Callie and I were best friends." I flinched at my use of the past tense.

"I see. Well, that does put a new light on things, doesn't it?"

I edged closer to spouting off when hearing his smug tone. "Maybe to you. I look at it as further evidence to clear my name. Why would I kill someone I cared for?" My voice quivered as both my anger and desperation grew out of control. Fingers curled around the phone with a tighter grip. "Do you have the results from my DNA?"

"Not yet. We're still looking. There's a lot of evidence from that grave to compare it to."

"I see. If I might make a request? I know you have to send someone to inform the family. I'd prefer you send Bree Davis to Callie Logan's house. Let her tell Callie about Reese. Bree knows the family well."

"I was planning to inform the mother. That's protocol."

"Forget your damn protocol," I snapped and then took a moment to breathe. "Mrs. Logan hasn't been well. Not since…Please, go to Callie. She has a right to tell her mother about Reese, in her own words." I ended the call before Parker said anything more and before I broke out in tears.

Those came after I set down the phone. They welled up until everything became a blur. Afterward, the anger built. I paced once more while the cry of rage in me

pounded and raced until it escaped my mouth in a scream.
I grabbed the coffee cup and slung it across the room. It
hit the wall and shattered, pieces of china flew everywhere.

I stood frozen with hands clenched into fists as I
stared at the bits of white scattered across the floor and at
my feet. Within seconds, my rage was spent. I sat down
once again and cradled my head in both hands. Eventually, my breathing settled into a steady, calmer rhythm.

I couldn't stop the hurt, but I could stop letting it
control my actions. What I'd had with Reese wasn't deep
and meaningful. It was physical. To put it bluntly, it was
a consequence, made when Nash left town. Nothing more
than the classic fling, a way to fill the void. I knew it was
stupid and immature, but I did it anyway. I was angry
with Nash for leaving, though I hadn't any right. He was
a close friend who wanted a change. Who was I to stop
him? Then Reese was there, willing to take on the role of
friend and casual lover. The sad part was, he'd felt more.
My bottom lip quivered. With a trembling hand, I
stooped to pick up the shards of china. The raw truth?
Face it. I used him. He never told me how he felt, and if
he'd have tried, I would have refused to listen, but he
confessed to Callie. It was one of the reasons I had lost
the close relationship with my best friend. We'd fought
about it, after the fire, when overwhelmed with emotion.
Those brutal and cross words, like daggers, cut too deeply.

No matter how hard I fought it, circumstances would
reopen those wounds, causing the rift between us to grow
wider and deeper until there'd be nothing left to call
friendship. I wiped my cheeks dry. For now, I'd tuck
those emotions into a corner and start concentrating on
what was more important. If it was possible to do anything to repair all those scars, to repay him and his family

for the hurt I caused, I needed to find out what happened to Reese Logan. Add to that, Toby Clearwater. The question was, where to go next?

I searched the room. The dream catcher was a start. "And Papa," I whispered.

A quick change of clothes, a travel mug of coffee in hand, and I was ready to go. I stuffed the dream catcher into my handbag, snatched my keys off the counter, and ran out the door. First, a minor detour to Uncle Chaz's place. A brief good morning and good day was all he'd get. Work on the project could wait until later. Time was crucial. Parker's news proved that. The thought of Elias Jamison came to mind. First things first. I would stop by the bar to speak with Nash after my trip to Salamanca.

My shoulders slumped. A mix of emotions stirred inside that left me racing with excitement and panic at the same time. I let jealous rage take hold when Nash flirted with the blonde last night. My jaw clenched. I swore at the insecurity teasing my brain and heart. This was me being foolish. I had to trust him, or there was nothing worth fighting for.

Reaching the front of Chaz's house, I forced a smile and called out from the bottom step. Opal pushed open the screen door and leaped up to slather my face with a kiss. Chaz sat in the doorway. After a brief explanation of my morning plans, I accepted the scowl on his face without comment and left.

I gave the gas pedal a generous push and headed north. As soon as the exit sign for Broad Street and the Seneca Casino came into view, I checked my watch. While making a left turn toward downtown Salamanca, I picked up my phone to call Papa.

"Hope I didn't wake you," I started when he answered. Despite my deflated mood, a grin formed.

"And you know better than anyone the answer to that.

Up when the sun first peeks its head to bring on the day. Now, what made you call me? Other than to hear my bright and cheery voice." He cackled, bringing on a coughing fit.

"Ha. Take a few sips of your fourth—or is it fifth— cup of coffee while I talk. I'm less than five minutes from the museum. I hope you're there?"

"Of course."

"I have something to run by you." I chewed on my lip and hesitated. "I had an experience last night. It was strange and…I just need somebody to listen."

"I'll put more coffee on to brew and bring out the breakfast pastries. This calls for plenty of sugar to sweeten your mood."

I opened my mouth to say thank you, but Papa had ended the call.

I neared the center of town. Traffic on Broad Street was sparse compared to my last visit. Of course, the day had barely started. Shoppers would filter out to browse the shops and restaurants this afternoon. Many who visited the area came to gamble at the casino and stayed awake until the wee hours of morning. Sleeping past noon was a common occurrence.

A white banner with red letters stretched above and across the road. I leaned forward, my face tilted upward to read the announcement of this weekend's pow-wow. First, Saturday events kicked off with the opening ceremony and the color guard. The announcer would invite onlookers to participate in the inter-tribal dance, and so it went. I had the agenda memorized. It was the same every year. Another block and I swung the truck left into the parking lot. In ten short steps, I was inside to meet Papa at the entrance. With one arm extended, he handed me a large mug of coffee while the other hand offered a plate of donuts.

"Welcome to Papa's, where the coffee is fresh brewed and the pastries are…" He shrugged. "Probably stale, but still tasty."

I chuckled. "I'll take it. You're right. I could use the sugar." I hid the frown behind my coffee mug. After a few sips, I walked to the table and set the mug down. Turning, I braved a smile at Papa and began. "I found this last night." I pulled the dream catcher from my handbag. "On the side of the road, a few hundred yards from my place."

Papa put on his reading glasses and studied it. "Nice work," he said.

"Yeah, but that's not all." With a slow start, I struggled to explain the event leading up to my discovery. The expression on Papa's face didn't reveal what he thought, although his brows did come together and his forehead wrinkled.

"I admit I was tired and may have imagined it all. Maybe it was an animal crossing the road." *An animal that looked like an old woman*, I thought.

"Maybe." Papa nodded. He studied the catcher once more. "I've seen these colors and design before. It's from the Seneca tribe. Plenty of them around these parts. Somebody traveling down your road might've dropped it."

"That's what I figured." My mouth felt dry. Neither one of us wanted to dig deeper or to consider whether I did in fact see a person. Or what it meant. "I went to visit with someone in Kane yesterday. Sage Bluehawk. She recently passed away, though."

"Yes, I knew her. Extraordinary lady. Why did you want to see her?" Papa handed me the dream catcher.

"I hoped she'd offer more information on the nine-teenth-century feud between the Bluehawks and Clearwaters. Uncle Chaz and I read about it in the book you gave us," I explained.

"A feud, huh? I might have a book on that." Papa shifted his gaze back and forth, searching the shelves. After a moment he shrugged an apology. "An ounce of patience is worth a pound of brains. I will find it eventually."

"That doesn't sound like an Indian proverb."

"No, but it works. All people need patience."

I grinned, more at ease, and sat down on a stool. "Here's the funny part. When I got to Sage's house, guess who answered the door?"

"We are playing games? Okay, let's see. Woman or man? Give me a hint."

"Oh, stop. The one who answered was none other than your assistant, Jemma Bluehawk." I sat back and waited for a puzzled reaction, but none came.

"Makes sense. She told me how she moved to Kane because she inherited a house."

I deflated with disappointment but wouldn't let go. "Don't you find it a weird coincidence?"

"Fate plays a strange hand sometimes. Besides, she married a Bluehawk, but I'm sure you thought of that." He looked sly.

I snorted without comment.

"Didn't she offer to help you with the research? Perhaps this was meant to happen. Man sees just the present, but God sees all—"

"Okay, enough," I interrupted. "I get it." Tired of skirting around the uppermost thought in my head, I added, "Interesting that Sage Bluehawk's favorite color was purple." I waited once more to see if Papa's mind would travel in the same direction as mine. It did.

"Purple. Magic and power. She certainly was mysterious, Sage Bluehawk." He sipped his coffee while he stared at me. "You sense a weird connection, don't you? Between the purple dream catcher and your visit to Sage Bluehawk's place?"

I shrugged. "It's not what I *want* to believe." And I didn't. I fought the notion with every sensible fiber of my being, although my being was out of sorts these days.

"Coincidence is often mistaken for what is intended. That's what I believe. But you came for another reason, didn't you?"

It unsettled me the way he managed to do that. "The sheriff got an ID on the body I discovered. It's Reese Logan. And then this morning, Toby Clearwater was found in the Pleasant View Cemetery. Shot through the head and buried in a grave." My words came out in a flat, even tone.

"Ah. And so it goes. Reese. Toby. Next, maybe Elias? Who was the body that died in the fire? Many, many questions."

"There were some herbs next to the grave marker. The sheriff said it looked like they had been burning." I frowned. "Do you know why?"

Papa sat down next to me. "Smudging. The Native Americans burn sage during a ritual to cleanse the body and rid the surrounding area of bad spirits and influences."

I tapped my empty mug. "I remember. It's supposed to fill you with good thoughts, keep the anger and hate from poisoning your heart."

Papa nodded and wrapped his arm around my shoulders. "The sheriff suspects you all the more, doesn't he?"

"I suppose, but at the moment, I don't care about that. If Elias is the next target, I have to figure out a way to stop it from happening." I didn't mention what else drove me.

"You should let the authorities do their job to catch

the real killer. This is too dangerous, Little Mac. Your uncle will say the same."

I ignored the warning and its common sense. "You know, since this all came about, I hadn't given much thought to who died in the fire until now. What if Dillard Hopewell's story is a lie? What if he's hiding some gruesome details? Maybe he knows the true identity of who burned to death. In any case, he and maybe Elias are the only ones alive to talk to about it."

"And I'm sure the sheriff will come to the same conclusion. He'll find Dillard and question him. You should leave it be." Papa's face grew heavier with concern.

"I don't plan on traipsing out to who-knows-where alone to question Dillard Hopewell. Not since he may, in fact, be the killer. I'm not as crazy as you suspect." I'd persuade Nash to go with me, instead.

"How is the handsome Nash Redwing these days?"

My one eyebrow rose. "Ah, he's fine. Still works at the bar and sings for the customers."

"You two ever going to get hitched?" Papa asked with a playful jab to my arm.

"Papa!" I slid off of the stool and walked over to the front desk and nearer to the window. The breeze cooled my flushed face.

"Tell you what. I'll ask around town, see if anyone remembers what Reese, Toby, and Elias had been up to before the fire. Maybe somebody will recall."

I turned to give him a hug when I caught Jemma walking down the hallway. When she spotted me, she stopped.

"Oh, sorry. I don't want to interrupt." An apologetic smile surfaced on her face. She hurried forward to hand Papa a book. "You were looking for this?"

Papa took it and squeezed Jemma's hand. "Thank

you. And you don't need to worry about interrupting. I think of you as family."

I read the concern in Jemma's eyes, but Papa seemed unaware. I struggled to dismiss what felt like an awkward moment.

"Still, I have lots of work to do before the next tour group comes. You two have a nice visit. Good to see you again, Mac." She tipped her head and then disappeared.

"Such a good person. Smart and hardworking. Jemma is a real gem. Get it?" He laughed.

"Uh huh, well, I'm glad you're pleased with her. She does come across as a tad mysterious, though. Has she told you much about her past?"

Papa lifted his chin and reflected for a moment. "Nope. But a person's past should be left there. It's what they measure up to at present that matters."

"I guess. Well, I should go. Thank you, and I'll see you in a couple days."

"Yes, the pow-wow. Can't wait to bend your uncle's ear."

"I'm sure he'll love that." I said and with a wave of my hand, I walked out the door. I had enough time to get back to the bar before heading home for supper. Enough time to meet with Nash to discuss Reese and Toby and to suggest he contact Elias. With any luck, the rest of my day would be minus the stress and emotion from this morning. I fingered the dream catcher sticking out of my handbag, and after a second, got into my truck, and pulled out onto Broad Street.

Chapter 15

Nash stocked the bottles onto storeroom shelves while I shared my news. I started with the easy stuff, how I found the dream catcher. All the while, he seemed to half pay attention. It bothered me and puzzled me at the same time. I fidgeted with the catcher and nearly frayed the yarn. I tossed it to the side and tore open a crate to hand bottles to Nash instead.

"I all but convinced myself she was real." I swallowed. "For a second, she reminded me of Sage Bluehawk. Crazy, right?"

"Your mind was on the woman after your visit, that's all. I hear from relatives living on Cole Hill Road they've sighted black bear. Going through trash bins, mostly. Maybe that's what you saw." He finished shelving and wiped the dust from his hands on his pant legs.

"I guess that's possible," I said, thinking, no, it *wasn't* possible. A woman with silvery black hair wearing a colorful skirt couldn't be confused with a black bear. I'd sooner believe I dreamed the whole incident, but that wouldn't explain the dream catcher.

Nash walked over to stand next to me. He wore the

scent of musk. I didn't back away, though the panic started to build again. The muscles in my legs twitched. I
willed myself not to move. My breath held as he leaned
closer. His arm brushed my side as he reached around me.

"You should hang this over your bed. Maybe your
luck will change." He placed the dream catcher in my
hands and smiled.

I shivered at his touch and closed my eyes for a second. When I opened them, I found him walking to the
doorway. "I have more news," I announced before he left
the room. "A call from Sheriff Parker."

Nash turned, his head tilted, the smile gone.

"They've got an ID on the body. It's Reese." The
struggle to keep my anxiety and fear at a distance lost its
battle. I wanted to tell Nash what happened back then,
after he'd left town. Yet, I still couldn't decide whether or
not I owed him an explanation.

"You figured as much. Have you told your uncle?"

"No. I rushed out this morning to visit with Papa. He
offered to do some digging and find more on what Reese,
Toby, and Elias were up to before the fire. And that's the
other bit of news." I paused. This didn't seem real, like I
watched some horrible play where everyone around me
kept dying. My body trembled. I had no flip comment, no
trivia facts to match the situation, nothing but the cold
truth. "Toby is dead, found in Pleasant View Cemetery
and buried in a grave. He was shot, like Reese."

Nash sucked air through his mouth and clenched his
jaw. "Two murders. And you in the middle. I don't like
the feel of this."

"And you think I do?" I made my way across the
room to be next to him when I added, "I'm worried about
Elias. Maybe you should call him? With both Reese and
Toby murdered…You know there has to be a connection.
And that includes Elias. It only makes sense."

"I suppose you're right. I haven't spoken to him in months. Don't know if his number is the same. He mentioned how his luck turned sour. Something like Trey suggested when we spoke. Only Elias had a more colorful way of putting it. Not enough gigs, too much booze and women." Nash chuckled without the smile.

"I pray he can explain why this is happening." I took a seat on one of the crates stacked next to the door. "It's awful to think this, but if Elias isn't a target—"

"Let's not go there." Nash leaned against the wall, his arms crossed his chest. "The killer could be anybody. Your messenger, Spirit Talker, for one. I don't care for him."

I shrugged. "It's possible. But if you throw him into the suspect pool, I'm adding Plum Steelwater."

Nash stared down at me. "You're serious?"

"It's a hunch, like one of those itches people have about something being wrong. He gives me that itch every time I see him. Add to it his scary talk of skeletons in family closets? Oh, I don't know. Silly, right?" I groaned and dropped my head into my hands.

"Fine. You can add Plum to the list. Might as well toss in Elias. Anyone else?"

I slid a thumbnail between my teeth. I sorted the bits and pieces of my conversation with Papa. "How about Dillard Hopewell? Learning Reese wasn't the one who died in the fire makes me question Dillard's alibi. There has to be more to it. He may have left town that night. I'm sure authorities checked. But the rest of his story may be one big lie. What if Reese contacted Dillard recently and threatened to expose him? That's a pretty strong motive for murder."

"Then Toby does the same thing so Dillard murders him, too? It's a stretch. And we can't be sure Dillard was responsible for whoever died in the fire. Boy, I wouldn't want to be Sheriff Parker."

"Yeah, having to figure out who died all those years ago. They may never find out."

Nash walked over to sit on the bench next to me. "Funny how nobody reported a missing relative or friend. You'd think John Doe had somebody who'd have noticed when he disappeared."

"Maybe a hobo? Some homeless drifter who found shelter in the warehouse that evening. Wrong place, wrong time. That sort of thing." I stared down at my feet. Next to Nash's they looked tiny and vulnerable.

"Hmm. Good call. In that case, you're right. Parker may never find out who he was."

"He reaches a dead end. Cold case closed."

"Ah, not so fast. He still needs to find out why Reese wanted folks to believe he was dead, and why he needed to disappear. Not to mention where he'd been the past ten years."

I glimpsed the shift in his expression. The anger was building, and it hit me. Nash must feel as betrayed as I did. I nearly forgot Nash and Reese had been friends, too. My heart thudded, and the weight of guilt swept over me, uncontrollable, until I began to shake.

"Hey." Nash wrapped his arm around me and squeezed. "It'll be fine. You'll see. I'm here for you. So are Chaz, Papa, Emmie, and even Deena. We'll keep you safe."

His words added to my grief. The tears started as my shoulders quaked. Even his tightened grip failed to keep me still.

"*Shh.* It's okay. I'll protect you. I'll be your dream catcher," he whispered in my ear but stopped there. No intimate kiss this time.

I sniffed and chuckled simultaneously. It came out in

a snort. "Thanks, but there's something I need to tell you. I—"

The tinkling of the front door bell interrupted. "Hello? Anyone here?"

Nash pulled away and stood. "Clive. He's right on time." He started toward the door but suddenly stopped. "You wanted to tell me something?"

I rubbed my thighs to smooth out the nervous tremor and shook my head. "It's nothing. I think I'll head over to Callie's place before going home. I'm sure she's heard about Reese."

"She could use a friend," Nash agreed.

"Yeah. That's me." I heard the hollow tone of my words. Some friend. Right now it was a toss of a coin. Either Cassie would welcome me inside or slam the door in my face. I needed to prepare for the worst, which was exactly what I deserved.

With a nervous smile, I said goodbye, and instead of exchanging social quips with Clive, I left through the service entrance. After a brief call to Chaz to let him know I'd be late, I was on my way down Scandia Road.

By five, the heat of the day had reached its pinnacle. Birds fluttered about to find their evening meal, along with the squirrels chattering as they scurried up and down trees and leaped from one limb to another. A doe with her two fawns nibbled on sweet grass at the side of the road. Sunlight filtered through the branches of trees to design the pavement with a speckled pattern of white and shadows.

The houses along Cobham Park Road were a mix of old and older. No one in this section of town bothered building new; they merely renovated, updated, and refurbished that which existed. As a result, treasures of past history remained for folks who appreciated such things.

I gripped the steering wheel as I slowed the truck to

pull into Callie's drive. A dim light in the kitchen shown through the front picture window. As I well knew, at this hour, Callie would fix herself a meal, maybe leftovers from Sunday dinner. Callie loved leftovers. She'd combine various meals to create a new and different dish. Some failed, some hit the success mark. I remembered when we'd all get together. It made me smile.

Once out of the truck, I forced my legs in motion. Neither my physical or mental side wanted to do this. It was the hurt Callie must be feeling that pushed me. I stabbed the doorbell button once and immediately dropped my arm to my side.

After a long, agonizing moment, the door lock clicked. I stood tall and smiled as Callie opened the door. "Hi, Callie," I said in a tone not much more than a whisper.

Callie froze. I feared the worst. Any second, she'd close the door on me and the chance of renewing our friendship. Maybe she'd been offended the other night at the bar when I'd left the table. I hadn't really answered her questions. Out of guilt, I'd kept my distance, and she'd been hurt by it. I could tell. And now, learning about Reese and my part in it? I stepped sideways, ready to leave, when Callie broke out of her still posture and stepped onto the porch. She grabbed me in a strong embrace and began to cry.

I joined her. And that's the way we stayed for nearly ten minutes. Until both our faces were soaked with tears. They weren't just for the moment; they were ten years' worth of sadness and regret.

"Please. Come in. Sorry I don't have anything to offer except hot tea. I was making myself a cup when you came. Would you like some?" Callie sniffed as she led me by the hand into the house.

I frowned. The room was darkened with all the

blinds closed. Nothing was like I remembered it. The walls had been stripped of most decorations, except for family photos, mostly of Reese. The drab, colorless look of the place made it seem like the house mourned along with Callie.

Callie nodded. "You'll have to excuse the clutter. I didn't get a chance to tidy up this morning."

The emptiness in her eyes mixed with something else I didn't recognize. "It's fine. The place looks how I remember it," I lied.

"No, it doesn't." Callie argued with a poor attempt to smile. "You never could keep the truth from me."

"No. You're right. I never could." I rubbed the goosebumps on my arms. "I'll take a cup of tea since you're having one." I peered at the framed photos. They filled the fireplace mantle, secretary desk, and the wall above that. Drawn to them, I crossed the room to take a closer look. Most were posed shots, but several caught candid slices of Reese's life. From toddler to graduate, he'd grown as any boy would grow. Happy, healthy, loving, caring. I missed the innocence we all had during our youth.

"My favorite is this one. We all jumped into the lake. Remember that day?" Callie laughed as she returned to the room.

I studied the photo. Callie and Reese, along with Nash and I stood on top of the giant rock, hands on hips as water dripped from our drenched hair. "My dad took the picture, didn't he? It was a fun day but freezing cold." I took the cup from Callie's hand. "November? The weekend of Thanksgiving, right?"

Callie nodded. Her eyes glistened as she spoke. "What could have happened, Sarah? Why did he do such a cruel thing? Leaving us like that, making us believe he was dead. It's so incredibly wrong."

I gripped the cup between my hands, soaked in the warmth, and wished it would seep inside to warm my heart. "I don't know the answer, but I intend to find out." At once, my anger grew stronger, and it felt good. It helped me push for the truth.

"I've been thinking. My mind won't rest until we have answers." I tugged on Callie's sleeve and led the way to the sofa, where we sat facing one another. The glimmer of hope in Callie's eyes gave me courage. "I visited the library and read the articles about the fire and Dillard's testimony, which I'll get to later. Anyway, I came across something that raises a question. You remember how Reese's personal belongings were found at the fire, next to whoever died there? Well, the article I found mentioned the belt buckle and watch, but not the silver turquoise ring. I gave him that ring for his birthday, remember? He told me he would never take it off." I stopped. The words struggled from my mouth. "If I'd paid attention then...but I didn't. I'm so sorry."

Callie sighed. "*I* should have been the one to notice. Can you guess how many times I pulled those items out to look at them? I was eaten up by grief." She shook her head. "Well, it doesn't matter now, does it? We still don't know why he did what he did. Why he was so desperate to disappear."

"No, but we will. I promise." I put on an encouraging smile for her. "Say! I got an idea. Why don't we take a ride to Dairy Delite? A cold treat sounds perfect."

"Sure. Why not?" Callie shrugged, but her face brightened. "I'm glad you stopped by."

"Me, too." Hope grew in my heart. Maybe my luck was changing. "By the way, there's something I should tell you." I stood and threw my handbag over a shoulder.

"If it's about Sheriff Parker, I know. Bree mentioned it. How can he suspect you?"

I winced. The news should have come from me. "Sorry. I couldn't mention it sooner."

"Ha. Don't worry. I told Bree it was hogwash, and if Parker didn't start looking for the real killer, I'd campaign against him next election."

I pressed my lips together but failed to keep the laugh bottled up. Without the heavy weight of worry and guilt stomping on my chest, I almost enjoyed the moment. I'd underestimated Callie, who managed to remain strong, no matter the tragedy laid at her doorstep. And our friendship was something she needed as much as I did. The realization warmed my insides.

I pulled the truck out of the drive and steered toward Dairy Delite. Chaz would have to keep supper warming in the oven because I was going to arrive late and with less or no appetite.

"What's this?" Callie picked up the dream catcher.

"Ah, there's a great story to go along with that," I said.

"A dream catcher." Callie laughed. "I remember Reese and I used to hang these over our beds. As kids, we swore up and down that we never had a bad dream because of it."

"And did you?"

"Well, yeah. Maybe a few. Honestly, I can't remember." Callie shrugged while she fingered the catcher. "I do recall how Reese gave me one as a birthday gift. Same design, as a matter of fact. He'd started collecting all sorts of Indian relics during his senior year. He even went to a few pow-wows and spent hours online to research local Indian history." Callie set the catcher down on her lap.

"I never knew." I studied the dream catcher. "You said it's the same design?"

"Yes. See how the woven pattern goes? Zigzagged

around the sides and with the top and bottom a solid shade of purple? Mine was orange and green, though. And see the webbing? Some catchers have several beads while this has one."

"Holy smokes, that's it." My hand smacked the steering wheel.

"What's it?"

"The design. Papa Birdsong mentioned how each tribe tended to have their own design to make craft items or tools. It's a signature of sorts." I snapped my fingers. "I came across this before. Families do this as a way to honor their ancestors and keep their heritage alive. If your catcher and this one came from the same tribe, even one family—I know this is pure speculation—but what if Reese knew Sage Bluehawk? What if he bought your dream catcher from her?"

Callie's brow pinched together. "I guess that's possible."

"Did he ever mention where he'd buy those Indian artifacts? Maybe where he purchased yours?"

"Not really. I assumed he found them at the pow-wows he attended. Why? Do you think it's important if he met Sage Bluehawk?"

I shifted and sorted the pieces of information to create a clearer picture. Yet, there were too many holes and parts missing. "I don't know. There is one connection, though. Reese used to work with Elias Jamison and Toby Clearwater during their senior year for that delivery company, Polson's. And Papa Birdsong claims Reese, Elias, and Toby not only worked together, they spent quite some time outside of work going to the bars. Which reminds me, did you know Reese played drums at the pow-wow in Salamanca?"

Callie's brows arched. "I didn't know about the pow-wow. Maybe it only happened once. Anyway, I knew they worked together. That's when the three of them became close friends. They'd show up at the house once in a while. Don't you remember?"

I shook my head. "Somehow I missed that, or maybe I wasn't interested. To be honest, I didn't notice much about Reese's life outside of high school and our little circle. I kind of suspected he had a few secrets, though. I knew he worked for Polson's, but he never talked about it. In fact, we didn't talk much at the time. It was more...well, you know." I blushed.

Callie smiled and patted my arm. "It's okay. You don't have to be embarrassed, silly. I'm over it, and you should be, too. Seriously though, Toby and Elias were older. It makes sense how they never hung out with our high school gang. I do recall one evening I found them in the den. They were looking at some photos of their getaway place. Reese explained to me they'd go there when they wanted to...you know...party?"

I grew curious. "You never mentioned it."

"It didn't seem like there was much to tell." She shrugged.

"Where was this place?"

"I'm not sure. I heard them talk. An old hunting cabin in the woods, north of here. It belonged to the Hopewell family, I think. Never used much since Dillard's grandpa passed on. Anyway, the shots included these rock formations, kind of what you'd see at Jake Rocks? They laughed about how one reminded them of a gigantic mushroom." Callie smiled.

"A mushroom?"

"Yep. A huge flat rock, nearly ten feet wide, they said. And it sits on top of one that's half its size. Weird, huh? Anyway, Reese commented on how the cabin was located close to the rocks, like maybe five minutes away. He said they'd get lost sometimes if they visited late at night. They'd come to the fork in the road and go right, which of course was the wrong way, then argue a blue streak about who to blame for getting them lost." Callie's attention drifted as she turned to look out the window.

I pulled into the Dairy Delite parking lot. What Callie said prodded my brain. The description of the rocks seemed familiar, those rock formations like the ones at Jake Rocks. And if there was truth how the cabin belonged to the Hopewells, I now had one more detail to connect Dillard to the other three.

A crowd of customers hovered around the dairy and many sat at tables enjoying their treats. "Both Reese and Toby are murdered. We don't know about Elias. Nash agreed to try and get in touch, make sure he's okay, and tell him what's happened. Something that connects the three of them, something that happened back then. There must be an answer to explain these murders. Right?"

Callie shivered. "Oh, Sarah. I'm worried. It sounds dangerous. Maybe you should stay away from this investigation. Let Sheriff Parker handle it."

I groaned. "Not you, too. Look. I appreciate the concern, but like I told Nash and Uncle Chaz, I can't stop. I have to do this for all of us, including Reese. After what happened between us in the past, it's important. And then there's the obvious reason. I need to find out who murdered your brother and Toby in order to clear my name." There. I'd said it. If Callie wanted to drudge up the past hurt, this would be the time. But she didn't. Once again, I underestimated her.

"If you insist, but you can't do this alone. Let me help you," Callie said with a firm nod.

A wide grin spread across my face. "Callie Logan, you are one special lady."

"Aw, shucks, ma'am. Thank you kindly." Callie laughed. "Now, let's get some ice cream. Maybe those chocolate crunchy treats we used to buy. Remember those? We'd order them with tons of sprinkles."

"Sure. And I confess, I always get one when I come here."

"You do? Well, then, chocolate crunchy ice cream, for old times' sake."

I wove an arm through Callie's, and we walked across the lot. Bits of sunlight still filtered through the trees, though the colors deepened into orange and russet. One tiny moment of happiness. That's all it took to give me hope.

Chapter 16

By the time I left Callie's, it was close to eight. Uncle Chaz would be steaming. Six would have been late enough. Seven passable. But eight was unforgiveable. Even worse when he made his sweet potato and sausage casserole. And this was Thursday's special. Lord, forgive me.

Still, I was grateful for my time with Callie. All seemed right with the world, at present. Despite the murders, the killer at large, and me being a suspect, I was happy. Nothing changed that, not even a grumpy uncle.

I picked up the phone. Might as well ease into the unpleasant situation. When the call reached the seventh ring I pretty much gave up. Maybe he was outside with Opal on the porch and didn't hear.

"Hello?"

"Uncle Chaz. It's me, and before you go ranting about being late, I want to tell you I have a perfectly good explanation. I visited with Callie. She needed me after what she learned today."

"It's fine. Take your time. I need to reheat the casserole, and it'll take a half hour or so."

I pulled the phone away from my ear and scowled at it. What was this? "Aren't you going to yell and complain? This isn't like you."

"Makes no difference. The food will be here. Like I said, take your time. I need to go light the oven. See you when you get home."

"Huh." I stared at the phone again. Not so much as a "missy" or "sweetie" thrown into his conversation. "And he didn't ask about Callie. Something's wrong." I pushed down on the gas pedal. Odd how Opal didn't bark. Whenever the phone rang, she would make a ruckus. I would certainly have heard her in the background.

Speeding around the curve, I passed Egypt Hollow Road. Twenty minutes to go—less, if I took the road at a reckless pace. I moved my foot to break. It wouldn't help anyone if I ended up in a ditch. And, of course, I'd be the fool if all that greeted me was a hot meal, a happy dog, and Chaz back to crabby. Most likely, it was nothing. Just one of his sentimental, sullen moods when he dwelled on the past and told me stories about everyone he missed. That mood. It happened on occasion. After a bit, he'd drift back into his old self.

The truck bounced as I pulled into his drive. It was weed covered with plenty of chuckholes and little gravel. Chaz stopped his regular routine of yard maintenance over eight years ago, and I had little time to help. Once the truck ground to a stop, tires hit the railroad tie put there to block anyone from driving closer. I jumped out and landed with both legs running toward the door.

"Uncle Chaz! Opal!" I bounded up the stairs and shoved the door open. "Oh, my lord."

I hurried to the wheelchair. Chaz's body was slumped over. Reaching down, I placed two fingers on his neck and found a pulse, weak but still there. Blood trickled down the back of his neck. I winced when my fingers located the lump on the top of his head. "What happened to you, Uncle?" I whispered.

At the sink, I wet a towel to clean the wound. Without giving too much thought to the idea, I reached for the bottle of Wild Turkey and poured some onto the towel and then applied it to his head.

"Ouch! What in holy saints are you doin'? That burns like Hades," Chaz growled and sat up straight.

"Oh, thank you, God." My legs gave way and I landed in the chair next to him. My eyes widened. The table was empty, cleared of all his papers and books. "What did you do? Clean house?" I stared, baffled. "What's going on?"

"I was robbed, that's what." He touched the top of his head and grumbled a few expletives. "I tried to warn you. I figured all my sugary kindness would trigger your suspicions." He turned and scowled. "I wish you called the sheriff. Who knows? He might've caught the scallywag. Miracles do happen."

"Huh. *Now* you like the sheriff. And who's the scallywag?"

"How should I know? I wouldn't be callin' him scallywag if I had a name." Chaz smacked his hand on the table with a thud. "All my research is gone. Why ever the scum bucket took it, I can't figure."

"Okay, so the scallywag, scum bucket took your research. Is anything valuable missing?" I searched for familiar items, like Moe's photos and mementos he'd given to Chaz. I eased my shoulders after a mental check list added up to account for them all.

"What do you mean, valuable? You don't consider my research valuable? We spent months on it, collectin' each and every bit." His fist slammed the table.

"I know. I'm sorry. It's—Did you get a good look at the scallywag, er, scumbag?" I pressed a hand to my forehead to stop the pounding. "We should call the station anyway. Maybe if we give them a description, they can track down the vehicle. Did you see what he was driving?"

"Not a single peek at him, and I have no idea what he drove." Chaz picked up the towel and held it to his wound.

"I don't understand. He was here and close enough for you to see."

"He wore a gunny sack over his head. You know, with holes cut out for the eyes, nose, and mouth. Reminded me of those photos we researched. The ones hanged by marauders durin' the war? And all I can say is he's skinny, tall as a bean pole."

"What about his voice?"

"Sounded disguised. Like he was talkin' through a machine."

I got up and walked to the front window. Opal's leash lay on the porch floor. I spun around, filled with fear. "Where's Opal?"

"Calm down. She's fine. I let her out to chase a rabbit right before the scallywag came burstin' into my house. I'm sure she'll be home any time now."

I held a hand to my throat. "Okay. I'll call the sheriff. Then we are going to the hospital to get you checked out. And don't argue. On the way we can share some ideas, like why the scallywag, scumbag or whatever you call him would rob you and then—Why did he knock you out? I mean, why bother? It's not like you could do anything." I pressed my lips together, willing myself to shut up. Instead, I grabbed his jacket and draped it over his shoulders. He didn't argue as I wheeled the chair outside and down the ramp to the truck. I picked up the phone and made the call to Sheriff Parker and, within minutes, we were on the road to Warren.

"You mean, how I can't chase anyone? You don't have to skirt around the fact, missy. And I'd say it was because I tried to do something. It wasn't smart but seemed right at the time."

"Oh, Uncle Chaz. Whatever for?"

"Takin' chances runs in the family, I guess. Anyway, when I tried smashin' the back of him with my bottle of Wild Turkey—a true sacrifice I must admit—he spun around, snatched the bottle out of my hands, and cracked me on the head with it. Last thing I remember."

"Foolish and dangerous."

"Done and duly noted."

I sorted through ideas of what could have happened. "Did he say anything? Tell you why he wanted your papers and all?"

"Nope. Hardly spoke. Just stormed in through the door and aimed a gun at my head while he gathered up the Clearwater book and papers, and then he stuffed 'em in a tote bag. That's when I did what I did. End of story."

I drummed my fingers on the wheel. "Why'd he let you answer the phone when I called, I wonder?"

"I imagine to keep anyone from worryin', and then come bargin' in to find me. Sort of like you did, but a couple minutes late, thank the Lord."

"Wait." I frowned. "A couple minutes, you say? I didn't pass one car on Roper Hollow. How's it possible he left your place and I didn't see him?"

"Unless he came on foot."

"Or went down to the boat launch."

"Maybe Cornplanter Road, which of course leads to a dead end. Only one farm down that stretch."

"But there are plenty of cabins along this road and down to the launch. Could be staying in any one of those." My shoulders sank. We had no description, no idea in which direction he fled, and not so much as one clue why he took what he did.

"At least I kept a few papers hidden in my sock drawer," Chaz announced.

I slouched. "Great, but the Clearwater book? We'd barely gone through it." I hoped things might change, and was more hopeful after my visit with Callie. This complicated matters again. I didn't want to believe the robbery had anything to do with the murders. All of it became one big, tangled mess, each and every detail. Why expect this to be any different?

"Probably be midnight before I get to bed. Can't see what any white coat will do to make it better. A good night's sleep. That's all I need."

"Glad you feel back to your cantankerous self, but we're going to see the white coats as you call them, so you can stop arguing. I promised your wife I'd take good care of you, and that's what I'll do."

He slapped his leg. "Saints alive. You rile me sometimes, you know that? Just like your aunt. I can't seem to get away from bossy women. All the time, tellin' me what to do, how to dress, what to eat, it's plain embarrassin'."

"And all the time, gripin' and complainin', can't get away from it. Just plain aggravatin' is what it is," I teased.

"Oh, sure. Make fun of the cripple from hill country. That's real respectful," he grumbled.

I grinned. There was a hint of a smile on his lips.

Medics wheeled him into the ER, and I sat in the lobby to wait for the doctor's report. Why steal something that had no true value? The book and papers, most of them notes taken from research, wouldn't be useful to anyone. And another question nagged at the back of my mind. How did his thief know about the book? I squirmed in the seat as I ticked off the numbers in my head. Besides me and Chaz, Papa, and Nash. Four. That's all. Unless one of us had blabbed, and I sure hadn't. Truth was, there'd been little opportunity to mention it to anyone else. *I'd like you meet someone. She's a real sharp lady.* I frowned. Make that five.

Pulling out my phone, I stepped outside the ER and called Papa. He answered on the first ring.

"Is everything okay? Not like you to call in the evening," Papa answered.

"Yes and no. Uncle Chaz had an accident of sorts a little bit ago." I explained the break-in and theft. "I'm sorry, Papa. I know you wanted the book returned when we were through with it."

"To have peace and love is more important than anything material. Your uncle is okay. That's what counts."

There was a catch in my throat. "You are a good soul, Papa Birdsong. Tell me. Did you happen to mention the Clearwater book to anyone? I mean, other than me."

"No one except the seller. But she is old and feeble and had no longer a use for it. Why?"

I didn't want to take my mind in the direction it was determined to go. One answer might put it to rest. "I need to ask. Did Jemma work this evening?" Thursdays were long days at the museum.

"Yes. She works most every day and many evenings when we are open. Again, why the questions? Is something bothering you?"

"Not anymore. You have a good night, Papa. We'll see you Saturday." All at once exhausted, I sagged against the hospital wall to keep my legs from collapsing. What if we never identified the intruder? Scarier still, what if he decided to pay a return visit?

I stepped back inside the ER. Right at that moment the attending doctor came out from the examination room. A nurse followed, wheeling Uncle Chaz into the lobby.

Despite my down mood, I chuckled to see the sour expression on his face.

"Good news. We haven't found any signs of acute trauma to your uncle's head. No swelling or contusions or bruising. I suggested to him we complete a CT scan to make sure there's no bleeding on the brain, but your uncle was quite adamantly opposed to that idea." The doctor shook his head. "I've prescribed pain medication. Watch for any vomiting or severe headaches. Symptoms such as those would indicate he's getting worse. Also, it would be wise to wake him a couple of times during the night. Nothing excessive, once or twice would do."

"Thank you, doctor." I glimpsed at Chaz. The sourness hadn't disappeared. Nodding at the nurse, I followed behind her as she wheeled the patient outside and to the truck. I kept my silence until I was behind the wheel. "You act like an obstinate, bratty child. You know that? Why can't you for once cooperate with the situation?" I said as I pulled out of the parking space.

"If you'd been poked at and prodded as much, you'd be actin' the same, missy." He hunched down in his seat and crossed both arms.

"Fine, but I'm spending the night. The doctor instructed me to wake you every few hours, and I will."

"What in tarnation for? I'd like to get a good night's sleep. That's what we old folks do," Chaz snapped.

"I guess you'd rather go into a permanent coma. And since when do you ever sleep through the night?" I shook my head. "We'll follow the doctor's orders. That's final." A slight chill made me tremble. The idea of losing him, my one remaining close relative other than Aunt Grace, wasn't an option.

He sniffed. "Just get me home."

Without a response, I made the call to Sheriff Parker and let him know we'd meet him by nine. Of course, he suggested we stop by the station, but I was prepared for that one. "No. I'm getting him home and to bed as soon as possible. We'll meet you there." I grew tired of arguing and giving into other people's ideas.

"The man is useless. I bet he can't fight his way out of a paper bag, let alone solve a case," Chaz said.

"Okay. Isn't it time you tell me why you're sour toward Sheriff Parker and critical of his abilities?" I poked his arm gently. "Hmm?"

"Just don't care for his demeanor," Chaz insisted.

"You can't slight his skills as sheriff because of that, can you? Come on. There's more to this, isn't there?" I pushed. Getting to the core of Uncle Chaz took some work.

"Fine. Might as well pass the time we'll be wastin' with a good story. It happened one evenin' before your aunt Grace left. She and I had another disagreement."

"You mean argument." I grinned.

"Same thing. But this turned into a shoutin' match. It was the night she told me she was through, done listenin' to my gripes. I tried to reason with her. I promised to change, but she didn't buy it." Chaz shrugged. "I didn't, either, when I said it, but I was desperate. Anyway, Zeke was haulin' some timber out of the woods next to our place. He heard the shoutin' and worried enough to call the sheriff's office."

I nodded. "Zeke had reason."

"I guess. Anyway, here comes Sheriff Dutiful, marchin' up my porch steps and poundin' on the door. Grace opened it to invite him in. By then, she and I had calmed down, but that was no matter. He was miffed because he'd had to drive clear up the mountain to our place. I'm sure of it. Grace tried to make amends. She offered him a beverage and a place to sit and rest his feet. All the man could do was complain how we were disturbin' the

peace and such. Grace tried to talk reason, explainin' how
we'd had a long day. All couples have those moments,
she said.

"What he said next, I still refuse to forgive. He told
her he didn't care about our marital differences or her
petty excuses. Next time, he'd throw us both in jail."
Chaz rubbed his jaw. "Nobody disrespects my wife that
way. Nobody."

I stared with wide eyes, never expecting such a
comment from Chaz Mackenzie. A rare glimpse of his
soft heart peeking through warmed me as I witnessed it.
"Well, I'm sure you had a fitting response to share with
Sheriff Parker, and it's nice that you defended Aunt
Grace's honor, but I suspect she'd want you to let it go
and forgive the man by now."

"Humph." He shifted his attention to outside the
window.

"I've yet to meet a kinder or stronger person than she
was. I'd say having her in our lives has been a privilege
and an honor, even if for a short while." He didn't answer,
so I concentrated on the road once more. It took all kinds
to make a world, and Chaz Mackenzie was a unique one.

We made it home by nine, and still Parker didn't
come for another half hour. He claimed the trip was a
long haul, though I traveled the same route as often as
three times a week without complaint. He took the report
in his usual methodical fashion, avoiding much eye contact with me. Dislike and distrust. The feelings were en-
tirely mutual.

Of course, Uncle Chaz had another approach. He
wouldn't stop glaring at Parker. The situation was entertaining to say the least, and I was sorry to see it end.

"Well, I can't say this is much to go on, but we'll do
our best. I'll call if we find out anything." He tipped his
hat and left.

"Guess it's too late for supper. Otherwise, I'd heat up the casserole," Chaz said.

I studied him for a second. He struggled to hide the tired look, with his eyes glazed over and lids barely able to hold themselves open. "You're right. It's past ten, and I'm too exhausted to chew food. I'll make the sofa bed and sleep out here."

"You don't have to stay."

"Yes, I do. Doctor's orders. I'll need to wake you in three to four hours," I argued.

"Fine and dandy. Make it four. Most assured, I'll wake myself. Can't sleep well and you know it."

"I want to play it safe, that's all." My eyes welled up. I blinked until they cleared.

Chaz glanced down at Opal who sat next to the wheelchair. "You want Opal to sleep with you? It don't matter either way to me." There was hopeful expectation in his eyes.

"I think I'll sleep better without her hogging the bed," I said.

Chaz latched onto her fur and drew her close. Opal sighed and rested her head in his lap for a few seconds until he wheeled toward the bedroom.

Opal stood in her place and turned. I shook my head, pointed, and mouthed the word go. Opal snorted before trotting off to the bedroom. Whether he'd admit it, Chaz needed Opal. More often every day.

Chapter 17

I woke to stiff joints and a sore neck. I'd interrupted Chaz once. The other times, it had been him waking me, wheeling the squeaky chair around in the kitchen, clattering dishes, and pouring drinks into glasses and snacks into bowls. How did he ever manage to stay awake during the day? It astounded me.

After a quick peck on the cheek and his mumbled response that announced he was still among the living, I tiptoed out of the house. At least somebody in this family was considerate. I'd planned my morning, not wanting to waste a second. Time seemed to be our worst enemy because there wasn't enough of it. Elias could be in danger. The thought nagged at me and wouldn't let go.

"First stop, Deja Blue." I threw the truck into gear and sped down the road. Nash covered the bar every Friday morning to accept their weekly delivery of supplies, mostly alcohol, but also paper items and cleaning products. Food deliveries came every afternoon, and those were handled by Cisco. I'd have enough time to talk before the truck arrived.

The lot was empty. Pulling around back, I parked

next to the rear exit and got out. When I reached the door, I frowned. A white sheet of paper nailed at the top of the door fluttered in the breeze. I grabbed hold and snatched it from the door. A slight uneasiness rippled through me as I read the words scribbled on the note:

The closer you are,
the stronger the flame becomes,
and it will burn.
~ Spirit Talker

I turned a one-eighty, searching the grounds but finding nothing. I folded the note and stuffed it into my pocket. Once again, the message seemed ambiguous. A flip of the coin and it became either a threat or a friendly warning. I knew which side Nash would take. And Uncle Chaz. I patted my back pocket. The note would stay hidden.

I turned, hearing the crunch of tires on gravel. Nash pulled into the back lot and parked next to my truck.

"Good morning." I forced a smile and swore away all thoughts of Spirit Talker.

"It is. What brings you out at this hour, boss?" Nash grinned and raised a finger to tweak my nose as he passed by to the door.

I followed him inside. "I couldn't wait to ask if you got in touch with Elias."

"I tried." Nash shoved bundles of supplies to one side of the shelf, to make room for the morning's delivery. "No luck."

"Nothing?" Exasperation filled me.

"I did talk to Trey, again. He reaffirmed Elias had been slipping."

"I remember you mentioned that before, but you didn't learn why."

"This time I asked. He'd been coming in late to practice, or not showing at all. And he missed one performance, which made the group boot him out. Last they heard was Elias left town. But no one knows for sure where."

"You don't suppose there's a chance he's come up this way?"

"Just as much chance of that as he went some other direction." Nash cleared one last shelf before he sat down on the bench across from me. "Maybe he's heard about Reese and Toby. If it were me, and I learned of the murders, I'd find a place to go where nobody would find me, especially the killer."

"Doesn't he have friends living in the bayou?" I focused on our conversation and the danger Elias might be in, rather than Nash's brown eyes and that cute dimple in his chin. It deepened whenever he smiled. *Nope. Not paying attention to that.*

"Yep. Marsh water and gators all around. It'd be the safest place to hide."

I tapped my thighs with splayed fingers. "But what if he didn't know? What if he came home under false pretenses?"

"You mean if the killer contacted him and concocted some story to convince him to return?" Nash scratched his jaw. "That's a scary thought."

"How about someone he knows? That would make the story more convincing."

Nash creased his brow. "If that's the case, we might know that person, too."

I had the same worry. The idea of it. How the person who'd taken the lives of people we liked or loved was someone we talked to, laughed with, or even shared a meal with? It left a queasiness in my gut.

"Hello? Anyone at home?"

Both of us stood when we heard the voice and rap on

the door. Nash crossed the room and opened the back entrance to find Deena. "Cousin, what happened? Did you get lost?"

"Ha. Good one. Fact is, I come to see Mac. You are just a bonus. How you been? Never come around to see your poor auntie or me," Deena chided.

"And your dozen plus brothers and sisters? Once a year at Christmas is enough," Nash teased.

She gave him a playful swat. "Still just nine of them at last count. But seriously, you should stop by. Mom asks about you all the time."

"More like cursing how I ruined your older brother's life. Not my fault he chose to follow me to Baton Rouge," Nash argued.

"Mine, neither. And I got no more time for this conversation. Stop by next week. Give the old woman a break."

"We'll see. I've got work to do." He slipped me a sympathetic sigh. "Enjoy."

I chuckled and sat down before patting the bench. "Come and sit. You look ready to burst with whatever you have to say."

Deena took cautious steps closer to me. "You won't be laughing in a minute."

"It's hard to be mad when you're around, Deena. You brighten my day, every time," I said, trying to hold my smile in place.

"Well, there's always a first." The bench quaked slightly when she sat down. "Me and my Grand Canyon of a mouth let something out I shouldn't have," she started.

"I see. As they say, it's better to rip off the bandage and get over the pain. So, rip away." A dozen thoughts whirled and tossed around in my head, each one worse than the one before it.

This was Deena, and catastrophe followed her around.

Deena spread her fingers out and rested each hand on a leg. "Let's see. It started when Sheriff Parker came into the lobby. No, wait. That's not how. It was when Paula and me discussed the bodies. You know, Reese and Toby? Anyway, Paula carried on how she knew Reese and Toby better than anyone. How John—that's her brother, the older one—and she hung around with them all the time."

Deena stopped talking and drummed her fingers on the bench.

"Deena?" I urged.

"Ah, well, that's when Sheriff Parker came into the room. He had one foot in the lobby. One. And I didn't see him. I swear. It was such a stupid mistake. I want to crawl into a hole, bury myself in it because that's where I belong."

"Deena. Come on." I rubbed her shoulder. "It can't be all that bad."

"Yes. It can." Deena sniffed. "I told Paula that other people were close to them, too. I told her that you and Reese were dating at the time. Serious dating." She narrowed her eyes and nodded. "You know. And that's what Parker heard. He heard everything. Sarah, I'm so sorry."

"Shh, shh. It's nothing. So what if he knows? That can't prove anything. Besides, I'd be surprised if he hadn't learned of it before that. Somebody was bound to tell." I tried to console her, but in truth, I needed to convince myself. I twisted around to grab a tissue box off the counter. Nash stood in the doorway. My breath caught and my heartbeat stilled. His stony expression felt worse than if he looked hurt or fired up to anger. I stood and kept my gaze on him as I shoved the tissue box at Deena.

"Oh. Oh no. Not again," Deena cried. The tears erupted once more.

While Deena sobbed, I walked toward Nash. "Please. Don't be angry with me," I began.

"I'm not. It's none of my business." He turned away.

I caught his arm. "It happened right after you left for Baton Rouge. I was lonely and hurt. I mean, not that you owed it to me to stay just because of our friendship, but…" I struggled to read his eyes. He always kept his emotions well hidden, and this time was no different.

He shrugged. "I had no claim on you. Like you said, just friendship. I left, and you found Reese. It happened." He tried to pull his arm loose, but I clung to him.

"I thought it didn't matter. We didn't mean—*I* didn't care for him like that." Suddenly, I knew why I hadn't told him, why I never explained to anyone what I had with Reese. I heard it in my words when I said them aloud. The shame washed over me. The tears I prayed to hide came.

"Listen to me." Nash grabbed my shoulders and shook them. "You don't owe me an apology or an explanation. What happened between you and Reese is in the past. I don't care about that, and neither should you. You can't change it, but you can learn from it." He let go of my shoulders and walked away toward the bar. This time I let him go.

"Oh, Sarah. I'm really sorry," Deena whispered behind me.

My lips quivered but formed a smile before I turned. I reached out with both arms to give Deena a hug. "Don't. You told the truth. There's no sin in that. Say, why don't I make us some tea? Maybe add a little Irish whiskey for luck."

Deena laughed, despite the tears trailing down her cheeks, and nodded. "Sounds good. Thank you."

෴

An hour later Deena had recovered from her emotional crisis and left. I stayed and attempted to thaw the tension that chilled the room. Nash hadn't said a word while Deena sipped her tea in between words of apology. He'd gone about necessary business, stocked the delivery supplies when they arrived, and then disappeared behind the stage. I heard the strum of his guitar with the notes it played, deep and soulful ones that sparked my emotions.

"Did I ever tell you the story of why every member of the Mackenzie family inherited the middle name Blue?" I took light, measured steps into the dressing room where Nash and the others practiced.

He didn't look up. His head was lowered, nearly touching the neck of Koko T with his chin, while his fingers arranged themselves on the fret board to play sweet chords. "Yes. More than once. From you and your uncle, and maybe from your dad. I can't remember."

I slid a chair closer to him and sat. "I bet no one ever told you why my dad named the bar Moe's Deja Blue."

Nash shrugged. "Don't need to hear it to get it. Common sense tells me."

I grinned, despite the awkward moment. "Okay, know-it-all. Why?"

Nash looked up and stopped strumming. "Moe's, because he started it. Blue, because your dad enjoyed blues music and his middle name was Blue. Deja? I'd imagine he used Deja Blue as a play on the words, déjà vu."

I scooted closer, grinning wider. "That's all you got? You left out the most interesting part of the story."

Nash's eyes warmed along with his smile. "Okay, tell me. Why'd he name it Moe's Deja Blue?"

"As you know, the first Mackenzie to carry the name Blue was indeed a musician from the old country. Scotland. He played and sang the blues, which in his small hometown was not commonly heard. People started calling him Blue, but he already had a first name. It was Dejan. I know. Unique and strange, but a carryover from Grandma Mackenzie's Slavic roots. I guess she wanted to pass down something from her side. Dejan liked the idea, especially on stage, and he became Dejan Blue Mackenzie."

"But the bar is Deja Blue, not Dejan Blue," Nash pointed out.

"What sort of person names a bar Dejan Blue? Seriously, what would people think?" I shook my head and attempted to look surprised. It took no more than five seconds before we both were laughing.

I stood. "I guess I should go. You, too. No point hanging around all morning. I'm sure you have more entertaining things to do than listen to me tell boring family stories."

"Not boring at all. And neither is the company." Nash held my gaze for a moment and then looked away.

"Yeah, right," I scoffed before turning to leave.

"Wait," Nash called out. "What are your plans for the rest of the day?"

I wasn't sure, but I suspected this question wasn't what he intended to ask. "I thought I'd take a trip north, out on Bone Run Road, near Onoville Marina."

Nash frowned. "Why?"

"Maybe visit the Clearwater family. Hear what they have to say about Toby's death."

"Mac. Don't." His fingers raked through his hair. "It's not your job. Leave it be before you get hurt."

"I can't, Nash. I need to do this." The pulsing rhythm grew louder in my head.

"Because you want to clear your name? Again, let Parker handle it. He'll get to the truth."

"Will he? You must have more faith in his law enforcement skills than I do. Anyway, that's not my main reason for wanting to see this through." I pushed past him to reach the door, but he held onto my arm.

"What's the reason? You think you owe somebody? Is that it?" Nash glared as his eyes grew wild. "You don't have to feel guilty. I told you. It's in the past. You don't owe him anything. He let everyone think he was dead for ten years! If anyone should have felt guilt, it should have been Reese." His voice had grown loud and his face so angry it frightened me.

"If I decide to keep pursuing this, it's my business. Not yours." I pulled away from his grasp. "And you should stay out of it."

"But I won't." The harsh lines of his face softened, and he no longer shouted. "I told you I don't care about the past. I care about what I feel now." He stroked my cheek. "And I hope you feel the same."

I tensed as he drew closer. The golden specks of color in his eyes sparked. I breathed in his heady scent. It reminded me of wood smells, pine, and dew-covered grass. I didn't pull away, but my heart raced, knowing what would happen. And it did. The touch of his lips when they met mine, the soft caress of his hands on my neck and throat. The passionate moment built up my emotions, and I almost didn't hear the footsteps approach.

Nash groaned and let go of me as he stepped back. "If that's Deena again, I'm going to—"

I touched a finger to his lips. "You won't do anything. And it's not Deena. I'm sure of it."

"Hello? Is anyone here?"

The voice was high pitched and sounded rather timid. It didn't belong to Deena. "Back here," I called and waited until a woman appeared.

She was small built, petite, with short, dark curls framing her face. The eyes reflected sadness while her hands clenched the straps of her bag, as if she was scared.

I smiled encouragingly. "Hello."

"Hi." She hurriedly extended her arm. "My name's Anne. Anne Lowell." After a brief handshake with Nash and me, she took several steps back.

"Well, Anne Lowell, I'm Sarah Mackenzie and this is Nash Redwing. What can we do for you?" I said in as cheerful a tone as possible to set the woman at ease.

Anne wasn't beautiful, but attractive in an exotic way. Her eyes were round like the shape of almonds and the deepest green, the color of seaweed. Slight lines of wrinkles feathered out from the corners, but not enough to make her look older. She nodded and dug into her handbag. "I was told to come here, if something happened. He said you would know what to do." She extended a sealed envelope to me.

"What's this?" I frowned at the envelope with my name scribbled across the top. The writing looked vaguely familiar.

"It's a letter, I think. From my husband, Ray." She shifted her gaze from Nash and back to me. "Is it all right if I sit down? I feel rather shaky."

"Of course," I hurried to say. "Nash, would you?" I nodded at the chairs, which he brought over and placed one next to Anne.

I sat in the other while Nash stood behind me. I stared at the envelope for a moment and then back at Anne. "Do you know what's in the letter?"

Anne shook her head and looked ready to cry. "No, and I'm worried. Ray hasn't been home for over a week. He told me he'd return after the festival. He attends most all of them. The pow-wows, you know. But he hasn't been in touch. I can't think of anything but the worst," she sobbed.

I signaled to Nash.

"Right. Tissue box. Be back in a second." He hurried out of the room.

"Have you contacted the authorities?" I said.

"Yes. Several days ago. It's not like him. He always wanted to be home in the evening to tuck Reese in. He's our son. Only eight years old." Anne dabbed her eyes with the tissue Nash handed to her.

I swallowed hard to dissolve the growing lump in my throat. "Reese?"

"Yes. Ray said it was a family name. Of course, I don't know much about that. He never spoke of them, said it was too painful."

"Open the letter," Nash said. The flat tone of his voice underplayed the emotion I sensed was building.

I hesitated, dreading to know, but still wanting to know, if that made sense. My hands shook until Nash reached down to take the envelope from me and ripped it open. He removed the letter and placed it in my lap.

"I suspected all along that he kept secrets," Anna said. "More than once, I caught him in a lie where he'd changed his story about his past. I love him so much, and I trust him enough not to question him. He's a good man. Kind, giving, a loving father and husband." She wept while her attention fixed on the letter in my lap.

I finally opened it. At first I read in silence, but quickly jumped to the end to find the signature. "It's him. It's from Reese," I whispered and looked over at Nash, my face pleading for help. I couldn't handle it. Not alone.

He put an arm around my shoulders and knelt down. "Go on. Read what he wanted you to know."

I finished the letter, but to myself. I knew it was self-ish, but I didn't want to share his words, not until I knew what Reese asked of me. I finished and then laid the letter back in my lap. I looked up to stare at Anne. Her face was full of curiosity. Probably mine was too.

"I need you to come with me. We're going to meet your sister-in-law. Where is your son? I think he'd like to meet his aunt."

I smiled sadly at the thought of what time and circumstances had done, all the memories they'd never experience. Man and fate, they sometimes made a cruel couple.

Chapter 18

I promised Nash I'd share the contents of the letter with him after I took Anne to visit Callie. He needed to be patient, I told him. And he agreed. Anne, too, wanted to know what her husband had to say. I cringed at the thought of telling her the worst news but pulled myself together and explained that it would all come out when we got to our destination. If anything, I needed Callie's help with what might turn out as an emotional catastrophe. After all, how do you ease into a situation like this, to let someone know the person he or she was married to was not that person, and that he had died? I prayed Anne was stronger than she looked.

Anne's gaze shifted sideways toward me on the drive to Warren. "You know my husband's family, then? Is that why he wrote to you?"

I reached down to pat Anne's hand. "Yes, I know them. And I promise you'll love Callie and her mom."

Anne sighed and her shoulders slumped. She had refused to call and talk to her son who stayed with his aunt. She explained how he didn't know his dad was missing. She'd told him that Ray had to make an important trip out of town but would return home as quickly as possible.

"We're here," I announced as the truck pulled into Callie's drive. I'd called ahead to make sure she was home. Despite her questions, I couldn't tell her the reason for the visit, not with Anne standing there listening to the conversation.

Callie was waiting at the door and opened it when we started up the walkway. "Mac. It's good to see you again so soon." She looked questioningly at Anne.

"Callie, this is Anne. May we come inside? It's hotter than blazes out here and...we need to talk." I gave her an apologetic smile. Callie stepped aside and motioned us in.

"Would you like some iced tea? That should cool you off," Callie offered.

"Sure. That would be nice." I gestured Anne toward the sofa. "Why don't you sit next to me?"

Anne's movement was slow and cautious as she took her time to sit down. Her eyes darted from side to side until they fixed on the fireplace mantle. She gasped. "Ray." She started to rise from the sofa, but I grabbed her hand.

"Wait. Please? I need to explain something first." I nodded and held on until Anne settled back in her seat.

"Here you go. Tea with lemon and lots of ice to keep it cool." Callie smiled and set the glasses down on the coffee table. She took a seat across from us and then leaned forward. "What's this about?"

I recognized the hint of worry reflected in her eyes. She had reason to be. "Okay. Well, as I told you this is Anne. She's...Reese's wife." I slowly nodded.

"No. My husband's name is Ray. I told you that." Anne shifted in her seat.

"I don't understand. Reese was married?" Callie's voice quivered.

Maybe this hadn't been such a great idea. I shifted my attention from one to the other. Letting them know the truth would be like watching a ping pong tournament. "Look. If you'll just listen, I'll explain. Anne, your husband's real name is Reese Logan, not Ray Lowell. He disappeared from Priest Hollow ten years ago and now we know he ended up marrying and moving to...upstate New York, didn't you say?" I sat back and released my breath. This would take a while.

"All right. Let's say I believe you. I admit he keeps secrets. I always felt that. But it doesn't explain where he is now."

I shot Callie a nervous glance. There was no easy way to tell Anne, no words that buffered the blow.

"My brother, your husband, was found dead several days ago." Callie managed the news without a hitch.

The tension splintered through my spine. I waited until the inevitable came.

"No. You must be mistaken. Maybe this Reese Logan isn't my husband. I—" She blinked before turning to the mantel. She walked as if in a trance, glided across the room until she stood in front of it. In silence, she picked up each frame to study the images and then carefully set them back in their places. Afterward she returned to the sofa. "My husband is dead?" She searched our faces as if she expected a different answer, a brighter outcome.

"I'm sorry," Callie whispered and walked over to reach Anne and embrace her.

They stood like that for several long and uncomfortable minutes as I rubbed my hands across my pant legs.

After they pulled apart, Anne nodded at me. "There's a letter Ray, I mean Reese, wrote."

I reached into my handbag. "He told Anne that if anything happened to him, she should deliver this. I think he meant for all of us to hear it." I unfolded the letter and waited until my heart slowed its pace. Then I read.

"'I know this will be a shock to you, but trust me, this was the only way. At least at the time it felt like my only choice. I hope you don't judge me too much, or hate me. It was a weak moment in my life. I made some incredibly poor decisions, but as Anne will tell you, I've been trying to make it right ever since, to redeem myself, if that's possible.

"'It started after high school. Lots went on then. You know that, Mac. We acted crazy at times. Impulsive immaturity, I'd call it. What we had together... I'll always remember it as one of the few decisions I made and never regretted a minute of it. I know you never felt the same. In time, I came to understand that. Like I said, I had a weak moment. It started before there was us. What I did had nothing to do with you or how you ended it. I beg you to believe me, if you believe nothing else I write. Please.

"'Toby, Elias, and I became buddies back when we worked at Polson's. We hung out together quite a bit after work. One day, Toby suggested this idea he had to make some quick cash. It was supposed to be a onetime thing, but one turned into several and a day into months. I knew it was wrong, but I didn't know how to get out of it. Toby had a strong temper. It was dangerous to cross him. And Elias did whatever Toby told him to do.

"'We broke into cemeteries and dug up the graves Toby picked out. If we found any valuables buried along with the dead, we'd steal them. It was a hit or miss thing, but we managed to find and steal quite a lot. I hated myself for it. I became as angry as Toby, but for different reasons. We'd sell the artifacts on the black market and deliver them using Polson's trucks. There were always plenty of buyers. They didn't seem to care where or how we got the items. And Toby was right about one thing.

The money was good. Then one evening we were spending time at Dillard Hopewell's cabin. We drank a lot and talked too much. Elias let it slip about our scheme and Dillard heard it all.

"'Next thing I knew, Dillard contacted me and demanded a cut or he'd talk. I didn't know what to do, so I told Toby and Elias. We had a huge fight. It ended with me agreeing to meet Dillard at the Polson warehouse and talk a deal. You know partly what happened that night. Dillard never showed and the fire burned the place down. Everyone thought it was me who died, but it was some unfortunate homeless guy I ran into a few minutes before the fire. I passed him on my way to the rear of the building where I arranged to meet Dillard. He never showed, of course. The homeless man sat in a corner finishing off a bottle of whiskey and was nearly passed out. I'm sure he didn't even notice me.

"'When the explosion happened and fire started, I ran back to get him out of the building, but by then it was too late. There was a metal beam that rested against the wall and it fell on top of him, crushing his body. I'm not sure what made me think it, but all at once I had this horrible feeling. Maybe it was a foolish notion, but I thought since Dillard didn't show, he might've created the explosion and fire, wanted me dead for some crazy reason.

"'It was insane, I know. It made even more sense if Toby or Elias wanted me to die, along with Dillard, since they assumed he'd be there to meet me. One or two less people to divide the profits with, right?

"'In one second, I made a decision. Since the fire was getting worse, I didn't have time to change my mind or think how crazy it was. So, I pulled my watch off and placed it on the guy's wrist, and then my belt. They had my initials. It was a gamble, of course. If the body burned badly enough, everyone would look at my things and decide it was me who'd died. I had to disappear. You have to understand that was the hardest part. It hurt the most to think of how my mom and Callie would feel. It killed me inside, but the fear I had of somebody wanting me dead was so strong.

"'Or maybe I was too weak and had to run. What I am certain of is how sorry I am. I can never give you all back those years, or erase the suffering, but I have tried to do better. Ask Anne. She's a beautiful person and we have a beautiful son. I hope you'll give them a chance and get to know them.

"'Since you're reading this, I know something has happened to me. I always felt I'd need to pay for my sins one way or another. I wrote to Toby and Elias to explain that by the end of this summer I planned to turn myself into the authorities and confess our story. I encouraged them to do the same. To carry around the guilt of what we'd done is too heavy a burden.

"'Enjoy your life and don't ever regret the choices you've made, Sarah Blue Mackenzie. You are a strong and moral person. No one can take that away from you, if you don't let them. Give my love to Callie and our mother. I've missed them all these years, more than they'll ever know.

"'Love, Reese'"

I finished and stared at the page for a moment before looking up at Anne and Callie. "That's it," I said.

"Oh my," Anne said then turned and ran out of the room.

I started to follow, but Callie stopped me.

"Leave her be. She needs time alone. I know." Callie sat in her chair and wrapped her hands around the cup of tea. She rocked back and forth in silence.

"It sounds like he had a good life." I paused, not knowing what else to add.

"Anne seems nice. Maybe we can meet the boy. What's his name?"

"Reese." I bit down hard on my lip. "It makes sense."

"Hmm." Callie set her cup down on the table. "I know he explained it, but I don't think I'll ever understand why he did it. Not the Reese I knew. It's awful."

"But he changed." Anne had come back into the room. Her eyes were dry and she wore a proud face. "To me, he's nothing like the man he described in that letter. My Ray never hurt anyone. He always gave everything he could. He…" She sniffed and turned her head away.

"He mentioned trying to make things right?" I urged her to go on.

"That's true. I was never sure why, because he always remained secretive about certain parts of his past. But he claimed it was his duty. He'd go to the pow-wows and fairs and flea markets. He'd buy certain artifacts, pay good money for them, and then turn around to donate them to museums. Sometimes he'd manage to track down the families he'd researched and give them artifacts he'd purchased, saying he was giving back what was rightfully theirs." Anne chuckled. "He often told me that the Indian spirits might look on him more kindly if he did that."

Callie sighed. She reached out to Anne and hugged her. "Despite the tragic end to Reese's life, I'm glad it brought us together. You and your son, my nephew, should come and stay with me for a few days. All right? You have lots of relatives to meet. Say! We can have a family reunion. I'll call—" Callie stopped when she caught my look. "Too soon?"

"Yep. Start small. You'll get to the big stuff later." I threw Anne a reassuring nod. For a moment, she'd looked terrified, but then relaxed after I spoke.

"Oh! I nearly forgot. He also wanted me to give you

this." Anne reached inside her bag and pulled out a box.

I took it and carefully pried the lid with my fingers. I opened the box and uttered a slight gasp. Inside I found the ring, the silver still shiny, without a scratch, and no discoloration. The turquoise stone was larger than I remembered. The wavy coloring of green and blue showed its worth.

I lifted it to see the engraved words along the inside of the band. "Honest and Loyal Spirit," I whispered.

"I never knew," Anne exclaimed.

I searched her eyes. Confusion, hurt, wonder, sadness—they were all inside Anne. I'd felt them myself. "It never was like that. We found each other at a time when neither one of us had figured out yet who we were and what we truly needed. It lasted for no more than three months. I found this when I visited my aunt in Export. It reminded me of Reese. The artisan who created it told me the story of his family, generations of artisans, jewelry makers. I knew Reese would appreciate it. Honestly, there was nothing more to it." I set the box down on the table and continued. "I told him we couldn't stay together. It had to end. This was right before the fire. And I've carried the guilt ever since. I wanted to stop, but I kept wondering if maybe he wanted to die, to stay there in that fire—" I stopped. My throat was dry and there were no more words. An arm wrapped around my shoulder, and I looked up to find Callie. "I'm sorry. I wanted to tell you. So many times I tried."

"It's okay. There's nothing to forgive. Do you know how often I worried it was me? That I pushed him to do it? We didn't always agree, and we'd argue. About...many things—" She broke off, not finishing her comment.

I nodded. "Like me? I knew. He told me, but I never listened. You were my friend, and I didn't hear the common sense in your words."

Callie gave my shoulders a firm squeeze and then let go. "Instead of all this talk about past regrets, we need to concentrate on the present."

"And Reese's killer," I added.

"Yes, but I don't think we should do more than discuss it. If we come up with something, we should hand it over to Parker, right?" Callie narrowed her eyes as she spoke.

I hesitated before commenting. "I guess. Anne? You mentioned Reese left to attend a pow-wow. Do you have any idea where exactly he went that day?"

Anne twisted the tissue in her hands. "It was in upstate New York, that's all I remember. He said it would be an hour's drive and that he'd be home by nightfall."

I connected my phone to the internet. "All right. And what day was that?"

"Saturday, last Saturday."

I searched for a pow-wow in New York on July fifth and found one. "Bingo! There was an arts and crafts festival in Ogdensburg."

"Oh, I recognize that city," Callie said. "We've been there. It's along the Saint Lawrence River and New York border."

"Well, that might be it. Seems too much of a coincidence not to be. You say it's about an hour's drive?" I said.

Anne frowned. "Yes."

"We should call the sheriff's station and let them know. Maybe that's where he met his killer," Callie suggested.

"Or maybe not." I argued. "He could have run into the killer at any time. That day or night on the way home."

"But it's a place to start. Maybe authorities can ask around and find someone who saw him that day or maybe found something suspicious." Callie remained insistent.

"It's not enough." I slumped down in my seat. "But you're right. It's a start." I didn't say aloud how I worried this would take too much time, especially for Elias, if he was in danger of ending up like Reese and Toby.

"Why don't we discuss it over lunch? I've got chicken salad made. What do you say, Anne? Can you stay longer?"

The pain in her face faded. "That would be nice."

"Good. Mac?"

I considered it. After all, I may have promised to show the letter to Sheriff Parker, but I could do more. And that meant returning to the bar as soon as possible. I needed to speak with Nash. He'd be anxious to learn what was in the letter. Afterward, I'd ask him to come with me to Onoville Marina. Talking to Toby's family might help us learn more. Maybe Toby himself shared some concerns with his mother. Most likely, when he received the letter from Reese, it panicked him. Since everything led to Toby not being Reese's killer, there had to be more to the story. It's what I hoped to learn from the Clearwaters.

"Sure. I can stay for lunch, but afterward I need to get back to the bar. Sorry, Anne."

"Nonsense. I can drive her later on to get her car. We should have some girl chat and exchange stories about Reese." Callie smiled at Anne who lit up.

"It would be extremely kind of you," Anne said.

"Good. Then it's settled." Callie marched off to the kitchen, leaving us in the living room.

"Again, I'm sorry about your husband. I know this can't be easy," I said.

"No. It's not. But, you know, I've worried all week this would end badly. I've had time to prepare." Anne stared off toward the mantle.

"Even if it takes a lifetime, we'll figure out who did this and make him pay. I promise." I squeezed her arm, and we stared at the photos together.

Chapter 19

The hour approached three when I returned to the bar. On my way from Callie's, I'd given Nash a call to see if he was free to meet me. He wasn't scheduled to come in until five but hadn't anything else planned.

Priest Hollow didn't have much of a downtown. Just a crossroads with maybe a dozen businesses—a gas station; two grocery stores; a few boutique shops that sold craft items or clothing; a discount outlet; two restaurants, neither one fast food; and two bars. Moe's Deja Blue Bar and Grill opened soon after Kate left home, close to sixteen years ago. Abe's Roadhouse started up a couple years later. Surprisingly, it remained in business, though most locals stopped at Moe's on any given night. Abe lived in a room behind the bar. He owned the building and turned the front half of his home into the Roadhouse bar after he and Moe had a falling out. It was a firecracker of an argument, or so I'd heard, and it had turned them into enemies. In the years since Moe's passing, I'd found Abe at the cemetery a time or two, standing by Moe's grave.

The Deja Blue sat on the outskirts of town, rather than the center where everything else lined up, crowded side to side. Moe bought the land dirt cheap. He built the inn with his own hands, along with help from relatives and few close friends. Hardly visible from the main road, the building sat nestled in a forest of tall pines, the majority Northern White and Candlewood. Moe couldn't have chosen a better spot.

In my review mirror, I watched as Nash's car cruised into the lot. I got out to meet him and relaxed as he walked toward me. Though I was seldom able to read his facial expressions, his body language often told me plenty. This time he walked with casual ease, a sure sign he wasn't upset. "Thanks for coming," I said.

Nash raised his hands. "Boss, you know I can't refuse you."

I almost sensed, before I noticed, the smoldering fire in his eyes. And it wasn't from anger. I shivered and rubbed my arms. "The temperature must be falling."

"I don't think so. Thermometer reads eighty."

He stepped closer, almost too close. I spun around to walk toward the building. "Maybe I'm coming down with a cold or some other bug. Let's go inside and talk. I've got lots to share." I rushed to get through the door.

"The letter?" he said as he stepped in behind me.

"Yes. The letter. Reese explained everything. Why he left, the crime he, Toby, and Elias had committed, and the real story about Dillard, which doesn't surprise me. I'd say you should take a seat. It will be a while before I finish."

I read the letter to Nash, even the more personal parts. No longer would I keep secrets from him. I related Anne's explanation of the day Reese went missing, and what Callie thought they should do. When I finished, the letter went back into my handbag. "I'll make a copy but give this to Parker. Reese didn't get an opportunity to come clean, but his letter will show how he intended to do so."

"The part about Dillard will raise an eyebrow or two," Nash added.

"Yeah, it looks more and more like he could be a suspect. Why hide the truth about his reason for meeting Reese unless he had something to do with the fire?"

"Maybe he was afraid he'd be arrested for blackmailing Reese." Nash picked up an empty beer bottle from the table and rolled it between his hands.

"And the police would think he had motive or an opportunity to kill Reese because Reese refused to pay," I added.

"But Dillard had an alibi."

"Hmm, yeah, but not for these recent murders. At least none that we've heard. I'll say it again. What if Dillard got wind of Reese's intention to come clean and tell the authorities?"

"You mean hearing from Reese? I thought he only sent letters to Toby and Elias." Nash set the bottle down next to him.

"Yeah, that's true, but maybe he ran into Reese. You know, a weird coincidence, but it could happen. Maybe...Dillard went to the festival in Ogdensburg." I sprang up from my seat. "We need to trace Dillard's whereabouts that day, maybe every day since last Saturday. It might prove Dillard is the killer."

"Don't look so eager. We can't forget Elias. He has as much motive, maybe more. And we don't know where he is or what he's been up to in the past couple weeks." Nash moaned. "What a mess."

"I know. Did you try calling him again?" I struggled to not lose hope, despite growing more confident of my hunch that Elias was an intended victim rather than a cold-blooded killer.

"Number's been disconnected." Nash picked up the bottle again and tossed it into the trashcan.

"Great," I mumbled. "Well, I should get moving if I want a chance to catch Sheriff Parker in his office before his supper break. Deena claims he never misses his wife's home-cooked meal." I snorted. *Hunger trumps duty.*

Nash stood up, directly in line with the back door and blocking my way. "Will you be back this evening?"

"Ah, yeah. I did plan to take a quick trip north. I still feel a talk with Toby's family might reveal something important." I eyed Nash nervously and expected his reaction.

"Not alone. All sorts of Clearwater relatives around there. And most of them aren't too friendly. I know firsthand. You'll be greeted with a shotgun pointed at your head. Rough bunch. I'll come along if you insist on going."

I stood inches away from him, now. He didn't budge. "Are you going to let me by?"

He crossed his arms over his chest. The muscles in his neck knotted and pulsed. "Not until you promise you won't go alone to visit the Clearwaters."

I held my breath for a moment and finally released it. "Fine. I won't go. Now, would you let me pass?" My voice quivered and it took extreme effort to speak. My mind fought a duel with my emotions. I wanted him to kiss me, but prayed he wouldn't, wondering if this was the way it would always be between us. I wanted a relationship that moved smoothly, where I eased through the motions—kissed without thinking, talked without it being painful or awkward, so it was as natural as breathing. At least most of the time.

"We should talk. Soon." He leaned down to brush

my cheek with his lips before stepping aside.

This time, I didn't budge. Though frazzled nerves and anxiety willed my legs to move, I refused. Not until I reached up and kissed him on the lips. "We will. I promise." My words came out in a hoarse whisper. Afterward, I bolted to the door, too scared to look back, surprised at what I'd done.

୧୬୧

I handed the letter to Sheriff Parker—pleasing or annoying him, I wasn't sure. His reaction didn't reveal which and his silence indicated even less. "It's all there. Everything I've told you. I think it clears up a lot of this mystery, don't you?"

"Hmm. I already sent someone out to Dillard's place to bring him in for questioning. Especially in light of the latest news."

My brows arched. Parker wasn't hiding anything. His face displayed a whole lot of concern and worry. "Oh? What news?" In the next few seconds, my stomach dropped. I sensed what he was about to tell me before one word escaped his lips. I prayed it wouldn't be this way, but I'd expected as much all along.

"Elias Jamison. Found his body in Heart of Hope Cemetery outside Kane. Same as Toby Clearwater, buried in a grave with a stone resting on top and a small pot with burnt sage. This one says 'sins of the followers.' Make sense to you?"

"Yeah, I think it does. Sort of," I said. The words in Reese's letter, especially Toby's idea to become grave robbers, made me think of it. "Elias always did whatever Toby asked him to do. That's what Reese said. It makes him a follower, whether the act is right or wrong, which the killer thinks is a sin. The stone on Toby's grave said 'sins of revenge.' And Reese's, 'sins of the soul.' I'm guessing whoever killed them must know them and about their past. He got Elias right. And he thinks Toby acted out of revenge." I paused.

"And Reese?"

"I guess he betrayed his soul by going along with Toby's crime, even though he felt guilty afterward and spent his life trying to seek absolution." I shrugged. "Who knows how to figure out the mind of a killer? Maybe he's insane. You'd have to be, at least a little, to shoot and kill three people like this. Right?"

"Two people. Elias died from having his throat slit."

"Oh, my." I grabbed a seat in the nearest chair and fought off the nausea rising to my throat.

"And there's more. The coroner found a letter tucked inside Jamison's pocket. It's from Dillard Hopewell. He wrote a short note to Elias saying he knew what he had done and if there was justice Elias would pay for his crimes. Mighty incriminating. We also found gas receipts in Elias's wallet from stations in Charlotte, North Carolina, and Akron, Ohio, dated two days ago. I'd say something urgent drew him to come here, maybe the letter Reese Logan mailed him."

I shook my head. "Reese would have written those letters at least a couple of months ago. Why wait until now to travel north if the letter was the cause?"

"Unless he hadn't received the letter until this week. Didn't you mention Nash found out no one's seen Elias for a while? Let's say he got back home after a long visit out of town and went through his mail. He found the letter. Bingo, here he comes."

"Yeah. I guess. But if this were you, and you found out what Reese planned to do, wouldn't you stay away from here? Why come home to be arrested? That doesn't make sense," I argued.

"I suppose. He may have wanted to try and stop Reese, talk him out of it." Parker turned when a deputy walked up to him. "Barkley?"

"Ah, sir, Deputy Severus called. They didn't find Dillard Hopewell at home. And his wife claims she doesn't know where he's gone, but says he's been out all day."

Parker frowned. "Thanks, deputy."

"He must've heard you found Elias," I suggested.

"Well, innocent people don't run and hide. I'd say this makes him look like the number-one suspect." Parker narrowed his eyes, but a smile teased the corners of his mouth. "You know, I got to a point in this investigation where I worried you were the killer. And this morning, I was ready to let you have a piece of my mind after hearing you and Reese Logan were more than chums. You kept that bit of information from me and I thought for sure I had you pegged. But then Elias ends up dead with Dillard's letter in his pocket."

"So, I'm off the hook." I smirked, knowing this moment would come.

"Not so fast. I still haven't heard back about DNA results. Those lab geeks take their time doing a thorough job. Until then..." Parker tipped his hat. "It's time for my break. Supper's calling."

"Enjoy. Maybe I'll go look for Dillard. I bet I can figure out where he's hiding." I couldn't resist.

"Now, I hope you don't interfere. This is sheriff's business." He scowled until seeing the smile on my face. "Ah. I deserved that one. Let's call it even. Miss Mackenzie, you have a pleasant remainder of the day, and please, stay out of trouble." He shook his head and walked out the front entrance.

"We'll see," I whispered. I had my phone out in a second and made the call to Nash. "Change of plans. We need to find Dillard. He's disappeared, and I think I know where to find him." I ended the call and headed out to the parking lot. Face to face, I'd do my level best to convince Nash we should go in search of Dillard this evening. It would be past midnight, but that was an advantage. Dillard wouldn't expect anyone to show up that late.

I pushed another button on my phone and waited, but got his voicemail. "Hey, Uncle Chaz. I can't stop by this evening. I expect a real late night at the bar and most likely I'll want to head straight for home and bed. Love you. Night."

This wasn't the way I'd planned to spend my evening, but I worried waiting until tomorrow would give Dillard a chance to get too far away, and we'd never catch him. If he was guilty, which I decided remained at fifty-fifty odds, he had to be caught. Callie, her mom, and all of us, needed justice. And if he wasn't guilty? Well, then, somebody needed to rescue him before the killer added another notch to his belt.

Telling Parker my hunch of Dillard's whereabouts was out of the question. Wrong as it might be, I didn't trust his overzealous approach to law enforcement. Circumstances might turn ugly. I pictured him and his deputies storming the place and Dillard running so deep into the woods, no one would find him. No, this was better kept to myself.

It was funny how, just a short while ago, I'd believed either Toby or Elias was the killer. And here we had new events leading us to Dillard. We were playing a game of whodunit, but fast running out of suspects. I didn't forget my personal messenger, Spirit Talker, either, but for all I knew, Dillard and the messenger were the same person. In any case, Dillard had a lot of explaining to do, starting with the letter found in Elias's pocket.

The quiet drive gave me time to think more, playing

devil's advocate. When I considered all the facts it almost seemed too convenient. If Dillard killed Elias, why would he leave a letter signed by him there on the body for anyone to find? Unless he'd panicked and never thought to look. I muttered a few strong words under my breath. At every turn, there were more questions than solid answers.

At least I figured out the general location of Dillard's cabin hideout. Callie's information had been sketchy, but her description of the rock formations was the perfect detail. All I had to do was sift through the multitude of facts stored in my brain and there it was. So obvious and easy to locate. I pulled the truck into the parking lot. "Being a trivia geek does have some serious advantages," I admitted aloud.

My feet crunched on gravel as I crossed the lot to go inside. My speech was ready to deliver. And with or without Nash, nothing would stop me from seeing Dillard tonight.

Chapter 20

Nash strummed his guitar. "Let's play an upbeat tune to warm your mood."

"You know, if you'd come out and say it, maybe you two—" Emmie started.

"It's more complicated than that," I interrupted but kept my attention on Nash as he sang and played. "Earl King."

"What?" Emmie said.

I tipped my head toward the stage. "He's playing Earl King's song, 'Time for the Sun to Rise.' It's a game I started the first year Nash performed on our stage. I try and guess the song in a few bars, kind of like that TV program? Earl King. During the fifties, he was a strong influence in the New Orleans music scene with his R and B. He even wrote songs for such big names as Fats Domino. Died in 2003 of complications from diabetes."

"Impressive, but now back to you and Nash," Emmie persisted.

"Enough about that. I see a scuffle sparking between Clint David Sanger and Carl Mackey. Maybe I can say something to divert their attention before it grows into a bloody fist fight. I swear, every time he has one or two beers, Carl itches for a confrontation."

Emmie laughed. "And since it's between those two, I'd bet the topic has to do with the property line bordering their yards."

"As always. You'd think one of them would've moved away from the other by now," I added while taking off my apron.

"And not have something to gripe about? Not a chance." Emmie wagged a finger when she added, "And don't think that gets you off the hook. We *will* finish this conversation."

"You just keep thinking," I said as I walked away from the bar.

I glanced at the stage to find Nash staring at me. A slight shiver gyrated through my body. I froze, my gaze locked onto his for several heart-pounding seconds until the song ended and everyone clapped. Shouts and a cheering crowd broke my trance. Quickly, I moved on toward Clint David and Carl who, by this point, stood nose to nose. Any minute there'd be shoving involved. Everyone around paused in their own conversations and focused on the explosive exchange between the two men.

"I *know* what my policy says. No matter whose tree it is, once it hits the ground, whoever owns that land is responsible for the dad-blamed thing. And the law will back me up," Clint David argued.

"Your poor excuse for a tree is riddled with ash borer beetles. Why, most every branch is diseased. You should've had that pesky eyesore cut down over a year ago. I know my rights. I can claim negligence. First thing tomorrow mornin', I'm callin' my agent. And the law, if a have to, you stubborn old coot," Carl snapped, his face turning blood red with anger.

"Now, boys," I said as I came between the two men. My hands gently rested on each one's arm. "The Deja Blue is a place to relax, kick back, have a beer or two, and be entertained by Nash and the band. Right?" I lowered my head to shoot them a stern expression.

Carl waved his arm wildly at Clint David. "This idiot thinks he can cheat me out of payin' for what he should be doin'. Well, it's not about to happen that way. I can tell you that."

I sighed and held up a hand palm in front of Clint David's face before he took a turn. "Eh, eh. I'll call the sheriff myself if you two don't stop this ruckus. And I can tell *you* that. Now, how about beers on the house?" I smiled and watched the two of them scowl at one another before nodding. "Good. It's settled. Try to be civil, okay?"

I started back to the bar when Nash cut me off. "Hello." I grinned. "Going my way?"

"Yes and yes."

"What's the second yes for?"

"Agreeing to go with you to find Dillard. I never said when we spoke before," Nash explained.

"Oh. You mean after using up all your wind to argue me out of it?" I quipped as we reached the bar.

"Funny. I figured you'd go alone. I know how you are." Nash swigged on his water and then tossed the empty bottle into the trash. "Hey, Emmie."

"Good evening, Nash." Emmie greeted him before she gave me a smile and a wink. "I liked your song choice. All about love, isn't it?"

"More like finding it, but then it vanishes at sunrise. Kind of how it happens sometimes." Nash shifted his gaze sideways to glance at me.

I ignored the exchange. Emmie wouldn't stop, no matter how much I disapproved. "It's nearly one. Emmie, do you think you and Cisco can finish closing the bar? Nash and I have an errand to run, and it can't wait until tomorrow."

"Ooo, right." Emmie laughed. "You two go on ahead. And have fun." She winked again and wiggled a finger wave.

I groaned. "It's business."

"Of course it is," she said, followed by a cough.

"What's that all about?" Nash let me lead the way but stepped closer with his hand touching the small of my back.

"Absolutely nothing. Just Emmie being her nosy self. Did you plug in the information on your GPS like I asked?" I wanted to keep the conversation going in the other direction.

"Yep. You'll see for yourself when I turn it on. The map shows we have a little over an hour's drive. I have to ask. What makes you think Dillard's place is in Olean?" Nash opened the passenger door of his car for me to get inside. "I'm driving. No buts."

"Wasn't going to argue. I need to keep an eye out for Balancing Rock." I slid into the seat and waited until Nash was situated behind the wheel. "When Callie mentioned there was a nature park nearby with rock formations similar to Jake Rocks, it teased my memory. Then last night it hit me. She said one looked like a mushroom." I grinned at Nash. "I remembered Balancing Rock is this huge rock sitting on top of a smaller one. A mushroom. One of a kind."

"Mushroom, huh?" Nash shrugged. "Well, who am I to argue with that? Let's go."

We traveled into Warren and then out of it, going east on Route 59. After a half hour, I turned on the radio to fill the silent void. Yes, I'd promised a talk with him, but somehow it didn't feel like the right moment.

"Seriously?" Nash reached over to switch the station before I could stop him. "Not in my car and not for my ears." He stopped pushing buttons when the sounds of Bob Brozman and his guitar came from the speakers. "That's better."

We'd hit the last leg of our trip. I scanned each sign as we passed them, looking for the right one. "There! The park. Slow down. I want to shine some light on the rocks," I ordered.

Nash tipped an imaginary hat my way. "Sure thing, boss."

"Funny you. I think the fork in the road is close by. We'll veer to the left after passing the mushroom rock." I rested the spotlight along the bottom edge of the window. Pivoting it from side to side, I searched for the landmark.

"There it is. Now let's hope the fork in the road is close by."

"And if it's not? Won't be easy searching in the dark," Nash commented.

He was right, but I had to trust my memory. It was all there in my head, the Rock City Park photos I'd come across a couple of years ago when Chaz did a travel article on the natural attractions of the Allegheny region. The overview map had shown every trail, rock, and road. "This has to be it. I'm certain."

Nothing but inky darkness covered the view in front of us. Even the bright glow of headlights failed to cut through it and provide a clearer path. I shined the spotlight anyway and squinted to read the signs. "Try going slower, Nash. We're close to the fork. I'm sure of it."

Nash groaned. "There's no way you can be sure. Unless you've grown psychic overnight."

We viewed the GPS, but it didn't help much at the moment. Lots of dark patches indicated the wooded terrain.

"I think…it's there, a few hundred yards ahead. See the split in the road?" My pulsed raced.

"And? We go to the left, but then what? If there's more than one dwelling along the road, how will we know?"

"We look for Dillard's car in the drive. That yellow monstrosity has to stand out."

"How dumb would that be? Why leave it in plain sight when he's trying to hide?"

I lowered my head and scowled at Nash. "This is Dillard, right? The same kid in school who fell for every trick you or anyone pulled on him? I think you're giving his brain too much credit. And if we don't find his car, we'll go door to door until we find the right place."

"Fine. Yellow car it is." He steered left and, at once, the tires crunched over the rough gravel. Though night veiled our surroundings, the tires left gray clouds of powdery dirt in their wake.

After a mile, I felt the first twinge of failure. I may have suggested it, but admittedly didn't want to go up to some stranger's door and ask for Dillard. Who knew what sort of people we'd run into?

At the next curve, Nash pulled the brakes to a stop. "Did you see that?"

Flashes of light burst into the sky from beneath the line of trees, like a festival of fireworks. My eyes followed the scene upward and then back down. "Look below, there, through the trees. Something must be on fire." My jaw dropped as I turned to see the expression on Nash's face. "Dillard."

Nash tromped down on the gas pedal and the tires spit out gravel and dust as the car sped forward. We reached the turn and he stopped, letting the car idle. Smoke billowed and trailed through the trees and toward the road.

Even from where we sat I heard the crackling flames. I jumped out and started to run, but Nash caught my arm. "Wait. We can't barge into the woods like that. These pines won't take much heat. The whole forest will be up in flames within seconds. Let's call it in and wait here."

"But what about Dillard?" I bent over and coughed. The air thickened with a smoky vapor.

"We don't know for certain. This might have nothing to do with him."

I tucked in my upper lip. "You don't believe it and neither do I. I swear, if he dies and we did nothing to try and save him—I can't live with that." I struggled to free my arm from his grip but he kept a tight hold. "Nash, please."

At that moment, a spot of light bobbed up and down while a flash of red and blue moved in and out of the trees. It weaved through and made its way toward the road. All at once, a figure broke out of the tree line and into the path ahead of them.

"Nash. It must be Dillard," I cried and with a hard yank freed my arm from his grasp. "Dillard, wait!" I ran toward him, and Nash stayed right behind me.

The figure paused for a second to stare our way before running across the road and disappearing into the grove of pines. But the moment was long enough for me to recognize Dillard's face. "Damn. He's gone." I stomped my foot.

"And my car will be, too, if I don't drive it away from here," Nash added. He tugged at my hand, leading us back to where we parked.

"Now we've lost him for good. If someone set his cabin on fire, he'll be scared enough to run as far away as he can get. Maybe clear to Canada," I said. Bent over, I grabbed my knees and drew breath until my heart stopped pounding.

"He can't get too far on foot. And I have an idea." Nash unlocked the car. "But first let's clear out before the fire comes any closer."

We retraced our steps and headed toward Rock City Park with the distant sound of sirens erupting behind us. Nash reached over to turn on his GPS. The screen lit up and he pressed a few buttons.

"This will show us where the woods lead out to and maybe a road where we can cut him off. He has to come out at some point," Nash suggested.

"Seriously, Nash. Those woods are massive. Over five hundred acres. I know. We can't possibly figure out where he'd appear, if he even tries to come out of the woods. He may find another house or cabin or sleep under a tree all night." I wanted to cry. Frustration hit its peak.

"The fire is too much of a threat. He'll want clean out of those woods. Besides, we've got nothing to lose by trying. There." He pointed a finger at the screen. "Barrow Road. It runs along the south border of the forest." He turned off at the next road and headed the car south.

"I still say this is pointless. Failed mission. I surrender. Let's go home," I pleaded.

"Since when does a Mackenzie give up?" Nash smiled.

"Yeah, whatever. Barrow Road, here we come." I forced myself to form a happy face. If we found Dillard, I'd be glad to admit I was wrong. But I had little hope. Of course, if we failed, the good news would be the killer may not find him, either. Hurray for Dillard.

We traveled down Barrow Road for five miles or more but saw no sign of Dillard. "It's no use. Let's go home. With any luck he'll find a safe place to hide," I said.

Nash didn't comment but turned the car around and

headed back toward the park. We came to the fork and spotted Balancing Rock in the distance. As the car drew near, I gasped and Nash put on the brakes.

"I guess we're all lucky," Nash said.

I nodded. No words to explain it. On the road next to the rock sat a bright yellow pickup, steam trailing up from the hood. Kneeling on top of the rock, with his head lifted toward the sky and his hands clasped together, fingertips pointed, was Dillard, praying. I said one of my own, thankful Dillard Hopewell was alive.

Nash turned off the car after pulling over to the side of the road. "Maybe we should wait." He laid his hand over top of mine.

"No time." I got out of the car and started toward the rock. At once, Dillard stood up, his rifle pointed in our direction. "Don't come any farther. I'll shoot."

"Dillard! It's me, Sarah Mackenzie," I called out but stopped moving.

"We just want to talk," Nash added and stepped out to stand next to the car. He held up both arms and waved. "See? No weapons. We want to have a word with you. That's all."

My feet planted in their spot, I froze, afraid I'd spook him, but Dillard didn't put the rifle down. "Please, Dillard. We know what happened and want to help you."

"Why should you want to help me?"

"Because we know you didn't do anything to hurt Reese or Toby," I shouted. I was uncertain whether or not Dillard heard about the latest victim.

"And Elias? I never wrote him a letter. I mean, why would I do that? I never killed anyone. I—" Dillard dropped the rifle. It landed on the ground with a thud. His hands reached up to cover his face while he sobbed. "I owed money and got desperate. I didn't mean for anybody to die."

Nash skirted around to the side and out of Dillard's sight. He grabbed the rifle and emptied it, tossing the shells out toward the road.

"Why don't you come down from there and we can drive someplace to talk?" I suggested.

Nash came back to stand next to me. We waited quietly. After Dillard stopped shaking and uttered his last sob, he nodded and climbed down. Without a word, he followed us to the car and got in the backseat.

"Your place is gone?" I asked, turning in my seat to look at Dillard.

Dillard nodded. "I was eating my supper and heard footsteps outside. Before I reached the window to look out, something broke through the glass. In the next second, I was blinded by an explosion. Flames lit the cabin and I grabbed my rifle and ran out the door. I swear, I don't know if I was more angry than scared, but I came out shooting. I wouldn't go down without a fight." His shoulders shook and he rubbed his jaw with one hand. "I ran to where I'd hid my truck, across the road and back in the woods parked in my neighbor's drive. That's when you spotted me. Damn truck. Never was a reliable vehicle."

"Dillard, you're lucky to be alive. Please remember that." I reached over to pat his arm.

Nash started the engine and headed into the park. "Maybe we can stop at the pub we passed a few miles back?" No one objected, so he continued down the road.

"I can't figure out why someone would do this." Dillard raked his fingers through his hair. "But I swear, I didn't kill Elias."

"Can you think of anyone who'd want to make you look guilty?" Nash asked.

Dillard shook his head.

I pulled up straight in my seat. "You mentioned how

you were desperate and owed money. What did you mean?"

Dillard swiped a hand across his mouth and chin. "I borrowed money from somebody who wasn't patient to get it back. I ran out of time. That's it. I figured if I put pressure on Reese—he seemed like the one who'd listen—I stood to make some quick cash." Dillard slouched, clutching his knees. "I panicked and didn't go to meet him. I left town to visit a sick uncle. In truth, he was, and it's what I told the police. I figured they'd check."

"But you told them the meeting with Reese concerned a business deal," I said.

"It was a business deal if you think about it. I just didn't tell them what the deal concerned." Dillard's eyes pleaded. "When I heard of the fire and how they'd found Reese's body...Do you know how much I've suffered these past ten years? I blame myself. I keep thinking if I'd gone to meet him, maybe things would have played out differently. Every day, that's what I'm thinking."

I pulled a water bottle out of my bag and handed it to Dillard.

"Why did you lie to the sheriff?" Nash turned into the lot of Ollie's Pub. Only three vehicles were parked there at this late hour.

Dillard nodded and glanced sideways out the window. "If you were me, wouldn't you worry it was you meant to die along with Reese in that fire? I've had plenty of time to think about it and finally decided odds were Toby and Elias started it. And now...well, I kept my mouth shut. It was the one thing I prayed could keep me alive."

"And the money you owed?" I reminded him.

A bitter laugh escaped his mouth. "I've learned life plays a cruel joke on folks sometimes. Right after the fire, my dad passed away. I imagine it was mostly from all the aches and pains he suffered because of me. Add that to my guilt. Anyway, the insurance policy covered my debt."

"I guess if we're to believe you, and with Toby and Elias dead, murdered at that, who does that leave?" I said, voicing my thoughts aloud.

Nobody answered.

"The one who wants to frame you, maybe wants you dead, is still out there," Nash said.

Dillard wagged his head. The shadows under his eyes seemed to darken more. "I have no place to go. If I return to my house, he'll be waiting for me. I'm sure of it."

"I have an answer to your problem. At least if you're willing to trust me," Nash offered.

"I'm in no position to turn down any suggestion. Not until I hear it, anyway."

"Good. The lady who owns this pub is a friend of the family. She would do anything to help."

"And why's that?" I puzzled over who the lady might be.

"Let's say she owes my family a big favor. She'd let you stay at the pub. Loretta has a bunk in the back, and nobody would know you're there or bother you."

Dillard scratched his chin while he remained quiet. After a long stretch he spoke. "You'll let me know when the killer's found. Right? I can't stand the waiting much longer, whether or not he'll come for me at any second. It's too much."

I smiled and patted his arm once again. "Of course we will."

"Good. It's settled," Nash said. "Let me go inside and talk to Loretta. She'll come around to open the rear entrance. That way, you don't need to worry about other customers seeing you." With that, he hopped out of the car and jogged to the building.

I turned to study Dillard's face. Worry and the fear of dying had taken a huge toll on him. Besides the dark shadows underneath his eyes, his skin paled with a sickening, yellow tone. The mere notion of how he could be Spirit Talker appeared ridiculous now. Still, I needed something to reassure me.

"You know, this reminds me of what a wise person once said. He told me the closer you get to the flames, the easier it is to get burned. Of course, he didn't mean it literally." I detected no reaction, other than a puzzled frown creasing his brow.

"Well, either way, I've been burned. Your wise person truly knows." Dillard closed his eyes and the creases in his forehead deepened. "Years and years of it. I've suffered and been burned."

It was difficult to feel sorry for him. He'd set in motion a chain of events that ended in tragedy. Even if he hadn't murdered Reese, Toby, and Elias, he needed to pay for his sins. Sins of the soul, of revenge, and of the followers. What would Dillard's stone say? Sins of greed? Hopefully, there would be no grave, no stone. Not until Dillard died an old man.

Nash returned to the car and announced Loretta was pleased to accommodate. "She'll come outside shortly. I'll take you to meet her. Mac, you may as well stay in the car. I'll be just a minute or two."

"Bye, Dillard. Take care. We'll be in touch," I said. My brows arched as a tall blonde exited the back and crossed to meet Nash and Dillard. It was the same woman who flirted with Nash the other night. "Great. And she's the one who saves the day."

After several agonizing minutes, Nash approached. Fortunately, Loretta wasn't with him. When he got in the car, I waited and hoped to avoid the embarrassment of asking for the obvious. When he turned the key without a word, I blurted it out, "Exactly how close of a friend is Loretta to your family?"

Nash began to hum a song and kept it going until I slugged his arm. "Seriously, would you answer me and quit acting childish?"

"Me? What about you? Oh wait. I'm sorry. You're not childish. You're jealous." He laughed and smacked his hand against the steering wheel.

This time I slugged harder. "Answer or you'll have a black and blue mark the size of Texas before I'm through."

He held up an arm. "All right, all right, I surrender. Loretta is my Cousin Brody's fiancée."

"The cousin in the army?" I wanted to crawl under a rock. I hoped Nash wouldn't gloat too much.

"Yep. The same. She's been staying with my aunt and uncle until Brody gets to come home, and that's next month. They're getting hitched in the fall."

"Hmm, how nice of them." What else was I supposed to say?

"What? No words like, 'I'm sorry, Nash, I was wrong for being jealous?' Or 'how crazy was I to think you and Loretta were a thing?'" Nash's eyes gleamed.

I groaned. "Okay, sorry. I was being jealous, but I do trust you."

"You do?"

"Yes. I do."

"Good. Glad to know. What did you and Dillard discuss while I was in the bar?"

"Nothing earth-shattering. I wanted to see if he'd react to hearing words from one of Spirit Talker's messages. All I got was a puzzled look on his face. Odds are, he's not Spirit Talker or the killer." I slouched down in my seat. My body ached from all the worrying. "Oh, Nash, what are we going to do? I'm out of ideas. Even if the killer is my secret messenger, we have no idea who he is or where to find him."

"Don't forget Plum Steelwater. You still consider him as a suspect, don't you?"

"Not any longer. In fact, I shouldn't have suggested him. Truth be told, he just crawls under my skin with that look of his and those comments. Can't say it's enough to make him a killer. This is such a twisted mess. Nothing leads anywhere," I griped.

"I suggest we try getting some sleep. The pow-wow is today. There will be time to worry about killers afterward."

I grunted. "What was I *thinking*?" My shoulders sank. The sudden thought of what I'd done left me feeling more miserable than before. "How selfish can I be? You'll have to perform in the dance with practically no sleep."

"Been doing that for years. We played gigs in New Orleans back to back with maybe an hour or less shuteye in between. Don't you worry, I can handle it." Nash winked at me.

"Still," I mumbled. If I were to justify my actions, it would be to claim saving lives trumped pow-wow competitions any day. The trouble was, with the way bodies were dropping like flies, we seemed to be going in circles and not saving anyone.

The ride home ended in dreams. I nodded off by the time we reached the New York border. The faint sound of rattles and drums kept time to the rhythm of my heartbeat, while somewhere far off, a voice chanted about the sins of man.

Chapter 21

The morning's cloudy haze melted and revealed brilliant sunshine by noon. On the drive to Salamanca, I listened to Uncle Chaz's continuous prattle warning me of demon spirits and bad medicine that surely intended to punish me for interfering.

I cast a reproachful eye at him. "Since when did you start believing in Indian superstition?"

"Since you've been nosin' around Indian cemeteries and findin' dead bodies, that's when," he snapped.

"I found one body. Singular. And as you might recall, I went to the cemetery researching for *your* project."

"Never mind that. I been tellin' you to leave it be. Let Sheriff Know-It-All handle the case. And now I hear you been gettin' these threatenin' messages from this whatshisname, Spirit Talker? I can't believe you'd throw common sense out the window to go chasin' after a lunatic killer," Chaz finished, grumbling under his breath.

I clamped down on my lips. If I'd have shoved my phone into my handbag instead of leaving it in the cup holder, the situation might've been avoided. As it was, the phone beeped and my sweet, well-intentioned, but very nosy uncle grabbed it to read the message. *Be watchful. The bones of dead ancestors are more than dust.* Though he didn't understand its meaning, he flew off the handle anyway, demanding to know how many of these messages I'd received, and on he went.

All the while, my mind tried for a few interpretations of its own. Of course, they led right back to where Uncle Chaz would go. The cemetery. And that's something I didn't want to admit. At least not to him, because it would only flame his anger. Besides, what was there to argue? Spirit Talker had to be the killer. With two of the original suspects murdered, and Dillard, who certainly looked innocent after someone blew up his family cabin, my messenger was the one person left. Uncle Chaz had a reason to be scared.

As we approached the pow-wow site, I slowed the truck to turn onto the dirt drive and pull in behind the line of vehicles waiting to find a parking spot. Throngs of visitors made their way toward the check-in booth, and beyond that several men and women walked around in regalia. Nash told me the thick deer hide leathers and heavy headdresses were cumbersome and hot. The day had pushed into the eighties and it was not even noon.

"Handicapped spot, please?" I said to the parking attendant.

He motioned to the front row on the left.

"I could've wheeled across the field. Don't see why there needs to be some special treatment," Chaz grumbled.

"You say that every year, and I give you the same response. In case there's an emergency." I refused to argue. Especially with all I had on my mind. I opened the bed door and dropped the ramp before wheeling the chair to the ground. Once Chaz was situated, we headed for the check-in booth. "I'll take you over to the main tent. Clint

David promised he'd meet us. Then I'll find Papa. He has something for me."

"Oh? And what's that?" Chaz scowled. "I hope it's not useless gossip about the murders."

My lips spread into a stiff smile. "Don't fret. Whatever Papa has to say is always worth hearing. Right?" I said without adding more.

He'd only criticize. Instead, I commented on the nice weather, the busy crowd, and the wonderful smells coming from the food vendors' booths. I let out a sigh of relief as I spotted Clint David by the tent entrance.

I smiled and waved with both arms to gain his attention. "Clint David!"

"Good mornin', lovely lady and homely gent." He leaned over to give me a peck on the cheek, followed by a hardy slap on Chaz's back.

"Talk about homely. I suggest you take a look in the mirror," Chaz growled but failed to hide the grin on his face.

"Well, I'll leave you men alone so you can continue throwing barbs at one another. I have business elsewhere." I tipped my hand and started off toward the museum stand.

"Nash told me to let you know he'll be waiting for you next to the dance competition tent," Clint David shouted.

"Thanks. See you during the opening ceremony."

Clint David was a war veteran and participated during the color guard presentation. During that procession, Chaz would wait next to the announcer's podium with a perfect view of the festivities. I had exactly one hour until the event started. That should be plenty of time to have my talk with Papa.

The buzz of conversations wrapped around me, along with the laughter and screams of children. The

pleasant aroma of fry bread wafted through the air. I in-
haled, as if the smell alone filled my appetite. A sudden
urge led me to one stand where I bought a plateful. I
munched on warm bread and continued on toward Papa's
booth.

"Have some." I shoved the plate at Papa who didn't
refuse.

"Good day, Little Mac. Give thanks to the morning
light. Give thanks to the food. And give thanks to the joy
of living. Tecumseh." Papa devoured a large piece of
bread and chewed.

"I'm sure you do all three. Now, what did you find
out?" I hungered for news. I would give lots of thanks for
that.

Papa swigged on his bottled water and set it down
next to him on the counter. "Remarkable news. In fact,
I'd bet you're in for a huge shock."

"Come on. Don't keep me in suspense," I urged.

"My assistant Jemma Bluehawk is a Clearwater."

I frowned. "But she never mentioned it. I mean,
when we discussed our research on the Clearwaters and
Bluehawks, she didn't say a word. Why?"

Papa shrugged. "Beware the man who does not talk.
I'd say she has something to hide. More than being a
Clearwater. The question is what?" He shook his head.
"And I thought she was such a sweet young lady."

"Did you confront her?" I reached over the counter
to grab a can of soda. From the far left of Papa's stand,
Nash was walking toward the dance tent. Feathers waved
in the wind and strings of beads bounced against the
leathers of his regalia. Several more dancers were scattered about, either chatting or eating while they waited
for the competition to begin. I smiled and waved, but he
didn't see me.

"No. I only found out this morning when someone

came to the museum looking for Jemma," Papa explained.

I looked around. "Where is she by the way? Shouldn't she be helping you run the booth?"

"I gave her the day off. She had urgent family business to attend to." Papa frowned. "But then her mother came to the museum. That surely made me wonder. She asked to speak to Jemma, her daughter. Of course I recognized the woman. I'd seen her many times with her family. It's Elsie Clearwater."

Soda sprayed from my lips as I coughed. "But that's Toby's mom."

"Yep. Toby and Jemma are brother and sister."

"How can that be? Wouldn't you have recognized Jemma when she came to you asking for a job?"

"I hadn't seen her since she was a little girl. Grownup Jemma looks a lot different."

"Somebody should've recognized her. Nash has been to the Clearwater place many times, I'm sure of it. Folks around town even. One of them would notice. Right?"

Papa shook his head. "She went away to school when she was twelve, a performing arts place in upper New York. She attended on a scholarship until graduation. Elsie implied things weren't pleasant at home. Jemma preferred to stay with her aunt and uncle, even during her summer breaks. She started coming home to visit after Toby left to find work in Pittsburg. But they were brief reunions, maybe stayed a day or two. After Greer Clearwater died, things got a lot worse. Elsie explained all the sad details to me. She'd lost a husband, and the kids had lost their dad. Of course, I never got past the news Jemma is a Clearwater. Still can't."

I heard the announcer call for the color guard members to meet at the dance tent. I glanced at my watch and relaxed. More than a half hour was left until the opening ceremony. "It's my turn. This news may shock you just as much, if not more. Reese married several years ago, and he has a son."

"Well, I'll be. That is a surprise. But how did you find out?"

I went on to tell Papa about the visit from Anne, and about the letter. He appeared alarmed by the news. "Papa, it's actually good, don't you think? The letter clears up several questions we had, and now Callie has a sister-in-law and nephew in her life."

"You're right. That is good news. But the artifacts? No more than a few months ago I received a shipment of Native American treasures. No return address. I assumed they were from a philanthropist or some other kind soul who wanted to donate his possessions to the museum. Now, I wonder."

"It could've been Reese. Anne insisted he'd given his all to finding as many artifacts as time and opportunity allowed. Then he'd either donate them or return them to their rightful owners."

"These are special. They belonged to the Longhouse collection, a direct lineage of the Seneca and Handsome Lake."

"I'd guess it must be from him, then. Reese had been doing tons of research, Anne claimed. He most likely traced the origin of those Longhouse items and donated them to the museum. He just had to make sure you got them without knowing who the sender was."

"Which brings me back to Jemma. What is she hiding?" Papa stared up at the sky before he added, "I think you must be watchful."

"I know. And I can't help wonder if she knew about Toby's illegal activity with Reese and Elias."

"Which, if true, makes her all the more dangerous. Before I forget. One more thing puzzles me. Remember how you questioned whether Jemma worked this past

Thursday evening? Well, it just so happens, one of my regular visitors, Ira Sandwell, came by yesterday. He passed by the museum Thursday around nine and claims the lights were out. He asked me if we had trouble with the power."

My fingers gripped the soda can. "It puts a different spin on things. Doesn't it?"

"I figured as much. You think it gave Jemma opportunity to break into your uncle's house and take the book? That's my conclusion." Papa nodded. "As I said, you need to be careful."

A sudden thought occurred to me. "Not only me. Callie mentioned this hunting cabin where the guys used to hang out. It belongs to the Hopewell family. Nash and I went to visit Dillard last night. Sorry to say, the cabin burned down. And, yes, it's a long story I won't go into. But I'm concerned about Dillard. He's connected to all the ugliness that happened ten years ago. Now, I'm sure the killer has made him a target." I sipped on my soda. "You know, I think I'll call Sheriff Parker. Maybe he can have a talk with Jemma."

"You're worried she may have something to do with the killings?"

"I don't know. Maybe she's in on it. Maybe she's totally innocent and the killer wants to make her look guilty. After all, it happened to me. Regardless, any information she has on Toby may lead to the killer. That's worth checking into." I admitted my suspicions led straight to Jemma, reasonable or not. She'd lied about her name and more. Beware the liar. Add that to Papa's sage words. And liars have lots to hide. What was Jemma hiding?

"It is something the sheriff needs to know. You want me to call?"

"Thanks, Papa. I'd appreciate that." I tossed the empty can into the trash. "I have to hurry. The ceremony will start soon. Meet us afterward?"

"Sure. By the dance tent. We can have a great reunion. I miss talks with your uncle." Papa waved as I walked away.

I picked up the pace and made a path toward the center of the fairgrounds. A huge crowd of spectators had gathered, but I was able to find an ideal spot to view almost everything. I spied Nash underneath the tent and near the band. He was talking with the two drummers and the flute player who were practicing. The excited squeals and chatter of young boys and girls rose above the din of drums. Some chased each other in circles while others kicked up their feet and waved their arms to dance.

The announcer tapped on his microphone before he made his first introduction. "Welcome everyone to the fiftieth annual Five Nation Pow-wow and our beautiful town of Salamanca. Today is a celebration. We gather once a year, all our brethren who come to honor the spirits and holy ones and pay our respects with dancing, the rituals of our ancestors. We sing, we dance, we eat, we share our stories, and much more. So, thank you, one and all for sharing this celebration with us. And to begin, we call on the color guard to open the competition. Color guard, come forward!"

The clap of hands and shouts resounded across the stands. I watched as Nash, along with several men and women, danced onto the field. His costume of leather, beads, and feathers blended with the others as they colored the scene like a rainbow-filled sky. The music of flute and drums kept tempo to the chanting and carried the color guard through their movements.

I clapped along with everyone as I searched the grounds for Uncle Chaz. The thickening crowd of people made it more difficult to see as much. I skirted around the field and to the other side, hoping to spot him from there.

I was weaving through several tents and chairs set up by the spectators when someone ran up to me. It was one of the costumed dancers I remembered standing near Papa's tent earlier when I'd spoken with him.

"You need to come with me. Your uncle is hurt." The voice was low and raspy.

"What? Where is he?" I tensed as the dancer tugged at my arm, leading me away from the ceremony and toward the outer edge of the pow-wow fairgrounds, closer to the rear exit. As he skirted around the last row of tents I asked, "Is he hurt badly?"

The dancer shook his head. He gave my arm a harsh jerk to lead me behind the last tent. I felt a sharp jab in my side while he hissed in my ear, his breath sour and warm. "Keep moving. Toward the parking lot. If you yell or scream or try to run, I'll shoot you."

I sucked in my breath. My gaze darted from side to side to see no others close by. What good would yelling do anyway? My mood fell to new depths. I couldn't think quickly enough. It was like I'd lost all ability to reason. Only panic was left. The gun shoved into my back dug deeper as my abductor urged me to keep walking alongside the back of the parking lot.

The announcer's voice echoed across the grounds and gave the final call for the color guard members to come to the dance tent. "I'll be missed. People are waiting for me." My voice sounded unfamiliar to me, weak and monotone, but at least I could speak. The gun jabbed at me hard, and I winced.

"Don't talk."

We finally stopped next to a blue sedan. The dancer yanked me to a halt, and I nearly lost my footing. The trunk popped open. A blanket lay inside, spread out neatly.

"Get in."

I shook my head. "No," I whispered, desperation in my breathless tone. Pleading with him, begging him to reconsider might work, but I doubted he would listen. My hands formed its fingers into tight fists. They opened and clenched, again and again. "Please, don't do this. You don't have to. Walk away and it's over. I haven't seen your face. No one has to know." There. I'd said it. The answer was a hard shove to my back.

"Get in. I'm not telling you again." The voice became more natural.

All at once I eased, my fingers relaxed. My breathing calmed and as if there was no reason to fear the situation, a sudden awareness flooded me with courage. I turned slowly to face the dancer and examined the clear and detailed images. The purple threading, the curved and woven design, the pattern of wolves across the middle. "You'll never get away. People know who you are and what you've done, Jemma."

"Shut up!" With one swift motion an arm swung up and around to slap me across the cheek. In the next second, Jemma grabbed hold of my arm and jabbed a needle into it.

My body went limp. It didn't take more than a slight shove, and I sensed myself falling, practically floating. I looked upward through heavy lids to see the patches of purple circling with blue and white in the background. My mind seemed to swirl along with the colors. As I grew tired, my thoughts refused to focus, becoming a jumbled, confusing mess like a black shade covered me, darker and thicker. I didn't know why, but when I heard the thud and click, everything went dark and my mind stopped thinking.

Chapter 22

A firm bump to the head stirred me awake. My eyes met with inky blackness. I rubbed my face and arms vigorously to break through the fog. My body jostled in constant movement. Car. Trunk. Needle. It came back to me in pieces. Dancer. Jemma.

I swallowed hard as my brain netted and weaved the details into place. Echoes of words, warnings from Uncle Chaz, from Nash, from everyone who cared, all of them resounded in my head. "Jemma Clearwater," I whispered.

My hand struggled to reach behind me and into a back pocket. I sensed relief as my fingers touched the top of the phone. I grasped it and brought it around to face me. With a swipe, I lit the screen and found the flashlight. I panned the perimeter of my tiny prison. Nothing. Not so much as a tire jack. The flashlight came to rest on the trunk lid. If I punched out one of the taillights, I prayed someone behind us would notice. As long as we traveled on a main road or highway, that is. With a hard thrust, I kicked. And again. Not even a crack.

The car tires hit a bump and the jarring bounced the phone out of my hands. I stretched out my arms and swiped them across the trunk floor until I found it. Another bump jarred me, this one not quite as forceful. The phone stayed clutched in both hands. Hope that we were traveling on a main road or highway began to wane. How long had I been unconscious? I lit the screen again. The pow-wow's opening ceremony started at one. It was past five o'clock. The sense of panic returned. Four hours. Surely someone was looking for me. Nash. Papa. Uncle Chaz would be squawking the most. I opened the phone to call, but there was no signal. I tried a text message instead. *Help. Jemma kidnapped me.* I hit send but the phone kept scrolling.

I suppressed a scream. Maybe if I surprised Jemma when she opened the trunk, but with what? Fingernails dug into my clenched fists. "Think." Jemma had a weapon. How could I get past that?

As if to signal an end to my thoughts about escaping, the car pulled to a stop. I drew in my breath, held it, and tensed. The ding of an opened car door sounded and a light footfall grew louder as Jemma approached. A click of the lock. The trunk popped open, and light blinded me as the lid rose. At once, I closed my eyes and froze still.

"Wake up," Jemma ordered.

Damned if I will. When I didn't respond, a sharp jab came into my side. I winced and my legs curled into my stomach. It was no use. I pried open my eyes to form narrow slits. The end of a double-barreled shotgun pointed at my head. Jemma had removed the face paint and headdress. Blotches of bright red covered her face, and sweat dribbled down her forehead. Her short hair was flat and plastered to her head. She looked like a young boy, but crazy and determined.

"Get out of the trunk. I know you're awake. The sedative wasn't that strong." Jemma motioned with the shotgun.

I crawled out, and my legs wobbled when I tried to stand. I blinked, stunned, as I recognized the scenery around me. The car rested at the end of a dirt road. In front of it was a sign hanging from either side on chain links. It swayed and twisted back and forth with the strong winds whipping around and up from the deep valley below. The words "danger, no cars or persons beyond this point" added their warning to all the others screaming in my head.

"Move." Jemma nodded toward a footpath overgrown with weeds and covered with scattered debris left by animals. A smaller sign trailed across the opening with a rope and stated no trespassing.

"Why did you do it?" Curiosity overcame my fear. "Why kill them?"

"I told you to shut up," Jemma hissed.

I picked my way over the cluttered pathway. I viewed the valley below. Pieces of twisted metal lying on the ground still remained, left as a memorial to the storm's wreckage. The Kinzua Bridge, or what was left of it, stood hundreds of feet high off the valley floor. More than a century old, its scarred structure jetted out from the hillside, towering over all, refusing to be beaten. I considered it for a moment. Under the circumstances, wouldn't it make more sense to take me to a cemetery? There had to be some kind of irony in that.

It took a long while, but we reached the end of the path and the bottom of the valley. Critters scurried out of our way as we trudged through the thicket of weeds and brush. The cry of a hawk sounded to break the silence. The squeal of a field mouse came from underneath a cluster of greenery.

"They'll come after you. You know that, don't you?" I dared to comment. What did I have to lose?

"I won't be caught. The spirits will protect me. They

always have. Keep moving." She pushed the lower part of my back with her hand.

We traveled toward the wreckage of metal beams. I kept turning my head from one side to the other, but caught sight of no one, no visitors to the bridge, no hikers on the trails. No one.

"You may as well stop looking. No visitors come to the bridge in the evening. I know."

My head reeled with thoughts, scenarios of what Jemma planned to do. The chattering in my head threatened to explode out of my mouth. It was hopeless to stop it. "The bridge is really something, isn't it? Standing there for over a hundred years. It was originally built in 1881 to ship coal and lumber, but then in 1900 they rebuilt it with steel. The railroad stopped using it to transport goods in 1959."

"Stop talking! What's wrong with you? Do you think I care about some bridge? That's all you've ever done. Build bridges and railroads and towns and everything to destroy what we cherished." Jemma's chest heaved. "It's so clear. There should be no crossing lines. You stay loyal to your family. Be proud of who you are and where you come from. That's the way it should be." She poked me with her shotgun. "Over there by the metal beams."

I desperately wanted to believe this was a dream. I walked forward, my steps dragging, heavy and slow. My mind replayed Jemma's words. "Someone betrayed you. Is that it?"

"It doesn't matter, now, does it? I had to make it right and bring honor to our families. It was the only way." Jemma motioned for me to sit. "Back against the beam." She came around behind me and set down the shotgun. She pulled rope from her backpack and grabbed my hands, tying my wrists and waist to the twisted metal.

"If you hadn't come to the cemetery, I would have

finished burying him and burned the sage. Instead, because of you, the angry spirits followed. You brought them. He'll suffer from this. You have yourself to blame for that." Jemma stood and walked around to stare at my face.

I shivered, recognizing the anger and hurt fighting the passion and fire in her eyes. "Why did Reese have to die? Please. I need to know."

"He stole what didn't belong to him. He was part of it. And Elias. And my brother. They all took from our ancestors, and they had to pay for their sins. Grandma Sage taught me. She saw the future." Jemma stared off toward the cliff. "Toby was a fool. He listened to our father, a bitter old man. He killed himself, you know." Jemma lowered her eyes to glare at me. "I told you. Consider yourself lucky. You have good family and friends. I never did."

I twisted my wrists to loosen the ties, but it was useless. "I heard an intruder shot him."

"No. He took his own life because of Toby. When he learned of the grave robberies, he blamed himself. He had Toby convinced the feud between our families destroyed the Clearwater name. He always spoke about it, and Toby listened. He listened until his anger exploded. It must've been the reason. I understand that much. He refused to sit still, to not do anything about it. But he was wrong. What good is revenge when it turns into greed? To steal from the dead because you think that will make everything right? And then profit from it? My brother disgusts me." Jemma squatted down in front of me. Her eyes softened. "Don't you see? I had to do this. They had to pay because the spirits were angry. Grandma Sage told me."

I shrank back when Jemma sprang up and paced back and forth in front of me. The crazed look in her eyes almost seemed haunting.

She finally stopped and shook her fist at me. "You shouldn't have interfered. Now, the spirits want you." Jemma opened her hand and held it up, her fingers splayed. "One more. And then I'm done." She picked up the shotgun.

Every muscle in my body tensed while my mind reeled. "How did you find him? No one knew Reese was alive or where he lived."

"When my mother told me about Toby, about the robberies, I knew. I knew he had been the cause of our father's suicide, not me. He brought us all the pain. And the shame. He was my brother. I looked up to him." Jemma wiped her eyes. "I found Reese by accident. I was at the festival in Ogdensburg. I recognized him from photographs my mother showed me. Fate and the spirits brought us together. I have to believe that. It came so easy. I didn't have to think. I never questioned or struggled with the idea. I simply convinced Reese how Toby wanted to see him. How he planned to turn himself into the authorities and tell their story. Your friend came with me, and I killed him."

A coyote howled and the sound echoed around and through me. I shivered as if the cold dampness clenched my very core. Sunset came early in the valley. Jemma's shadow grew longer and her mood darker. Nervous fingers twitched and rubbed back and forth across the trigger of her shotgun.

"My husband was a Bluehawk, descended from the man who fired the first shot to begin the feud against the Clearwaters. Still, that never mattered to me. Out of respect and forgiveness, I cleaned Joseph Bluehawk's stone whenever I managed to visit, and I laid flowers on his grave. I'm a Clearwater, yet I loved Sonny. And I loved Grandma Sage. She was pure and kind. You would have liked her." Jemma nodded. She took a step away from me and then stopped to add, "I'm sorry. You shouldn't have interfered. It was never your fight."

My shoulders dropped and relief overwhelmed me. A sob escaped my lips. I wasn't her victim, not today.

Jemma walked down the path leading across the valley floor. She was a ghost. She danced for the spirits. And she was mad. The understanding left me saddened. No matter how insane or how evil her actions had been, Jemma believed she was on the right path.

I stared after Jemma as she reached the valley wall and climbed up the path that led to the cliffs and higher ground. I turned away as a coyote appeared in her path. Its howl echoed a mournful sound. I heard Jemma answer with a loud cry. It was as if they were of the same soul. And then another cry brought me around to look back up the cliff.

My breath hitched. Jemma's arms flailed as she lost her balance. She fell more than a hundred feet to the ground. My heart beat faster, and I waited to hear another sound, maybe a cry for help, but nothing came. The coyote remained on the path. Still. Silent. Its head bent toward the valley floor as if it, too, waited to hear. When nothing but the stirring whisper of winds and the cry of a hawk came, the coyote tread with slow steps as it disappeared into the brush.

I slumped against the metal beam. My shoulders shook as I wept. There was a price to pay, driven by my passion to find the murderer. And I felt no different than Jemma. Both of us grew reckless and lost our reason.

My wrists bled as I twisted harder to free myself from the ties. The sun descended, swallowed up by the sky until a narrow slice of it showed. In the dimming light, nothing more than vague, shadowy images remained. I feared what the night would bring. Nocturnal creatures would hunt for prey and here I sat, tied to a rusting relic from a bridge built more than a century ago.

I caught sight of the coyote when it reappeared. His shadowed outline sat closer, near the bottom of the valley floor. I sensed his eyes stared at me. The image was fuzzy, but I knew. He raised his head to howl once more. An empty cry. I remembered the coyote on the road as it had stood there, ravaging the carcass of its prey. I eased back against the beam as I stared at the shadowy form. My hands and wrists stopped moving. Jemma was no fool. She left me here, knowing a shotgun wouldn't be needed.

Worry and fear exhausted me. I was no longer able to fight it. Maybe Jemma was right. The spirits wanted to punish me. My eyes drooped, the lids grew heavier. I let them shut tight, and my pulse slowed to find an even, peaceful rhythm. It was pointless to change fate. This one was mine. I fell asleep. The pain in my wrists and the howl of the coyote faded into dreams.

It seemed hours passed. I squirmed. A pungent odor stung my eyes and nose. Tears ran down my face and I awakened to see the bowl of burning sage. Its smoke rose and wrapped its scent around me. Chanting. Drumming. Echoing sounds in my head. I heard them call to me. A woman danced in circles. Her arms waved like wings, up and down. She blew the smoke toward me. It fed my lungs to speak in kindness. It tickled my ears to listen with my heart. The voice, raspy and quaking with age, spoke to me. Feet stepped hard, making clouds of dust rise. The rattles, tied to her ankles, sounded like tiny pebbles dropping on a glass floor. She dressed in shades of brown and purple. A long, fat, silver braid slapped her back as she danced and her voice chanted louder still. A coyote skin covered the top of her head. She smiled and nodded, then waved her arms at me. As if they grew longer, they reached out farther and closer until they touched my face.

I flinched as if the fingers left a mark. It burned. The ties once bound so tightly began to loosen, and the image of the braided dancer faded into nothing.

I gasped when my arms hung loose at my sides. In one swift gesture, I pulled at the rope around my waist. It fell away as if it had never been tied. I squinted to peer into the darkness. I was confused. What direction should I take? No matter. I refused to stay in the open where I'd be prey to any wild creature. Reaching into my pocket, my hand came out empty and I muttered a curse. My phone must've fallen out on the way down to the valley, but I didn't let it stop me.

Despite the dark, I trudged forward. I extended my arms in front of me, reaching from side to side. Prickly bushes sprouted from the ground everywhere. I tripped again and again, nearly stumbling into a ditch. There had to be a way out of the valley, a way to escape without killing myself. I laughed at the thought. How ironic that would be.

The coyote howled again, its lonely cry streaking across the valley, and I jumped at the sound. The moon drifted out from behind the clouds, lighting the valley floor for a brief instant before hiding once again. It was enough. I turned in the direction only a moment ago shown by moonlight, and I walked. My body shivered. The chill soaked into my bones. The temperature had fallen sharply when the last bit of sunlight disappeared beyond the hilltop. Dressed only in a flimsy T-shirt and shorts, the one thing keeping me warm was to continue moving.

"You can do this. Mackenzies never give up," I said, forcing confidence not to abandon me now.

My legs tired. I wasn't sure, but it seemed like I'd been walking for over an hour. Worry came and grew. I hadn't reached higher ground or found a path that might lead up and to the hills. My heart skipped when I made out the shadowy forms several yards ahead. I slowed and then abruptly stopped. My breath held. I watched and waited for the forms to move. I had nowhere to hide. If the shadows were a pack of wild animals, I was doomed to meet the fate Jemma and the spirits intended for me. Minutes passed. When nothing happened, I took one cautious step forward. The forms were like statues. Another step and another until I began to cry. The sobs turned into screams as I recognized the familiar iron metal beams and the ropes spread out on the ground.

My legs dragged forward until I reached the spot where I'd started. I crumbled to the ground and curled up so my head rested against my knees. I tucked my arms underneath them and rocked. It would be light soon. Maybe help would come. Maybe Jemma was wrong. I cried, softer and softer until the sound of protest became a mere whimper, and then nothing.

Chapter 23

I shivered as I opened my eyes. I'd slept, but didn't know how long. The cold, damp air had spread over my skin, coating it with a wet, dewy layer. Was it the coyote?

In my dreams it called to me. And now it was coming for me. I sensed it. I turned my face up to the sky. A scream rumbled in my lungs and forced its way out.

"I'm here!" I responded, not caring what happened now. The fear, the anxiety, the waiting. Let it all end.

"Sarah! Sarah, where are you?"

I moaned, longing to silence the sound. I dropped my head to my chest and covered my ears. "Stop. Please," I whispered. The coyote howled, louder and closer. The rapid patter of steps. Louder. Closer.

"Sarah." Nash rushed to my side. He wrapped his arms around me and squeezed. "I didn't think we'd—"

I sobbed, seeing his face. I relaxed against him, letting his body warm me. I couldn't stop crying, even when Nash tightened his grip and I buried my face in his chest. He rocked me, and still I cried.

"It's all right. I've got you, now." He spoke in a

whisper as his lips brushed the top of my head. "Shh. I'm here." He rocked me even harder.

The sun peaked over the hills. The light with pale yellow and pink hues streaked across the sky. Flickers of it touched the valley below.

At length, my sobbing stopped and I opened my eyes to find Nash. I reached up to touch his face. "It's really you."

"Yes. It's me. You're safe now, and I won't let go." He hugged me closer.

Voices chattered in a conversation close by. My gaze strayed from Nash to look behind him. Sheriff Parker stood next to Papa and Clint David.

"You gave us quite a scare, you did," Parker said. His voice carried the usual solemn and serious tone.

I sucked in my breath. "Jemma."

Parker nodded. "We found her. After Nash got your text, and I spoke with Mr. Birdsong, it didn't take much to put it all together."

"Of course, we had no clue where to look," Clint David added. "If it weren't for Plum Steelwater—"

"Hogwash. It was her phone that told us where to go," Parker interrupted. His scowl warned Clint David to keep the notion to himself.

"I never figured it was her, but she confessed everything. She murdered all three of them because she listened to the spirits. They told her what to do." I bit down on my lip to keep more tears from coming. "Jemma was insane. She had to be."

Parker shook his head. "I'll say. Talking spirits. What a tragedy. Maybe that's why she ended it all."

"No. I don't think she meant to kill herself." I pictured the coyote, how it leaped out from the brush and onto the path in front of Jemma. "Something scared her. A coyote. And she lost her footing."

"Maybe the spirits knew what they were doing after all," Clint David said.

"I guess this clears my name once and for all, doesn't it, Sheriff?" I struggled to joke, but in truth I wasn't feeling it.

"You go a long way to prove your innocence, Miss Mackenzie." A hint of a smile surfaced. "Sure enough, and lucky for you, DNA results came in last night. Nothing matched the scene, except for the tool brush of yours."

I nodded. It made sense. "Jemma placed it in the grave."

"We need to get you back to town. The paramedics are coming down with a gurney to take you to the hospital," Nash explained.

"Don't be silly. I'm perfectly fine. I can walk. Put some antiseptic and Band-Aids on these cuts, and I'm good to go," I protested, trying to force confidence into my voice, but Nash held me down when I pushed to stand.

Nash narrowed his eyes and kept a firm grip on my arms. "Not this time. For once, you'll listen to me."

I sighed. "Fine. *This* time."

Secretly, I didn't mind. Pride had made me object, but in truth, I was still shaken. Jemma was dead, and if not for the rescue party, I may have ended up the same way. I caught sight of the coyote poised on the cliff again. He stayed for mere seconds and then slipped into the trees.

"I worried when I spotted the coyote. We followed him into the valley, and then you called out. We're lucky we found you soon enough." Nash wrapped his coat around my shoulders. "The paramedics are here. We'll talk on the way to the hospital."

"You don't need to ride—" I began to argue. But stopped when I saw his face.

"No. I'm going. I won't let you out of my sight. Not for one minute." Nash kissed the top of my head and then stood up to step aside while the medics brought the gurney over.

Once the EMT van got underway, I closed my eyes. I tried to erase the images but they refused to fade. Giving up, I stared at Nash instead. He turned to face out the window, but I detected the taut muscles along his jaw and the rigid line of his mouth. He was angry and I couldn't blame him.

"I'm sorry I didn't listen to you," I said.

He shifted his attention back to me. A frown wrinkled his brow. "What? You think I'm mad because you almost ended up dead? Because some insane killer tried to take your life?" A cynical laugh escaped his lips as he shifted his head back and forth. "You're right. I am angry, but not with you. At myself, yes. But not you."

I reached out to take hold of his hand. "You shouldn't."

"Oh, yes, I should. I should've been more careful. I should've watched more closely and stayed by your side. That won't happen again. I swear. I'll never let you out of my sight." His hand gripped mine.

I laughed. "Such a chivalrous man you are. And it totally isn't going to happen."

His jaw dropped before he started to speak again.

"Eh, eh." I placed a finger over his lips. "Impossible. Impractical. You can't be with me every second. I won't allow it anyway."

"Only when you throw yourself at trouble. I'll stay by your side then."

"Ha. And that would be pretty much every day, it seems. We'll have to work on that. Okay?" I squeezed his hand for one more second and then let go. "Now, what was Clint David saying about Plum Steelwater?"

Nash smiled. "I'd agree, the man was right. Plum did give us a hint as to where you'd gone, even if Parker thinks it's crazy."

With all the nonsense Plum spewed concerning family skeletons and such, I might go along with him. "You mean as in Plum crazy?" I bit down on both lips to keep the laughter from escaping.

"Oh, good one, funny lady. But yeah, he claims a vision came to him. He saw you surrounded by tall, broken pillars, once mighty and strong enough to carry many until the great wind brought them crumbling down, weak and useless. That's how he put it. Right away, Clint David blurted out the words Kinzua Bridge. Of course, seconds after, your text message came through. Sheriff Parker got someone to track your phone, which, by the way, we found on the path leading down to the valley." He pulled it out of his pocket and handed it over. "Anyway, the rest you know."

"Huh. How about that?" I closed my eyes again and yawned. "The sedative must be working."

"Then you should sleep. Plenty of time for talk later." Nash leaned down to kiss my cheek.

I smiled and nodded. Soon, the gentle rumble of the van as it moved down the road toward Warren lulled me to sleep. I drifted and the rumbling turned into other sounds. It traveled in and out of my dreams, took me into a field where I danced and then soared into the sky with a hawk flying next to me. Below, coyotes formed a circle. They surrounded a grave, the mound of dirt freshly turned. Resting on top was a stone marker etched with crude lettering. The hawk coaxed me to follow and we dropped to the ground where I read the words. *Grave Maker.* The ghostly image of a woman floated up from the stone and opened its mouth to scream.

I gasped and clutched the rails of my bed as I awoke.

I searched the room and found Uncle Chaz and Nash sitting next to me. My heartbeat slowed until I finally relaxed. "Guess those drugs make for some crazy dreams." I shrugged.

Chaz smiled. "Maybe you should work your charm on one of those doctors and get me some. I could use it with all you're puttin' me through."

"Stop. You're crazy enough," I chided, but with a grin. I rested my eyes on Nash who didn't speak. But his expression, for once, told me plenty. "You been here all night, I bet."

"I slept some. Chair's not too comfortable, but it works." He stood up and stretched. "You want me to call the nurse? I can get you a soda from the machine if you're thirsty."

"Nope. I'm fine." And I was. The ghostly image didn't quite fade, but it didn't bother me. Not while I had the family and friends Jemma spoke of near me. I'd handle pretty much anything. "Anyone check on Dillard Hopewell?"

"Yep. He's home, and I'd bet as happy as one man can be," Nash said.

Chaz scowled. "He oughta be plenty happy. Got his name cleared, and unlike those other three, he's alive. Darn fool. He deserves to be behind bars after all he did."

"Maybe, but I'm guessing Parker will let it go. Spending hours in that rundown cabin of his? Must've felt like a ticking time bomb, scared out of his wits not knowing if the killer would find him. That's punishment enough," I argued.

"Sheriff Parker and his deputy paid a visit to Elsie Clearwater. She had quite a bit to say. And one thing she asked for was to see you." Nash sat back down in his chair. He drummed his fingers on his legs.

I scratched my head. "Why me?"

"I guess since you were the last one to talk to Jemma. Or maybe she wants to apologize for her." Nash leaned forward and placed one hand on the bed close to my side. "You don't have to."

"But I want to. You can come along, if you like."

He narrowed his eyes and leaned closer. "It's not really an option."

"Oh, for crumb sake, why don't you kiss the girl? I'm goin' for a ride down the hall. You two can smooch all you want." Chaz pivoted a one eighty and wheeled out of the room, still grumbling.

I laughed. "Such a unique sense of humor. Wouldn't you agree?"

"Humor? I can think of a dozen words to describe your uncle's demeanor and none of them begin with humor. As soon as you're released, I'll take you home and make you lunch. Then, if you're up to it, I'll drive you to see Elsie."

"Wow. You seem to have my entire day planned. I'm beginning to understand how Uncle Chaz feels. I'm not an invalid, Nash."

He nodded and drew back from the bed. "It's too much. I get it. And I'm learning. You want to be alone, then?"

"No, silly. I…" I shrugged. "Let's start over. I would love for you to drive me home. And *I'll* make lunch. We can visit Elsie afterward, if it suits me. Sound good?"

"It does. Okay, let me press the button for the nurse, aaand…" He smiled. "…maybe *you* should press the button."

"Now you've got it." I laughed. This felt nice. Natural, like breathing.

Chapter 24

S he was so angry." Elsie dabbed her eyes with a tissue. "I simply meant to ease her pain. She always blamed herself for his suicide. So much guilt in this family." She shook her head and sobbed quietly.

I sat across from Elsie Clearwater. A widow and now childless. Mothers shouldn't have to outlive their children. "When did you tell her about Toby?"

"A couple of weeks ago. She came home for a visit to check up on me, I guess. She never comes but once or twice a year. Anyway, she knew Toby had returned home to live. He lost his job in Pittsburg several months ago." Elsie reached for another tissue and her pack of cigarettes. "After his girlfriend kicked him out, he had nowhere else to go. I let him stay here. He is—*was*—my son."

Sheriff Parker's deputies trailed in and out of the house during our conversation. I watched one of them carry a box up from the basement. "I'm surprised you never knew about all that." I nodded at the boxes filled with Indian artifacts.

"The boxes were stored in Toby's bedroom in the basement. He warned me never to mess with his belongings. I respected his wishes." She tapped ashes into a coffee mug. "Jemma happened to be searching his room to find old photos. She just wanted to reminisce. After she opened one box, she stormed upstairs, demanding to know what all those treasures were doing in Toby's bedroom. I had to tell her. It's what Greer confessed to me right before...well, you know."

"And when Jemma learned how Toby robbed graves to get the artifacts, it made her angry enough to do what she did." I remained quiet for a moment, but I needed to ask. "You wanted to see me. Was it to explain Jemma's anger?"

"To apologize for her. It doesn't mean much, I know. But I felt it needed to be said." Elsie leaned back in the chair, her eyes empty and without hope. "Toby came home the night after Jemma stormed out of here. I thought he'd go mad when he found out what she'd done. He claimed those treasures were for his rainy day. He planned to sell them so we'd be set for life. Those were his words. I tried to convince him it was wrong, but he wouldn't listen. It was the last time I saw my son." She stared at nothing in particular as she rocked in her chair.

After a long moment of silence, I stood and glanced at Nash. "We should go. I'm sure you'd like time alone to rest, Mrs. Clearwater."

An expression of surprise surfaced, seeming surprised to still have visitors in her house. "My Jemma was such a bright girl, but always quick to anger. She and Greer seldom got along. They were too much the same, you know. Toby was more like me." She frowned and got up from the rocker to cross the room. She opened a drawer and pulled out the Clearwater tome and a smaller book.

"Here. Jemma left these. She said you would come, and I should give them to you. The journal belonged to Sage Bluehawk. Jemma warned me to keep both safe. If anything happened to her, she wanted your uncle and you to have them."

I frowned. "I don't understand. When did she say this?"

"Yesterday morning, she stopped by the house. By her voice, I knew she was upset, more than a little. That's why I visited Mr. Birdsong. I'd heard he hired Jemma to work at the museum. I knew in my bones something bad was going to happen. Why else would she say those words?"

She placed the books in my hands. I studied the cover of the smaller one. It showed dates and Sage Blue-hawk's name. I tucked it into my bag before giving Elsie a hug. "If you need anything, call me. Or Nash. Even Papa Birdsong would be glad to help." My hand gripped Elsie's arm for a moment, and then I turned to leave.

Nash gave Elsie's shoulder a squeeze before joining me. Once we reached the car, he spoke. "She'll need someone to stay with her. I'll ask my parents if they'll talk to her relatives."

"Good." Knowing what Elsie would go through stirred my own memories. "Maybe she'll move away. Everything in the house will form a reminder of what she can't change."

"I suppose. What do you want to do next?" Nash opened the car door, and I slid into the seat.

"I need to get home. I promised Uncle Chaz we'd wrap up his research. I have a strong hunch this may help." I pulled the journal out of the bag and placed it in my lap. Surprising as it was, Jemma never intended to kill me. Everything she'd done, forcing me to go to the bridge, leaving me alone and helpless, what else was I to think? It was as if Jemma, who put so much faith in the spirits, believed they had other plans. I wasn't supposed to die. Not yesterday, at least.

"Can we make a quick stop to see Callie, first?" The ring was still in my handbag. It was a day for exchanging gifts. Now, it was my turn. Reese gave me back the ring out of love, but it was wrong. Callie's love for her brother was genuine. She deserved the ring. It would be my gift to her.

"Callie's it is," Nash said and steered the car back onto West Bank Perimeter Road and headed south.

ᘓᑊᘓᑊᘓ

"This is more interestin' than I figured it to be." Chaz moved his reading magnifier back and forth across the pages of Sage Bluehawk's journal.

Time reached close to an hour since Chaz read the first page. He'd poured over the entries with meticulous effort, savoring each word while my fingers itched with anticipation. I'd had the chance to glance over a few entries on the way home, just enough to thirst my curiosity for more. However, this was his baby, his project. The research and building the story into his own words earned him the honor of reading Sage's thoughts first.

"Listen to this. 'I figured from what my Grandma Bluehawk told me that the feud sparked a bitter trail that would never end. Maybe if two innocent souls hadn't sacrificed their lives, two infants who never had a say in such cruel acts, maybe if that had been avoided our families would be friends.'" Chaz studied the page before he glanced up to face me with the questioning stare. "You figurin' what I am?" he said.

"Two innocent souls. Maybe one is Jacob Bluehawk?" I sucked on a licorice stick while searching through my memory. "I think I recall something. It was when I visited the library and searched through genealogy records on the Clearwaters. Not much more than birth and death dates, no details on their lives. Some were infants and young children. I assumed those deaths were mainly caused by diseases like dysentery or scarlet fever."

"Maybe you can pay a visit and check the dates?" Chaz squirmed in his chair and scratched his side. "This is purely guess work, but what if the innocent souls came from both sides of the fence?"

"You mean a Bluehawk and a Clearwater? Two children dying because of a feud. The story makes for a great movie, but in real life…" I shrugged.

"I'll keep readin' Sage's journal. She might say more." Chaz picked up the magnifier and returned to his task.

I settled more comfortably in my chair and absently scratched Opal's head. The irony of the situation would make me laugh, if only it wasn't so tragic. A feud which started over a hundred years ago—and, for the most part, ended soon after—was still claiming lives. Of course, the sins of those three men had stirred the hatred up again. Reese may have been young and naïve at the time, since Toby most likely kept the revenge element a secret, but that still was no excuse.

Elias wouldn't have cared, no matter what reason Toby gave him. He'd agree to it. Sins of the soul, revenge, and the follower. Yet it took little for Jemma to commit the worst sin. Murder.

"She would have done something like that in time, anyway," I said, voicing my assumption.

"What's that? Who?" Chaz asked.

"Jemma. Even if Reese, Toby, and Elias hadn't committed their crime, she would have eventually cracked and done something."

"A mad woman, that one. Somethin' sent her over the edge long before these three." Chaz nodded.

"Um hmm. Well, I'm off to the library. You need anything from town?"

"Just the information. I'll call you if I find out more." He grumbled his last words and buried his head in the journal again.

I gave Opal a hug and Chaz a kiss. "Be back soon."

On the way into town, I stopped at the bar to give Nash an update, but he wasn't in. Emmie had arrived early to accept a special afternoon delivery as a favor.

"He wanted to run an important errand. I didn't have the heart to say no." Emmie wedged the crowbar under one strip of wood and broke open the crate. Once done, she looked up to smile at me. "I'm sure you know how that is."

"Oh, for the love of Pete. Will you stop with the innuendos? Did he say when he'd be back?"

"This evening. Before opening."

I scowled. Emmie's lack of conversation was highly suspicious, but I didn't have time to poke for more information. "Fine. I have to hurry. If I'm not back, let him know I need to talk."

"I'm sure you do. Bye." Emmie did her finger wave and winked.

I groaned and mumbled a few curses about Emmie's knack for butting into personal issues as I left the bar. I'd stop by on my way back home if I found anything worth mentioning. Truth told, Emmie did get under my skin. Especially since the murder mystery was solved and the killer dead, I had more time to think. Of course, I refused to admit it to myself or anyone else. I had been building up the courage to speak to Nash ever since he dropped me off this morning. Silly as it sounded, I was waiting for some sort of sign, something to signal the moment was right. Yes. I was procrastinating. No doubt about it.

I drove out on the road and tromped down on the gas.

"You're letting Jemma's spirits get into your head, Sarah Blue Mackenzie," I griped. There would be no sign. I'd either tell him or not. Simple as that.

I mounted the steps to the library. It was near closing time. Budget cuts forced them to trim down their hours. If it weren't for Mrs. Quintero's persistence, Sunday wouldn't have been an option. For her efforts, the narrow window of three to five was agreed upon and library patrons were grateful.

I hurried up to the top floor and tapped on the glass partition enclosing the genealogy room. The library assistant let me in, and I went straight to the section where I'd found the records. It took no more than five minutes to get a match. In fact, the deaths of the two infants, Jacob Bluehawk and Samuel Clearwater, were a day apart. If Chaz found anything in Grandma Sage's journal to corroborate our hunch, it might explain the reason for the ongoing feud.

I thanked the library assistant and took the elevator down to the main floor. Giving Mrs. Quintero a wave, I pulled out my phone to call Chaz. I sat outside on the library front porch and waited for him to answer.

"I found it. Samuel Clearwater died one day after Jacob Bluehawk. Did you come across anything in Sage's journal?"

"I did. And it goes along with what you mention. There was one hellacious fire exchange between the two families and their kin. Impossible as it seems, both boys were wounded. Jacob died first. And when Samuel passed on, the feud was rekindled to the point neither side was willin' to make peace. A few years later, Joseph and his wife had another son. They named him Joseph Junior, as you already know."

"And the father died one year after that. Joseph the son must be Sage Bluehawk's father," I suggested.

"Yep. She writes a lot about him. And there're more stories about the early years. This was a valuable gift Jemma put in your hands. I'd say I'll have more than enough to finish my book."

I smiled. "Anything to make you happy and not grumpy."

"Well put, missy. Can't argue there. But I saved the biggest news for last. And this one will take a heap of explainin'. Remember that deed you were supposed to check into at the courthouse?"

I smacked my forehead. "Holy smokes. With everything that's happened, I forgot. I'll head over there first thing tomorrow. I promise."

"No need. I have it all explained here in Sage Bluehawk's handwritin'. And I quote, 'If only the land deeded to my great uncle had ended the feud. It was a magnificent gesture made by the Clearwaters, but when Jacob died none of this mattered. Still, the land stayed and passed on to my father, Joseph Junior. And then to me. I had no miracles to help make amends for all the sins of our kin, but at least there was one gift I could offer and did. I think it made him a little less sad. Losing a wife is never easy, just as it was hard for me to lose my Adam.'"

"All right. I see why the property exchanged hands. We already figured it out. But who is she talking about? She doesn't say, and I—"

"Just hold your tongue a minute. I'm not through readin'. The next line explains, if you keep an open mind. It says, 'In loving memory of Kate and Moe Mackenzie. May you enjoy what should have been yours all along.' You see?"

"No, I don't see." Impatience flooded over me. It made no sense at all.

"She gave your daddy the property where Deja Blue sits. The land given to little Jacob and passed on to his brother Joseph Junior by the Clearwaters. I swear, he covered up the story well. I never once doubted him when he claimed to have bought the property outright."

"Why in heaven's name would Sage say it should have been Moe's all along? I'm more confused than ever." And I was. Why would Moe hide the truth, if indeed the property was given to him, a gift from Sage Bluehawk, no less? Why keep it a secret?

"I don't have an answer to give you, but I can make a guess."

"Then, guess away, because I come up empty." I sighed.

"Remember how you been told you have a smidge of Indian blood in you? From your mama's side, that is. No one ever talked about it. Your daddy certainly didn't. Guess he kept lots of secrets. But what if—"

"Stop. Don't even finish your thought. My mother can't be a Clearwater or a Bluehawk or be connected in any way to Sage's claim. I'd know that much, wouldn't I? No, she's wrong. That's all there is to it." I gritted my teeth. Despite my protest, truth be told, Moe seldom mentioned the details of Kate's history. Oh sure, he lamented over her leaving him and her demise, especially after an evening spent with Jack Daniel's or Wild Turkey to console him. But really, what did I know when it came down to it? I was barely into my teens when Kate left. After more than fifteen years, my memories had faded to vague images and mostly the troubling ones remained.

"Are you sure of that, missy? Seems pretty coincidental how the property came to him right after your mama died. Well, I'll let it go. I've said enough. Now, I'm makin' turtle soup this evenin'. You stoppin' by?"

I wrinkled up my nose. "I think I may swing by the bar for a spell. I have some business to take care of." Relieved, I dismissed the whole story of the deed. It was nonsense and soon enough, I'd prove it, when I was good and ready. After all, I was the expert at fact finding, wasn't I?

"Suit yourself. I'll give Zeke a call. He can't get enough of my turtle soup."

"Enjoy." I chuckled and ended the call. As I rose from the bench, my phone buzzed. A text message lit up the screen. *The spirits are dancing to celebrate your great courage. ~ Spirit Talker.* I frowned, rereading the words. Jemma wasn't my messenger after all. Not unless she was sending this message from the afterlife.

Slinging my handbag over one shoulder, I stepped off the porch. I made my way down the sidewalk when, all at once, I caught sight of Plum Steelwater, who sat in his rocker smoking a pipe. He took one more puff and then stood. He tipped his head and smiled before taking a deep bow. As he straightened, his arm raised up to salute. I hesitated for a brief moment before returning a slight nod. "It can't be." I shook my head. The idea was too preposterous. I had no solid reason to think it was him, did I?

My phone was still in my hand. Glancing down, I read the words once more: *Celebrate your great courage.* I smiled and pushed a button. After three rings, Nate answered. "You're slipping. That took five rings," I teased.

"It was no more than three, and you know it. You okay?"

"Of course. Never better." I glanced at Plum Steelwater one last time before crossing the street to my truck. "Say, what special errand did you need to run? Emmie mentioned it."

"I went to visit with Elias's family. I figured some stories about their son might lift their spirits. I had a few to share from our days together in Baton Rouge. Of course, I had to clean them up a bit." Nash chuckled.

"You're a real nice guy. You know that?" I chewed on my fingernail. My courage was about to crumble if I held back any longer. *Now or never, Sarah.* "Would you be interested in going out on a date?"

"Sure. Who'd you have in mind?"

"Funny. No, I mean you and me and a real date." My heart pounded so loudly I barely heard myself speak. *Please let this be easy.*

"I might be inclined, if you promise to change out of those jeans and wear something nice. Like a dress."

"The guy with the jokes. I don't own a dress. I suppose I'd consider buying one, if you take me to a fancy restaurant." I laughed. "And you pay."

"You are one demanding lady. I like that."

"Enough to take me out?" My breath held as I gripped the phone.

"Yes. I would love to take you out." His voice softened enough to calm me.

"Great. Okay, then. It's a date." I relaxed my grip on the phone and said goodbye. A cool breeze tickled my neck, and I shivered from its touch. I glanced around me before getting into the truck. My thoughts wondered back to Nash, and I grinned. Easy and natural as breathing.

"Thanks, Spirit Talker," I whispered and made my way home.

The End

About the Author

Kathryn Long's passion is writing mysteries, creating the intricate details and weaving them together into the clues which the reader will enjoy collecting to solve the crime. However, she's worn many hats over the years—bookseller, teacher, mom, wife, and author. Many of her works include Native American elements and hints of the paranormal. She loves a scary ghost story!

Her writing inspiration began with reading about Nancy Drew and the heroines of romantic suspense authors such as Victoria Holt and Mary Stewart. Her first creations were short stories meant to entertain anyone who'd listen or read. Playing the guitar led to song lyrics, which she insists taught her the rhythm and pace of writing prose.

Writing took a serious turn several years ago when she had her first book published. To date readers can find her self-pubbed cozy, *Lilly M Mysteries*; her traditionally published work, paranormal mystery, *Dying to Dream*; and latest, a romantic suspense, *A Deadly Deed Grows* at online retailers and in bookstores. *Buried in Sin* is her first book with Black Opal Books. She keeps actively involved with fellow authors as a member of Sisters in Crime and International Thriller Writers.

When writing and the creative muse take a break, this author loves to travel, watch *Castle,* and of course, read mysteries. Oh, and there's always an author event or two she will attend in order to—you got it—talk about mystery. Long lives in the City of Green, located in northeast Ohio, with her husband and little pooch, Max.

CPSIA information can be obtained
at www.ICGtesting.com
Printed in the USA
FFHW012346260319
51196733-56672FF